RECKLESS ENDANGERMENT

Recent Titles by Graham Ison from Severn House

The Hardcastle Series

HARDCASTLE'S SPY
HARDCASTLE'S ARMISTICE
HARDCASTLE'S CONSPIRACY
HARDCASTLE'S AIRMEN
HARDCASTLE'S ACTRESS
HARDCASTLE'S BURGLAR
HARDCASTLE'S MANDARIN
HARDCASTLE'S SOLDIERS
HARDCASTLE'S OBSESSION
HARDCASTLE'S FRUSTRATION
HARDCASTLE'S TRAITORS

Contemporary Police Procedurals

ALL QUIET ON ARRIVAL
BREACH OF PRIVILEGE
DIVISION
DRUMFIRE
GUNRUNNER
JACK IN THE BOX
KICKING THE AIR
LIGHT FANTASTIC
LOST OR FOUND
MAKE THEM PAY
RECKLESS ENDANGERMENT
WHIPLASH
WHISPERING GRASS
WORKING GIRL

RECKLESS ENDANGERMENT

A Brock and Poole mystery

Graham Ison

severn House

This first world edition published 2014
in Great Britain and the USA by
SEVERN HOUSE PUBLISHERS LTD of
19 Cedar Road, Sutton, Surrey, England, SM2 5DA.

British Library Cataloguing in Publication Data

Ison, Graham author.
  Reckless endangerment. – (A Brock and Poole mystery; 13)
  1. Brock, Harry (Fictitious character : Ison)–Fiction.
  2. Poole, Dave (Fictitious character)–Fiction.
  3. Police–England–London–Fiction. 4. Murder–
  Investigation–Fiction. 5. Missing persons–
  Investigation–Fiction. 6. Detective and mystery stories.
  I. Title II. Series
  823.9'14-dc23

ISBN-13: 978-0-7278-8362-9 (cased)

All Severn House titles are printed on acid-free paper.

Severn House Publishers support the Forest Stewardship Council™ [FSC™],
the leading international forest certification organisation. All our titles that
are printed on FSC certified paper carry the FSC logo.

Typeset by Palimpsest Book Production Ltd.,
Falkirk, Stirlingshire, Scotland.
Printed and bound in Great Britain by
TJ International, Padstow, Cornwall.

ONE

The flight was scheduled to take off from Heathrow Airport at eight o'clock that July morning. It had been pouring with rain for quite a few days in London and the temperature had dropped to an unseasonably low fifties Fahrenheit.

When the passengers were settled, and the huge Boeing 777-300 had been towed away from the walkway and positioned for take-off, members of the cabin crew started to move through the aircraft, handing out newspapers and magazines, and ensuring that everyone was comfortable. Once that was complete, a steward described the safety measures that should be taken in the event of an emergency.

With a surge of power that thrust the passengers back in their seats, the Boeing left the ground, immediately creating the illusion that it had lost speed.

Once it had reached optimum altitude and the seat-belt warning light had been extinguished, the cabin crew explained how the in-flight movie could be accessed and enquired what else the passengers may need to sustain them for the long flight to Miami.

'Good morning.' The smiling man seated in the first-class section of the aircraft was in his late thirties, good-looking and a frequent traveller to Miami, where he had business interests. 'It's nice to see you again . . .' He paused while making a pretence of reading the stewardess's name badge. 'Sharon.'

'Good morning, sir.' The stewardess's name was Sharon Gregory. She was twenty-six years of age and a petite honey blonde. She returned the man's smile. 'Would you care for coffee, sir?'

'Thank you. That would be most welcome, Sharon.'

'Breakfast will be served shortly, sir.'

'I look forward to it. You're very kind,' said the man.

'We aim to please, sir.'

'And you do. I've always found your service to be impeccable, Sharon,' said the man, with a knowing look.

'Will you be staying in Miami long, sir?' Although it sounded like the normal trite enquiry that cabin crew staff made, there was more to it than that. The passenger and the stewardess were not strangers to each other; in fact, they enjoyed an intimate relationship, and one that was a closely guarded secret from the airline for which Sharon worked. At least, by Sharon. But he was far from being the only man in her life.

'Just for twenty-four hours. I have business meetings all afternoon.'

'Oh!' Sharon struggled to keep the disappointment from her voice. 'That doesn't leave you very much time for pleasure, then.'

'Oh, I wouldn't say that,' said the man, and smiled again. 'You never know what might happen in Miami,' he added in a whisper.

Nine hours later, the huge aircraft touched down at Miami International, taxied to the walkway and the passengers began to alight.

'Enjoy your stay, sir,' said Sharon to the man from first class. She was standing at the exit, a fixed smile on her face, bidding farewell to the disembarking passengers. 'I hope we'll see you again soon.'

'I'm sure you will,' said the man, his mouth twitching into a smile that hinted of the promise of things to come.

Once the enormous airliner was empty, the crew gathered their suitcases and left the aircraft, making their way to customs, and thence to the crew bus that awaited them at the airport terminal.

An army of cleaners descended on the Boeing and began the routine task of clearing up after the largely untidy passengers who had just left; the sooner the cleaners finished, the sooner they would be off duty.

A tractor moved the aircraft away from the walkway to its stand and the task of refuelling began.

Arriving at the Shannon Hotel, Sharon Gregory stepped through the automatic doors into the cool, tiled lobby and checked in. A bellhop immediately seized her suitcase and took the key to her room from the receptionist before leading the way to the elevator.

In contrast to London, the temperature in Florida was up in the nineties and the humidity had hit eighty-four, not that Sharon Gregory understood or cared about humidity percentages. She did, however, know that it was damned hot, but being the United States her room was cool and spacious, the air conditioning blasting out at full power. All of which made her grateful that the airline for which she worked always put their crews into this particular luxury hotel for stopovers. It was twelve noon Miami time and she now had eighteen hours in which to relax and enjoy the sun. And anything else that might take her fancy.

The bellhop put her suitcase on the luggage rack. 'I won't open the balcony doors, Ms Gregory,' he said, 'otherwise the room will get hot and stuffy pretty soon.'

'Thank you.' Sharon handed the young man a few dollar bills.

'You have a nice day now, Ms Gregory,' said the bellhop, adroitly pocketing his tip.

Dismissing the idea of having an early dinner – her body clock told her it was five in the afternoon – she stripped off her clothes and scattered them carelessly about the room. Walking through to the bathroom, she spent the next ten minutes luxuriating under the needlepoint jets of freezing cold water that struck her body from all angles. But she felt no cooler when she stepped out of the shower.

Dispensing with the need for a towel, she returned to the bedroom and, ignoring the bellhop's advice, slid open the balcony doors. For a moment or two she gazed down at the beach and considered, yet again, how lucky she was to have a job that took her to such an idyllic place. Some of her former school friends in her native Basildon worked as hairdressers, shop girls or checkout assistants at a supermarket, but such mindless occupations would not have suited Sharon. And the dismal selection of available men would have suited her even less.

Turning from the balcony, she opened her suitcase and took out a small leather bag. Inside was a collection of perfumes: Tommy Girl, Coco Mademoiselle, Chanel No 19, Prada Amber and Lancôme Trésor. Each of them was a gift from one of the several men in her life. And she always ensured that she wore the right perfume for the man who had given it to her when she was about to make love to him. Although uncertain whether the man she had spoken to earlier would appear, she nevertheless selected his favourite, Lancôme Trésor, and dabbed it behind her ears and between her breasts.

Her preparations were interrupted by the ringing of the telephone. She crossed the room and sat on the edge of the bed to take the call.

'Hello?'

'Fancy a swim, Sharon?' It was her crewmate Cindy Patterson calling from the room next to her own.

That was a bloody nuisance, thought Sharon, and presented her with a minor dilemma. Should she wait on the off chance that her lover would arrive, or should she go to the beach? He'd said he had meetings all afternoon. She made a decision; after all, she might find a hunk on the beach who would catch her eye, and she could hardly tell Cindy that she was waiting to get laid. But the sea water would wash off her perfume. Oh, what the hell. She had plenty more and she might only sunbathe anyway.

'Sure. See you on the beach. Usual place?'

'I'll be there in ten,' said Cindy.

Sharon took a moment or two to study her all-over tan in the mirror, a tan that had ensured there were no ugly white lines or patches. Donning a string bikini, she shoved her feet into a pair of flip-flops and slipped into one of the hotel's terry robes. Grabbing a towel, she was about to leave for the lift that would take her direct to the beach when there was a knock at the door.

'Just coming, Cindy,' shouted Sharon, assuming that her friend had decided to call for her rather than meet her on the golden sands beneath her window.

She opened the door and the first-class passenger she had served on the flight that morning entered the room. Before locking the door, he hung a 'Do Not Disturb' sign outside, as he always did on these occasions.

Sharon smiled. 'I thought you said that you had business meetings to attend all afternoon, darling.'

'I cancelled them.' The man moved closer to where Sharon was standing, arms at her sides, and slid the robe from her shoulders. Quickly untying the bows of her bikini, he allowed the microscopic pieces of fabric to fall to the floor.

'I don't have the time, darling, really,' said Sharon. 'Cindy's expecting me on the beach in a few minutes' time and she'll wonder where I am.' But it was a futile protest and she didn't mean a word of it.

'Cindy will have to wait,' said the man, quickly stripping off his clothing. 'Unless she'd like to join in.'

'Naughty,' said Sharon. 'I want you all to myself.'

Later, when the couple were lying side by side and perspiring freely from the exertions of their love-making, the man raised himself on one elbow and gazed down at the girl.

'You are a thoroughly wanton woman, Sharon Gregory,' he said. 'But you know that, don't you?'

'Of course I am, darling. And aren't you pleased? However, there's something I want to talk to you about. Something that will mean we can be together always.' And she went on to explain what she had in mind. But before her lover could respond, the telephone rang. Reaching across him, she deliberately lowered herself so that her breasts were pressing on his chest. 'Hello?'

'Where the hell have you got to, Sharon?' demanded Cindy crossly. 'I've been on the beach for nearly an hour already. What's more, there are some dishy men about: a crowd of hunky all-American six-packs in a variety of colours, for a start. It's not like you to miss out on an opportunity like this.'

'Sorry,' said Sharon. 'I had to take a call.'

'Oh, really? I wasn't born yesterday, Sharon,' said Cindy sarcastically, and terminated the call.

Sharon replaced the receiver and turned on to her back. 'I've got to go,' she said.

'Not yet,' said the man.

'No, please, I can't,' protested Sharon lamely.

'Liar!' said the man.

'No, really, not now,' she said, but nevertheless locked her legs tightly around his body.

The first-class passenger was not the only man in Sharon's life. He was just one of a select group of lovers who travelled on her flights and to whose advances she willingly surrendered, as she had today. She had to admit, if only to herself, that she was an insatiable nymphomaniac. But it was the man with whom she had just spent an hour in bed who interested her the most, and the one whom it was her intention eventually to ensnare. By whatever means.

Sharon Gregory had been born an only child in Basildon, but had been trying for almost the whole of her short life to eradicate traces of her 'estuary' accent and what the sneering classes scathingly described as 'Essex girl' characteristics. She had even considered taking elocution lessons, but decided instead that she would listen carefully to the better educated of her passengers and try to emulate the way in which they spoke. In this she achieved some success, although the occasional grammatical slip would betray her origins.

Sharon's parents still lived in Basildon, in the same depressing little house in which she'd been born, and in her view they had done nothing to improve themselves. Her father had been a train driver, but had been disabled in an accident and forcibly retired from his job with a meagre pension, and her mother was suffering from some awful debilitating disease. Sharon avoided visiting them, claiming that the demands of duty meant she was often away. The truth of the matter was that she couldn't abide being in the company of sick people, even when they were her own family.

But Sharon was a very selfish person, accustomed always to getting her own way. And most of the time she succeeded.

However, just over twelve months later there was to occur an incident that put paid forever to the reckless endangerment that typified Sharon Gregory's immoral and self-indulgent lifestyle.

It was a Saturday evening towards the end of July and it was hot, unbearably hot. All the windows were open in the Gregorys' house in Tarhill Road, West Drayton, less than three miles from Heathrow Airport, but it made little difference to the temperature, even though it was now ten o'clock at night. The odour of aircraft kerosene fuel that always seemed to pervade the area was even more pronounced because the humidity prevented it from dispersing.

Outside, the usual crowd of noisy Saturday-night revellers, young men and teenage girls mostly, were passing the house on their way to the pub, or making their way to the garish nightclub a few yards further on, the heavy beat of its sound system polluting the still evening air for miles around.

Sharon Gregory hated the domesticity of housework and was grateful that her job meant that she was rarely at home to do it. Nevertheless, she was pottering about in the kitchen, loading the dishwasher and clearing up after dinner. Because of the heat, her long, honey blonde hair was clipped back into a ponytail and she was wearing nothing but a diaphanous cheesecloth kaftan.

Clifford Gregory yawned, turned off the television and ambled through to the kitchen. 'I think I'm going to turn in, love. How about you?'

'I'm just making your cocoa, Cliff. I'll bring it up when you're in bed, and I'll come in with you a bit later on.' Sharon Gregory wished that her husband wouldn't call her 'love'; it was so working class. Even though she was working class herself, she had been trying to shake off that image ever since leaving her birthplace. But Clifford had never used any other form of endearment during their seven years of marriage.

In fact, she often wondered if he noticed her at all. She thought, as she had done over and over again, what a mistake it had been to marry a man fourteen years her senior; a man who had turned out to be a boring accountant whose only interest was watching sport on television and spending hours making his wretched model aeroplanes. There were at least twenty of the damned things hanging from the ceiling in the study and Clifford could identify each one and accurately describe the history of its original.

Clifford and Sharon had met on a short-haul flight from Glasgow to Heathrow, and he had asked her out to dinner that very night. At nineteen years of age, she had been completely besotted by a man she had seen as handsome, mature, sophisticated, attentive and amusing, and over the ensuing months he had wooed her and made love to her repeatedly. And he had been breathtakingly inventive as a lover. But once they were married, a matter of two months later, all that had changed.

Over the course of the seven years since, his once chiselled good looks had become fleshy, he had run to fat and developed a paunch that he was ill disposed to do anything about. Even more irritating, he had attempted to disguise the onset of his baldness by effecting a ridiculous fold-over hairstyle. And at ten o'clock each night when Sharon was at home, he would announce that he was 'going to turn in'. And that was it: never any compliments on her appearance, never any affection, and definitely never any sex. The marriage was empty and loveless. It drove her mad and she felt trapped.

'When are you on duty again?' asked Cliff, pausing on his way out of the kitchen.

'Next Wednesday afternoon, LHR to MIA, as usual.' Sharon knew it was a formal question and one that he asked every time she was at home. But she sensed that he wasn't really interested in whether she was there or not.

'*Where*?' Clifford raised his eyebrows.

'Oh for God's sake, Cliff!' Sharon snapped at her husband impatiently. 'Heathrow to Miami International,' she said, slowly and distinctly. 'I must have told you a hundred times what those codes mean. And to think you're interested in aeroplanes.'

'Oh yes, I believe you have, love.' Clifford seemed not to notice her censorious tone and smiled infuriatingly.

'I'll make your cocoa.' It appeared to Sharon that nothing would rile or excite her placid lump of a husband. Not even flaunting herself naked, as she frequently did.

Waiting until she heard him mounting the stairs, she put a single mug of cocoa in the microwave and switched it on. Once the cocoa was ready, she paused briefly to shed her kaftan and sling it over a kitchen stool.

Clifford was already in bed when Sharon entered the master bedroom. She handed him the mug of cocoa and sat down in a chair, waiting for him to drink it.

'Aren't you having any, love?' he asked, completely oblivious to her nakedness.

Oh, if only he'd show some interest in my body and ask me if I was coming to bed, she thought. *Or better still throw me on the bed and force himself on me. Oh God, how deliciously exciting that would be.* But she knew it was a vain hope.

'In a minute.' Sharon had plenty of time; she had been preparing for this day for over a year now. 'I'll have mine in the kitchen. I've one or two things to do downstairs. I've got to close all the windows for a start.'

'Oh Lord! Did I forget? Sorry, love, I should've done that.' Clifford slowly consumed his cocoa. When he had finished, he put the mug on the bedside table, settled down and turned over so that his back was towards his wife.

Sharon returned to the ground floor and walked around the house, closing the windows. As she was in the act of drawing the curtains in the sitting room, a youth spotted her, paused wide-eyed, and then whistled loudly. She quickly closed the curtains.

Finally she went into the sitting room and sat down on the settee. Glancing at her wristwatch – the only thing she was wearing – she settled down to wait the hour before the next part of her plan could be brought to fruition.

She firmly believed that she had thought of everything, but in that she could not have been more wrong. Whatever else she may have learned in her short life, modern crime detection methods did not feature highly.

TWO

I have no idea why it should be that murders always seem to be carried out at a time that is most inconvenient to the police officers who are assigned to investigate them. Perhaps I'm just unfortunate enough to catch the homicides that occur in the small hours. Doubtless a team of erudite criminologists at some obscure university has spent thousands of pounds – or dollars – conducting a survey on the subject and will eventually publish its inconsequential conclusions. Nevertheless, such findings would undoubtedly be seized upon by the directing staff at the College of Policing and enthusiastically moulded into a grandiloquently boring lecture. And repeatedly delivered by a member of the team of resident sociologists to every successive course at what is laughingly referred to as 'the policeman's university'.

On the occasion of my latest murder it was getting on for one o'clock on a Sunday morning in late July. For once I was in my own bed rather than that of my girlfriend. The day had witnessed the onset of a heatwave, and at close to midnight it was still very hot and I had gone to bed with just a sheet over me and the windows wide open. For an hour, I twisted and turned, but was unable to sleep, not helped by the noise of the main-line trains passing through the nearby Surbiton railway station almost beneath my window.

Eventually giving up the struggle, I got up, intent on making myself a cup of tea and watching a repeat on television when my mobile rang.

'DCI Brock, sir?' queried the voice.

'Yes, this is Harry Brock.'

'It's Gavin Creasey at the incident room, guv'nor. Did I disturb you?'

'No, I had to get up to answer the phone,' I said sarcastically. I knew that Creasey thought he might've been disturbing something else. 'What is it, Gavin?'

'A burglary and murder at Tarhill Road, West Drayton, guv. A private dwelling. One male victim.'

'Wonderful! Just what I need. Arrange for a car to pick me up, Gavin.'

'It's on its way, guv.' Creasey paused. 'You *are* at Miss Sutton's place, aren't you?' he enquired archly.

It was an open secret among the members of my team at Homicide and Serious Crime Command West that I was in a relationship with a shapely blonde named Gail Sutton, and was more likely to be in her bed than in my own.

'Strangely enough, Gavin, I'm in my own flat.'

'Oh, I'll get on the air and divert them to your address, sir,' said Creasey, sounding rather surprised. 'I've alerted the principal actors and the supporting cast in this latest drama, and they're on the way.'

'Thank you, Gavin.' The people he was talking about comprised Detective Inspector Kate Ebdon and Detective Sergeant Dave Poole, as well as the other members of my Murder Investigation Team. Dr Henry Mortlock, the Home Office pathologist, and Linda Mitchell, a senior forensic examiner, and her assistants, would also have been invited to the party. It was the standard turnout procedure and swung into action like a well-oiled machine.

The traffic unit car arrived five minutes later.

'Good morning, sir. A lovely morning for it,' said the driver, with an exuberance that I found quite nauseating.

'Matter of opinion,' I muttered, regretting that I'd been obliged to don a jacket and a tie, and was perspiring already.

The driver covered the fifteen miles from Surbiton to West Drayton in as many minutes, blue lights blazing and siren blaring, although neither seemed necessary at that time of the morning. Emerging somewhat shakily from the high-powered BMW, I concluded yet again that this near-maniacal driving was a deliberate ploy on the part of the Black Rats to test the nerves of CID officers. I shouldn't really worry; the Met's drivers are among the finest in the world. But I do worry. Only about my personal safety, though.

'Good morning, sir. Mr Brock, isn't it?' Amazingly, the smart young lady inspector holding a clipboard and pen recognized me. I couldn't recall ever having investigated a murder in West Drayton before and I didn't know why she should have known me.

'Yes, I'm DCI Brock.'

'Thank you, sir,' said the inspector, as she made a note on her clipboard. 'DI Ebdon, DS Poole and Doctor Mortlock are here already. And Miss Mitchell and the evidence recovery unit are working in the house somewhere.'

Obviously lady incident officers were more wide awake at twenty minutes to two on a Sunday morning than were their male counterparts. We could use someone like her in the Department, and that prompted a thought.

'Have you ever considered a transfer to the CID, Inspector?' I asked.

'Good God, no!' exclaimed the inspector, as though I'd just made an indecent suggestion.

I was saved from further discussion on the subject by the approach of a youthful individual dressed in an expensive linen suit.

'Morning, guv. I'm Tom Watson, the hat DI.'

When Watson described himself as 'the hat DI', he didn't mean that he wore a hat; in fact he was bareheaded. HAT is yet another of the many acronyms to emerge from the Metropolitan Police 'funny names and total confusion squad' and indicated that he was a member of the Homicide Assessment Team. Its members comprise a select group of CID officers who patrol around the clock and are called to the scene of suspicious deaths by the local CID.

It is up to the HAT officer to decide whether or not a murder is of sufficient complexity to require an investigator from HSCC. Like me. But they've yet to do me the favour of deciding that the murders that occur when I'm next on the list could have been dealt with by the local detectives.

'What's the SP, Tom?' I asked, culling a useful bit of shorthand from the racing fraternity, although to a CID officer it doesn't mean 'starting price' but 'what's the score?', or in English: 'Be so good as to bring me up to date on what has occurred so far.'

'It's a funny one, guv,' said Watson predictably.

'Aren't they all?' I replied, hoping that one day someone would come up with a newer cliché with which to start a conversation about a murder.

'A guy called Sidney Miller,' Watson began, referring to his pocketbook, 'put up a 999 call at eleven forty-five to say that he'd heard a woman screaming. He went outside and eventually found that it came from this house.' He cocked a thumb of indication. 'It belongs to a couple called Gregory. Miller's house is next door,' he added, pointing. 'Going to investigate, Mr Miller discovered that the front door was ajar. Just inside, on the floor in the hall, he found Mrs Sharon Gregory, the occupant, lying on the floor, stark naked and trussed up with rope. She claimed that she'd been attacked by a burglar.' He paused ominously. 'Miller took a look around the house to make sure that the intruder was no longer there, and found that Mrs Gregory's husband, Clifford, was dead in the couple's bed in the master bedroom. First signs indicate that he was bludgeoned to death. But so far there's no sign of the murder weapon. At least, it wasn't anywhere near the body.'

'Was Mrs Gregory attacked, Tom? Physically, I mean.'

'It would appear not, apart from being tied up,' said Watson, 'but she's still a bit shaken up.'

'D'you reckon she's fit to be interviewed?'

'I think so. She had a couple of brandies to steady her nerves. You'll find her upstairs in the second bedroom with a woman officer. Incidentally, the whole place has been trashed.'

'Trashed?'

'Every room, as far as I could see. The first officers on the scene thought that a rave party had been held here, but then they found the body.'

'Have you seen Dave Poole, my sergeant, Tom?'

'He's in the master bedroom with Doctor Mortlock. And the body.' Watson paused. 'That's a pretty smart skipper you've got there, guv. He got to grips with the job the minute he arrived. He certainly knows what he's doing at a crime scene.'

'Of course he does; I trained him. As a matter of fact, he's the best sergeant I've ever had working with me,' I said. 'And he's got a degree in English from the University of London.'

'What's he doing in the Job, then?' asked Watson, raising his eyebrows.

'He told me it's what he always wanted to do,' I replied.

'Must be mad,' commented Watson, appearing to take the view that anyone who had been to university would be insane not to seek better paid employment in a cushier sort of job.

Dave Poole is of Caribbean origin. His grandfather, a medical doctor, arrived in this country from Jamaica in the 1950s and set up general practice in Bethnal Green. Dave's father is a chartered accountant, but Dave, describing the pursuit of a professional career as a tedious occupation, joined the Metropolitan Police. He often claimed, to the discomfort of those who worried about diversity, that it made him the black sheep of the family. And just to pile it on, he frequently referred to himself as a colour-sergeant when talking to the more pompous officers. Like our beloved commander.

'Where's this neighbour now; the one who found the body? Sidney Miller, did you say?' I got the conversation back to the task in hand. 'Is he still around, Tom?'

'I sent him back to his own house,' said Watson, 'but I told him that you'd want to see him at some time. The guy's obviously a key witness. Not to the murder, of course, but he's the best we've got so far.'

'Where's DI Ebdon?' I asked, but Watson didn't have to reply.

'G'day, guv.' Right on cue, my Australian DI, Kate Ebdon, emerged from behind the Metrolamps that were illuminating the front of the house; not that I could see any reason for turning the crime scene into something akin to a *son-et-lumière*. Kate was attired in a set of white coveralls, a pair of overshoes and the sort of mob cap that made her look like an escapee from a TV hospital soap opera. She was joined by one of Linda Mitchell's assistants who handed me a similar set of garments.

'Come with me, Kate, and we'll see what's going on.' I donned the coveralls, but refused point-blank to wear the mob cap. 'I understand that Mrs Gregory's upstairs in the second bedroom.'

'Yes. It seems to be the only room that hasn't been turned over.'

'Turned over?'

'Whoever this drongo was, he's wrecked the place. I've never seen anything like it.'

I was gradually learning Australian slang – or Strian, as Kate sometimes called it – and gathered that the burglar to whom she was referring was a total idiot.

'Yes, Tom Watson told me it had been well and truly trashed.' On the way into the house, I stopped to examine the front door. There was a standard rim lock, but no sign of a forced entry. No splintered woodwork surrounded the lock area and there were no broken panes in the glass panels, one of which bore a Neighbourhood Watch sticker.

'Looks as though it was 'loided, guv,' said Kate, as she removed her mob cap and stuffed it in the pocket of her coveralls.

The form of felonious entry to which Kate referred was often used by spec thieves. Usually a credit card was inserted between the edge of the door and the jamb, enabling the latch to be pushed back. Providing the burglar struck lucky. These days most people were wise to it and had fitted a deadlocking cylinder night-latch. The Gregorys were no exception. I pushed at the tongue, but it moved easily.

'You might be right, Kate,' I said. 'There's a mortise lock, too, but neither of them has been engaged.'

'Perhaps the intruder had a key,' said Kate.

'Surely it can't have been that easy. It's more likely that the intruder left the door open or, as you say, it was 'loided.'

'Perhaps he left it open on his way out,' said Kate, 'but that doesn't explain how he got in.'

Leaving the enigma of the unlocked door in the hope that it might be explained by Mrs Gregory, I started by looking around the hall. There were a couple of lengths of rope on the floor, presumably those with which Mrs Gregory had been tied up. Nearby was a wad of material that I imagined to be a gag that the killer had used to silence the dead man's wife.

'I hope the lab people can find something of use among that lot,' I said, as Kate and I made our way upstairs.

Dr Henry Mortlock was in the act of packing the tools of his trade into his murder bag. Dave Poole was leaning against a wall, looking his usual chipper self, despite the fact that it was now two o'clock in the morning.

'Whoever he was, guv, he certainly went through this room,' said Dave.

I began a careful visual survey of the room. It was as Kate and Tom Watson had each said. The dressing-table drawers had been pulled out, their contents – mainly Mrs Gregory's colourful underwear – thrown all over the place. The fitted wardrobes were wide open, a man's suits and shirts and a woman's dresses and trouser suits strewn untidily about the room. An empty, open jewellery box lay on the floor near the bed.

In the bed was the body of a man, his head covered in blood.

'While Doctor Mortlock tells me the tale, Dave, go next door and have a few words with Sidney Miller, the guy who found Mrs Gregory in the hall. See what he's got to say. DI Watson will tell you which house is his.'

'Right, guv.' Dave made his way downstairs.

I turned to the pathologist. 'Good morning, Henry.'

'There's nothing bloody good about it,' muttered Mortlock. 'Why the hell can't people be murdered at a respectable hour?'

'My sentiments exactly, Henry. Is there anything you can tell me at this stage?'

'On a superficial examination it looks as though our friend here was bludgeoned to death with a blunt instrument, Harry. I'll be able to tell you more when I get him on the slab. It smells as though he was drunk, too. He reeks of whisky.'

'Blended or malt?' I could smell Scotch even from where I was standing.

'Undoubtedly cheap blended,' said Mortlock, making a point of deliberately ignoring my attempt at humour. 'A supermarket's own brand, I should think.'

'When are you going to do the post-mortem?'

'You chaps are always in such a terrible rush,' complained Mortlock, 'and I suppose you want it done ASAP. I'll make a sacrifice and do it this afternoon. See you at about two o'clock. Usual place.' His face took on a sour expression. 'What a way to spend a Sunday. I should've been playing golf.'

'Never mind, Henry,' I said. 'You'll be making holes instead of filling them.'

'Very funny,' said Mortlock, and with that pithy rejoinder he departed, whistling a few bars from Handel's 'Dead March' from *Saul*.

Linda Mitchell, the senior forensic examiner, came into the room as Mortlock departed. 'Can I start processing this room now, Mr Brock?'

'Yes, it's all yours, Linda. Will it be all right for us to have a look around downstairs?'

'Yes, the fingerprint and photographic people should've finished there by now, but get their OK before you start,' said Linda. 'Incidentally, the whole place is a real wreck. God knows what the burglar was looking for, but he made a thorough job of turning the place upside down.'

When Kate and I reached the sitting room I could see what Linda Mitchell had been talking about. We didn't touch anything because some of the scenes-of-crime guys were still there.

'It's all yours, Mr Brock,' said one of the examiners as he packed up the remainder of his equipment. 'It's a right bloody mess. I've never seen the likes of it.'

I was forced to agree. The cabinet beneath where the television set had stood was open and DVDs and CDs had been spread about the floor. The television set itself had been hurled from the cabinet and now lay face down on the carpet. Both occasional tables had been overturned and the lamps that had been on them thrown to the floor. Two uplighters had suffered a similar fate and were lying across the floor, their glass shades shattered.

The dining room was also a scene of devastation; drawers had been pulled out of the sideboard and left on the floor, and their contents – mainly table linen – scattered over the thick pile carpet. There were pictures on the floor, too, while those that had been left on the walls were askew. In addition, a wine bottle had been emptied on to the carpet. An open, half-full whisky bottle stood on the sideboard. As Mortlock had jokingly suggested, it was a supermarket brand.

Detective Sergeant Flynn appeared in the doorway of the room and for a moment or two stood surveying the substantial damage.

'Jesus!' he exclaimed. 'It's just like a bomb's hit this place. Looks like a job for the anti-terrorist boys, guv?' he suggested jocularly.

'It's one hell of a mess, Charlie.'

'Our intruder certainly had a go at this lot,' said Flynn, 'and the upstairs is probably the same.'

'Apart from the second bedroom, I understand. At least that's where Mrs Gregory is at the moment, so I'm told. I wonder why the burglar left that room undisturbed?'

'I suppose he must've found what he was looking for,' said Flynn.

'It took him long enough,' I mused aloud. 'And I wonder what he was after? I've never come across a villain who made this much mess. I very much doubt that he was a professional. No, Charlie, there's more to this screwing than the usual sort of break-in. He must've been searching for something specific.'

'Maybe Mrs Gregory can shed some light on it, guv,' said Kate. 'It could've been something that the Gregorys didn't want the rest of the world to know about, like a naughty home-made porno DVD or something the intruder could blackmail them with.'

'Slow down, Kate,' I said, although I thought she might have a point. But it didn't do to jump to a hasty conclusion before we'd analysed all the evidence. And there was plenty of that about.

We were joined by Dave Poole.

'What's this neighbour, Sidney Miller, got to say about all this, Dave?' I asked.

'He strikes me as being quite a good witness, guv,' Dave began. 'He said that at about eleven forty-five, just as he was preparing to go to bed, he heard a woman screaming. Being a hot night, all his windows were open and so, he later discovered, were some in the Gregorys' house, but only the upstairs ones. He quickly worked out that the screams were coming from the Gregorys' place. When he got here, he found that the front door was open and Mrs Gregory was lying on the hall floor just inside. He said she was naked and bound with rope around her wrists and ankles. He untied her, and she told Miller that about an hour earlier a man had broken in, grabbed her and then tied her up and gagged her. She then said that the man left, but it took her some considerable time to dislodge the gag from her mouth, and that's when she started screaming.'

'She said the man left?'

'That's what Miller said she'd told him, guv.'

'Did you take a written statement, Dave?'

'Not yet. Miller looked about all in, so I told him to go to bed and that someone would call on him later today to get it all down in writing.'

'Any idea what Miller does for a living?'

'I didn't ask, guv, but I expect he's something to do with an airline or a hotel. From what he was saying, it seems that a lot of the people who live in this area have jobs in and around Heathrow. In fact, he mentioned that Mrs Gregory is an airline stewardess, long haul, and is away from home more often than she's here.'

'What do we know about our murder victim?'

'His name's Clifford Gregory, and Miller thought that he might be an accountant, but he's not sure,' Dave said. 'However, he's fairly certain he's not employed by an airline because he works at home most of the time.'

'We'll see if he's got anything to add to that when we talk to him later today. In the meantime, I'll interview Mrs Gregory if she's sufficiently recovered. In the circumstances, Kate, I think it might be better if you came with me. She's probably a bit fragile after an experience like this and might be more responsive to a woman officer.'

'Maybe,' said Kate cynically.

THREE

We made our way upstairs to the second bedroom at the rear of the house. The curtains were open, as were the windows, and both the bedside lights had been turned on, casting a warm glow throughout the room.

But Kate wasn't about to have our interview stage-managed. She turned on the overhead light, left the windows open, but closed the curtains; it was a still night and there wasn't even a ripple of air to move them.

Sharon Gregory, wearing a white satin robe, her feet curled beneath her, was reclining elegantly on a velvet-covered chaise-longue set against a wall adjacent to the window. An attractive woman, probably in her mid-twenties, she had found the time to prepare for the interview by brushing her long, honey blonde hair and applying lipstick and eye shadow. Despite the fact that it was now half past two in the morning and the windows were open, she was perspiring quite freely.

The woman constable who had been posted there to keep her company was lounging in a nearby chair. She had slackened off the cravat at her neck and undone the top two buttons of her shirt.

'I'm Detective Chief Inspector Brock of New Scotland Yard, Mrs Gregory, and this is Detective Inspector Ebdon. D'you feel up to telling us what happened? From the very beginning.'

'Yes, certainly.' Sharon smiled at me, but then cast a nervous glance in Kate's direction. Kate Ebdon has that unnerving effect on people, especially women and villains, and particularly if the two are combined in one person. In Kate's view everyone is a suspect until proved otherwise.

'You can go now,' Kate said to the woman officer who was still seated, a lack of courtesy that had obviously irritated her.

'At last, thank God!' The PC stood up and stretched. 'I could do with a cup of tea. I'm parched. Well, I'll be off, then,' she said, directing her comment at Kate.

Kate followed the woman officer to the door, out of earshot of

Sharon Gregory. 'It's *ma'am* when you talk to me, young woman, and don't you forget it,' she said, in a menacingly low voice. 'And do up your cravat and button your shirt. You're a bloody disgrace to the uniform.'

'Sorry, ma'am,' said the PC, adjusting her clothing as she fled from the room.

Kate Ebdon could be very hard on her own sex, particularly those in the Job. A flame-haired Australian, she had honed her detective skills as a sergeant on the Flying Squad, where, it was rumoured, she had given pleasure to several male officers; but you shouldn't believe everything that policemen tell you.

Kate was attired in jeans and a man's white shirt, a form of dress that she usually adopted. It was this informal attire that had somewhat irritated our conventional commander when Kate had joined HSCC on promotion to DI; he took the view that an officer reaching the rank of inspector should behave like a lady. Not that there was any doubt that Kate *was* a lady, no matter what she was wearing. Certainly her appearances at the Old Bailey, in a smart blue suit, high-heeled shoes and gold earrings, turned a few male heads, including the judges and members of the legal profession. However the commander didn't see it that way, and when he had suggested that I speak to Kate about her outfit, I had jocularly warned him that this may be seen as either sexism or racism, or both. The commander, a keen devotee of diversity, had taken me seriously and had said no more on the matter.

'Perhaps you would start by telling me where you were when this man broke in, Mrs Gregory,' I began. 'Inspector Ebdon will write down what you say in the form of a statement, and I'll ask you to sign it when we've finished. Are you up to doing that now?'

'Yes, of course. To answer your question, I was in bed with my husband.' Sharon Gregory spoke confidently and seemed perfectly composed, despite the gruelling ordeal she had undergone, to say nothing of the brutal slaying of her husband. 'It must've been about ten o'clock when I heard this noise downstairs and I shook Cliff, but I couldn't wake him.' She paused and cast her eyes down. 'I'm afraid he has a drink problem and he'd had a lot to drink this evening,' she said in a soft voice that was probably intended to inspire sympathy.

But if she was hoping for consolation from Kate, she failed;

Kate wasn't much interested in Sharon Gregory's alcoholic husband, at least not yet. 'Is Cliff his given name?' she asked.

'No, it's actually Clifford, but he's always called Cliff.'

'I'll make that clear in the statement, if that's all right with you.'

'Yes, of course.'

'How long have you been married?' asked Kate, having included the deceased man's full name.

'Seven years,' said Sharon promptly.

'Are you saying that you couldn't wake up your husband because he was drunk?' Kate wanted to be absolutely clear on the point.

'I'm afraid so. He often went to bed in that state, I'm sorry to say.' A few forced tears rolled down Sharon's face and she reached across to a box of tissues. 'In the circumstances I had no alternative but to go downstairs myself, but I was a bit scared.'

'What were you wearing, Sharon? You don't mind if I call you Sharon, do you?'

'Not at all, Inspector. And I wasn't wearing anything.'

'I see. So, you went downstairs completely naked to find out what this noise was. Is that correct?' Kate stared at Sharon, clearly wanting to confirm what, in her view, was strange behaviour for any woman. Especially one who had claimed to be 'a bit scared'.

'I don't see that there was anything wrong in that.' Sharon lifted her chin slightly, almost giving the impression of defiance. 'My husband and I never wear nightclothes, especially in weather like this. It is awfully hot, isn't it?' She smiled and fanned herself with her left hand. The hand bore neither an engagement ring nor a wedding ring, not that that meant a great deal these days.

'And you didn't think to put on a robe?'

'No, why should I? I often walk about with nothing on. Anyway, it's our house, and I honestly didn't think the noise was anything serious. It was just something I'd heard. I thought it could even have been something outside because all the windows were open; we get a lot of noise from people going home from the pub. But I had to satisfy myself that everything was all right, otherwise I'd never have got back to sleep again. I'm sure you know how it is.'

'When you say that all the windows were open, did that include the downstairs windows?' asked Kate, who knew perfectly well that they were closed. At least, they had been when we arrived.

And when Miller, the next-door neighbour, had spoken to Dave, he'd said that they were closed when he'd arrived. But Kate knew the value of checking everything a witness said. And then checking it again.

'No, of course not. Everyone living in this area takes part in Neighbourhood Watch. And we've been told all about crime prevention by the local home-beat policewoman.'

'Oh, well, that's all right, then,' said Kate quietly, but her sarcasm was apparent to me if not to Sharon Gregory. Kate shared the view of most police officers: that the scheme was pointless and time-wasting. It had actually degenerated into a system of telling people about crimes long after they'd been committed, and that was of no value at all in terms of *preventing* crime.

'Please carry on, Sharon,' I said.

'I had a look round downstairs, and when I went into the sitting room there was this man standing there.'

'Did you recognize the man?'

'No, of course not. I'd never set eyes on him before. Anyway, he was wearing a mask. The sight of him terrified me and I screamed. Then he stepped towards me and put his hand over my mouth. He said that if I didn't be quiet he'd kill me.'

'What sort of mask was it?'

Sharon spent a few moments thinking about that. 'It looked as though it was a stocking what he'd pulled over his head,' she said after a short pause.

'What colour was it?' I asked. For no particular reason I made a mental note of her grammatical slip. 'Black, brown?'

Sharon hesitated. 'I'm sorry, but I can't remember. It was such a shock seeing him there in my house that I felt violated.' Once more, she cast her eyes down, but then looked up, a coy expression on her face.

'Did this man say anything else, after he'd told you to be quiet?'

'No. I asked him what he wanted and why he was there, but he didn't say another word.'

'What sort of accent did he have? Was it local, or maybe North Country? Scottish or Welsh perhaps, or even foreign?'

'I don't know. I didn't pay too much attention. I was so scared.'

'Can you describe him? What he was wearing, how tall he was, if he was stocky.'

'He was quite tall; about your height, I should think,' said Sharon, glancing at me. 'And he was quite slim. He was wearing a black sweater and jeans – genuine Levis, I think – and trainers.'

'D'you remember anything about the trainers?' asked Kate.

There was no hesitation before Sharon replied, 'They were black with light green soles. Oh yes, they were Nikes. They had, like, that tick trademark on the side what they all have.'

Again Sharon made a syntactic error and that prompted a question.

'Where were you born, Sharon?' I asked.

'Oh, I'm a Home Counties girl.'

'Yes, but where exactly?'

Sharon paused before replying. 'Basildon,' she said quietly. 'It's in Essex.' She spoke reluctantly, as though her birthplace was something of which she should be ashamed.

'What happened next?' I asked.

'He grabbed hold of me.'

'But hadn't he already got hold of you?' Kate paused and waggled her pen in the air. 'You said that he'd put his hand over your mouth.'

'Yes, but then he held me really tight.'

'How did he do that?' I asked. 'Did he take hold of your arms?' I was beginning to have doubts about this story. I had interviewed many victims of violent crime, and to my experienced ear her account sounded as though it had been carefully rehearsed. It was much more detailed than I would have expected. Then again, shock has some strange effects. Perhaps she was babbling on in a mistaken attempt to be helpful.

'At first, yes. He held me really tight,' she said again. 'I was terrified. Then he swung me round and got hold of me by the waist. At least, I think he did, but it all happened so fast. He picked me up – he was very strong – and carried me into the hall, stood me down and then forced me on to the floor. Then he tied me up and stuffed a rag in my mouth. It was dreadful, Mr Brock. I was frightened to death. I was sure he was going to rape me.' Sharon looked down demurely as she spoke of her apprehension. 'Or even attack me with a knife,' she added, looking up again. 'It was all quite awful. I was choking a bit and I think I must've fainted, but I can't remember how long I was out.'

'Did he have a knife, then?' I asked. 'You said you thought he might attack you with one.'

'I don't know,' said Sharon, 'but don't people like that usually carry a knife?'

'Is it true that you're an airline stewardess?' asked Kate. From the dramatic fashion in which Sharon Gregory was describing the events of the night, it had crossed Kate's mind that the woman might be an actress.

'Yes, I am. But we're actually called airline cabin crew. I'm usually on the long haul to Miami out of Heathrow.'

'Getting back to this assault, Sharon, exactly how did this man tie you up?'

'He knelt down and put a knee in my back and forced my arms behind me and then he tied my wrists and ankles together and then he—'

'Hold on. Slow down a minute.' Kate was recording Sharon's account on a statement form as fast as she was able to write in an attempt to keep up with the woman's story.

'Did he bring this rope with him?' I asked.

Sharon Gregory appeared to be nonplussed by the question. 'I suppose he must've done,' she said eventually. 'I honestly don't know where it came from.'

'Go on.'

'The next thing I heard was him crashing around the house as though he was searching for something.'

'Did you see him leave?'

'No, but I think I must've fainted again. When I came round I managed to push the gag out of my mouth with my tongue and I started screaming at the top of my voice.'

'Didn't you think that this intruder might still be in the house and would come back to attack you, or even kill you?'

'I wasn't thinking. Anyway, a few minutes later Sid came in through the front door and untied me.'

'My sergeant has spoken to Mr Miller,' I said, 'and Miller claims that you told him that the man had already left. Is that true?'

'Did I say that? I really don't know. I was so confused and frightened by the whole business that I didn't know what I was saying half the time.'

'How did this man get in?' I asked.

'I don't really know,' said Sharon. 'Through the front door, I suppose.'

'Wasn't it locked, then?'

'I thought it was.' Sharon looked directly at me. 'I leave that sort of thing to my husband. He always makes sure the house is secure.'

'Who closed the downstairs windows?'

'I did. My husband forgot.'

'Did he perhaps also forget to lock the front door?'

'I suppose it's possible. I didn't think to check.'

'Did the intruder take anything?' asked Kate, switching the subject again.

'My jewellery,' Sharon replied without hesitating.

'How did you know that? You were tied up.' Kate stopped writing and looked up, smiling to mask her suspicion – a suspicion that was growing stronger as Sharon's account unfolded.

'Well, Mr Miller had a look round the house to make sure that the burglar really had gone.'

'This is your neighbour, the same Sidney Miller, that you're talking about, is it?' I asked.

'Yes, he and his wife Janet are very good friends of ours. Of me and poor Cliff, that is.' Sharon stifled a sob. 'I followed him upstairs to the master bedroom and it was then that I saw Cliff. I was sure he was dead and Sid felt his pulse and said that he was. I must admit that I screamed hysterically at the sight of my poor husband lying there covered in blood, and I fainted.'

'You mentioned that this man took your jewellery, Sharon,' prompted Kate impatiently.

'When I came to, I saw that my jewellery box was on the floor near my head. It was empty.'

'You hadn't noticed it there when you first entered the room?'

'No, but I didn't really know what I was doing.'

'Presumably you'd put on a robe before following your neighbour upstairs, Sharon.' Kate was doing what she always did: returning to an earlier statement to see if the story had changed.

'I think so. Yes, of course I did.'

'Where was this robe?'

'Er, in this room.'

'Do you sleep in this room, then?' Kate glanced at the undisturbed bed.

'No, I sleep with my husband.'

'But the robe was in this room. Is that correct?'

'Yes, it's a spare one I keep in here.' Sharon plucked at the front of her robe. 'This one.'

'So there should be another robe in the master bedroom?'

'Yes, I'm sure there is. Well, there must be, I've got more than one.'

'So when did you come up here to get the one you're wearing?'

It was obvious to me that Kate was interested in this business of the robes. But knowing Kate, I sensed that her interest went far deeper than that.

'Straight after Sid untied me,' said Sharon.

'You didn't look into the main bedroom to see if your husband had been disturbed or even attacked?'

'No – well, I didn't know whether the man was still here.'

'Just now you said that Mr Miller had already had a look around the house and he'd told you the man had gone. Apart from which, Mr Miller told one of my officers that when he untied you, *you told him* that the man had gone.'

'Did I? I must've got mixed up.' Sharon started to cry again, and grabbed a handful of tissues. 'It's all been such a terrible shock,' she said, 'and you're confusing me.'

Kate looked at the ceiling in exasperation. Sharon Gregory's dramatic performance might've impressed a gullible man, but it wasn't having any effect on Kate.

'Did Mr Miller come up here with you?' asked Kate, when Sharon had recovered.

'No, he stayed downstairs until I'd got my robe and gone back down again. Then we started to look round the house together. I can't really remember what I did or what order I did it in. I was so frightened and upset about having found that this man had murdered my poor husband that I didn't really know what I was doing.'

'Did you hear anything after this man had tied you up, apart from the noise of him crashing around the house? Did you, for example, hear a car starting up, or perhaps later on, after you'd recovered from your faint?'

'No, I'm afraid not.'

'I think that'll do for the time being, Sharon,' I said. 'Now perhaps you'd carefully read the statement that Inspector Ebdon has taken down. You can make any changes you want to, and then perhaps you'd sign it.'

Kate handed over the several sheets of paper and a pen. 'Put in your date of birth at the top of the form, Sharon. You'll see a space for it.'

'Do I have to?' Sharon Gregory fluttered her eyelashes and once again assumed a coy expression. She seemed to be very good at coy expressions.

'Yes, please,' said Kate firmly, unmoved by the woman's shrinking-violet artifice.

Sharon Gregory took a few minutes to read the statement. 'I'm not sure about the bit where I said that I came up here first to get my robe. I think perhaps I was wandering around in the nude . . .' She glanced at me as she said that, and smiled.

'Let me get this straight. Are you now saying that you were walking around the house with your male neighbour, but you don't think you had any clothes on?' asked Kate sharply.

'I can't really remember. As I said, I was confused and frightened.' Sharon shot another shy smile in my direction.

Kate took back the statement and made the necessary alteration. 'There we are. Now perhaps you'd sign it at the bottom of each page, Sharon.' She handed the woman the sheaf of forms and proffered a pen.

Without another word, Sharon scribbled her signature in the places Kate had indicated.

'We'll undoubtedly have to talk to you again soon, Sharon,' I said.

'Yes, I suppose so,' said the woman, but I got the impression that she was not relishing the prospect of another interview.

'When are you next due on duty?' I asked.

'Not until Wednesday afternoon.'

'One other thing, Sharon,' said Kate, as we stood up to leave. 'Would you mind just pulling up your sleeves?'

Sharon didn't query this request and did as she was asked.

'And now your ankles.' Kate stepped closer and examined the woman's wrists and ankles. 'Thank you, Sharon,' she said. 'I should get some rest now, if I were you. Can I get someone to bring you a cup of tea?'

'That would be nice, thank you. Then I think I'll try to get some sleep.'

'Tell me, Sharon, was your husband's life insured?' asked Kate. It was the sort of barbed question that she was very good at posing, and she asked it almost as a throwaway query. As though it were of no real importance.

'Yes, thank goodness, but unfortunately it's only for twenty thousand pounds. Cliff took it out when we were married and I don't think he bothered to increase the amount. I've always left the financial side of things to him. He's very good at it, being an accountant. Still,' continued Sharon, 'this house is worth quite a bit and I'll probably have to sell it now. I really don't know what I'm going to do.' Her last statement was accompanied by a suitably sad expression.

We left it at that, but I determined that I'd get DS Flynn, who had previously served on the Fraud Squad, to look into the Gregorys' financial affairs.

I was unhappy about the statement that Kate had just taken. Somehow it didn't seem to hang together, and I began to wonder if we were dealing with something more complex than a straightforward break-in that ended up as a murder. The possibility that was foremost in my mind was that the so-called intruder was actually an accomplice and that he and Sharon had arranged the whole thing. But we had a long way to go before we could prove that.

FOUR

Downstairs in the hall, Kate sought out the woman PC who had earlier been sitting with Sharon Gregory. 'Get a cup of tea organized for Mrs Gregory and take it up to her, would you, please?' she said.

'Yes, ma'am,' said the WPC, and turned to go. If she thought that making cups of tea wasn't included in her job description, she had yet to learn that care of victims was an important part of police duty. But she didn't comment, probably from fear of annoying Kate again.

'Don't run away just yet,' said Kate. 'While you were baby-sitting Mrs Gregory, did she say anything about what had happened?'

'Only that she'd been frightened out of her life when the man appeared, ma'am. She said she thought he was going to rape her. And then she said she hoped he wouldn't come back again.'

'Did she say anything about having been naked the whole time this was going on?'

'She did say that she was naked when she first saw the man in the hall, ma'am.'

'In the *hall*?' queried Kate. 'She didn't say that the man was in the sitting room?'

'No, ma'am, she said he was in the hall.'

'Are you absolutely sure about that?'

'Yes, ma'am.'

'Give me your book,' said Kate, holding out her hand. 'Why isn't there anything here to that effect?' she asked, having read the last few entries.

'I didn't think it was important, ma'am.'

'And who the hell are you to decide whether it's important?' snapped Kate. 'For all you know, it could be vital evidence. Well, put it in your book now. And when you're called to give evidence at the Old Bailey or wherever, you'll say that I directed you to put it there and that you only put it there some time after the statement was made by Mrs Gregory because I had to tell you to do so. Clear?'

'Yes, ma'am.' The WPC spent a few moments making notes and handed the book back to Kate.

Kate read through the entry and then signed it, adding the date and time. 'You need to note everything a victim says to you, young lady, especially at the scene of a murder. Got that? And if defence counsel asks why you didn't make the entry earlier, you'll have to admit that you failed to do your job properly, won't you?'

'Yes, ma'am.'

'Good. Now get Mrs Gregory her tea.'

As I said earlier, Kate could be very hard on her own sex. But above all else, she was a good detective and knew the value of apparently inconsequential statements made by anybody immediately after a crime had been committed. Especially those made by the victim.

Linda Mitchell appeared in the hall from the kitchen. 'I thought I'd bring you up to date, Mr Brock.'

'Anything interesting so far, Linda?'

'There are obviously fingerprints all over the place and it'll take some time for Fingerprint Bureau to come up with any matches. And there's this.' Linda held up a plastic evidence bag. 'It looks like the jewellery that Mrs Gregory said was stolen.'

'Where on earth did you find it?' I asked.

Linda smiled. 'On a shelf in the garage behind some pots of paint, would you believe? I'll have it checked for prints, not that I hold out much hope of finding any.'

'But why would someone steal jewellery and then hide it in the garage?' I asked. 'What d'you make of that, Kate?'

'If he did,' said Kate. 'On the other hand, it might not be the real thing,' she suggested. 'And when he realized that it was value-less he dumped it.'

'But why bother to put it in the garage?' I asked. 'Why not just leave it anywhere. Having looked round the house, I doubt that he was too worried about being untidy.'

'I can tell you now that it's not valuable,' said Linda. 'The necklace might look like gold, but it isn't. The stones aren't diamonds either – they're crystal – although they have the appear-ance of being the real thing at a first glance. I'd say that she'd get away with it in a room with soft lighting, but an expert would spot the difference immediately.'

'Any other surprises?'

'Yes, I found a window sash weight in the garage as well, and what appears to be an almost new clothes line, but a length has been cut from it. They were also secreted on a shelf behind paint tins, along with the jewellery. I'll keep you posted on anything else we find.'

'Could the rope that was used to tie up Mrs Gregory have come from that clothes line?'

'It's possible, Mr Brock, but I shan't know for certain until the lab's carried out a few tests on it and conducted a comparison with Mrs Gregory's bonds that were found in the hall.'

'Thanks, Linda. Is it all right if Kate and I have a thorough look round the rest of the house now? We had a cursory glance earlier, but your chaps were still at work in some of the rooms.'

'They've finished dusting for prints now and the video chap's got all he needs. You'll find Sergeant Poole around here somewhere. I think he's made a start.'

We began with the ransacked sitting room and found Dave having a look around. Kate and I sat down on a sofa to compare notes and Dave took a seat in an armchair opposite us.

'What d'you think, Kate?'

'I think the widow Gregory's one carney little bitch who seems to have a habit of fainting every five minutes. And she was very composed when we were talking to her. Too bloody composed in my view.' Kate was clearly not taken in by Sharon Gregory's simpering pose. 'I think she's lying through her teeth. Her account was much too detailed. If she was as terrified as she claimed to be, she came up with a pretty good description of this mysterious guy's jeans and trainers. One minute she said she was scared out of her wits, but the next she said she didn't think the noise was anything serious. And if she didn't like the question, she claimed to have fainted. Again!'

'Do I get the impression that you didn't like her, guv?' asked Dave, addressing himself to Kate.

'Got it in one, mate, but overall I'm not too impressed by her story,' said Kate. 'She was a bit too vague when I pressed her, and she wasn't red-eyed as if she'd been crying her eyes out when she discovered her husband had been topped. And when I had a look at her wrists there were no signs of rope burns, which is what I'd've expected to find if she was tied up in the way she described and had attempted to escape. There were no marks on her ankles either.'

'Perhaps she wasn't tied up very tightly,' I suggested. 'What did Miller have to say about it, Dave?'

'All he said was that when he found her she was secured with rope around her wrists and ankles, guv, and she was lying on her side. He didn't enlarge on it.'

'We'll see if he can tell us a bit more when we have a word with him later on.'

'I told him you'd probably want to interview him this afternoon,' said Dave.

'I wonder what this intruder was searching for?' I said, turning back to Kate. 'He certainly tore the place apart, but he doesn't appear to have taken any of the things I'd've expected a burglar to take. The TV is still here and so is the DVD recorder, albeit both chucked on the floor. And there are some easily portable items around the house that he could have fenced without raising too much suspicion.'

'She did say that her jewellery was missing,' said Kate.

'Yes, but why turn out all the cupboards and drawers and throw CDs and DVDs about the place? And why overturn tables and lamps? Any housebreaker worth his salt would probably go straight for the bedroom if all he wanted was jewellery. Of course we shan't know whether he took anything else until Mrs Gregory's had a chance to see what's missing.'

'There's something else, too,' Kate said. 'This bit about her wandering around the house completely naked with Miller, the man from next door. Seems a strange thing for a woman to do, if what she said is true. Unless,' she added, 'she's having a fling with him.'

'Or he was the accomplice,' said Dave cynically.

'Perhaps she likes to show off her body,' I suggested lamely.

'But only if there's a man around to admire her,' responded Kate cuttingly. 'You're not going soft on her because she's a good-looking bird, are you, guv?'

'She's not my type,' I said. 'Although I could understand a lot of men being taken in by her. Sharon Gregory is certainly a woman who oozes sex appeal.'

'To repeat what I said before, in my opinion it's a put-up job,' said Kate. 'I reckon that this intruder, if he exists at all, was an accomplice. And, as Dave said, it might've been Miller. I haven't worked it out yet, but I reckon Sharon's scared of this guy, whoever he is, in a different way than she expressed. But if that's the case, what was the motive?'

'The murder of Sharon Gregory's husband,' said Dave bluntly, as usual encapsulating a valid reason in a few words. 'The classic elimination of one side of the eternal triangle.'

'Maybe,' I said thoughtfully. 'Let's assume that the mysterious intruder is having an affair with Sharon and they jointly decided to get rid of boring old Clifford. But we'll need a lot more evidence before we've got enough to arrest Sharon for conspiracy to murder. And it would be useful to know if she was cheating on her husband. And if so, with whom.'

'There's another thing,' said Kate. 'I had a look in the master bedroom and there wasn't another robe in there. So the one Sharon was wearing wasn't kept in the second bedroom. What's more, there was a pair of trainers in the bottom of the wardrobe that were exactly the same as the Nikes that she said the intruder was wearing.'

'The intruder wouldn't have taken them off and put them in there, surely?' I said.

'No, but for want of a description, Sharon probably decided to describe her husband's trainers just to bolster up her story.'

'Yes, you're right,' I said reflectively, 'she's lying, but I've yet to work out the reason.'

Leaving Kate to get DI Tom Watson's account of what he'd found when he'd arrived to do his preliminary survey, Dave and I began a detailed examination of the downstairs rooms. The result was much the same in each: the place had been thoroughly ransacked. And the more I saw of it, the less I was convinced that it was a professional job.

The study on the ground floor was clearly where Clifford Gregory had worked. A state-of-the-art computer was on the workstation, along with all manner of hi-tech equipment – far more than seemed necessary for an accountant. A small filing cabinet stood next to it, but it appeared that Gregory had tried to keep paper to a minimum in his office. I don't think our dear commander would have taken to him at all. It was mildly interesting that there were at least twenty model aeroplanes suspended from the ceiling, most of which were warplanes of the two world wars. I certainly spotted a Sopwith Camel and a German Fokker *dreidecker* among them.

'Looks like Clifford Gregory's into making model aircraft,' said Dave, stating the obvious. 'A bit of an anorak as well as a computer nerd, if that equipment of his is anything to go by.'

We finished touring the house, but learned little more that was likely to be of use to our investigation.

'It seems very strange that this intruder took the place apart, Dave,' I said once again, 'but apparently only took the jewellery. And then left it in the garage.'

'Left it in the garage?' queried Dave, who had not been a party to my earlier conversation with Linda.

'Yes, Linda found it on a shelf behind some paint pots, along with a window sash weight and a clothes line. But she reckons the tomfoolery is worthless. I've a feeling there's something not quite right with all this. And Sharon seemed perfectly in control of herself when she was telling the tale, but it didn't hang together somehow. I'm beginning to wonder if it was just that: a tale that she made up as she went along.'

'I think Miss Ebdon's right, guv,' said Dave. 'There's certainly more to this whole business than meets the eye. I reckon he took the jewellery and hid it along with the sash weight and the clothes line rather than run the risk of being stopped by police in the middle of the night with a bloodstained sash weight in his possession. That'd take a bit of explaining. And all of that points to the primary motive being murder, not burglary.'

'I think you're right, Dave. She knew the accomplice. When we get back to the office, see if you can track down the security officer for the airline Sharon Gregory works for. He's bound to be ex-Job, and he might be able to tell us something. I'd be particularly interested to know if he's heard anything about her having any admirers.'

'A racing certainty, I should think,' said Dave. 'Sexy young bird like that married to a fat anorak.'

Having decided that we'd done all we could for the time being, I rounded up the rest of the team and we headed back to the factory, as CID officers are wont to call their office.

It was almost half past nine on that same Sunday morning by the time we got back to Empress State Building. Two months ago, for some reason best known only to the hierarchy of the Metropolitan Police, but probably as a result of budget cuts, it had been decided to move our offices from Curtis Green in Whitehall, which was now rumoured to become the fourth Scotland Yard. Over a period of two days of glorious mayhem we had been shifted to an inaccessible monolithic abomination in Lillie Road, Earls Court. The only person to be pleased was the commander, who had acquired a larger office, and with it a second filing cabinet.

Detective Sergeant Colin Wilberforce, the incident room manager, had already arrived, early as usual, in order to relieve Gavin Creasey, the night-duty man. Always immaculately attired, Wilberforce was an administrative master with an encyclopaedic knowledge of the particular enquiry on which we were engaged. He had been completely unfazed by the move from Whitehall, and his little empire had been fully operational within an hour of our arrival in Earls Court. His desk was a classic example of orderliness and I had only to ask him for a particular statement or report and it was on my desk within minutes.

'I'm set up and ready to go on this Gregory enquiry, sir. But do you think we're likely to need HOLMES?' Wilberforce looked up enquiringly.

'Not at the moment, Colin, but we'll have to wait and see how this one pans out,' I said. HOLMES, the Home Office Large Major Enquiry System, was installed whenever the police were faced with an investigation that was likely to be complicated and wide-ranging. Its value lay in those cases where we were dealing with a suspected serial killer who might have committed several murders spread over more than one police force area. 'Although this particular job is unusual, I doubt that we're dealing with a mass murderer. Nevertheless, I'm keeping my options open.'

While this conversation had been going on, the other members of my team had been standing around awaiting further instructions. For those of them who had not been at the Gregorys' house in

West Drayton, or privy to the finer points of what we knew so far, I briefed them on the situation.

'Sergeant Poole is already tracking down the security officer of the airline Mrs Gregory worked for,' I continued, 'and I want the usual house-to-house enquiries made in the vain hope that someone might have seen something or heard something. It might also be useful to discover if any of them knew the Gregorys. If they did, ask what sort of people they were. Did they have fights, hold parties, or did they keep themselves to themselves? Speak to the local nick in case police have ever been called to a domestic, or another break-in. See if you can find out if Sharon Gregory had a reputation for putting herself about or if they had ever seen a man, other than Clifford Gregory, calling at the house at any time. There must've been people in the street at that time of a Saturday evening, especially as there's a pub nearby, and particularly as it was a hot night. Perhaps you'd oversee that, Len. You know the sort of thing we're interested in.' Detective Inspector Len Driscoll was one of the three inspectors on my team.

'Right, guv,' said Driscoll, making a few notes on a clipboard.

'This afternoon, Dave Poole and I will interview Sidney Miller, the neighbour who found Mrs Gregory all trussed up like a chicken – after we've paid Doctor Mortlock a visit at his carvery.'

'There's more to this death than was at first apparent at the scene, Harry,' said Dr Henry Mortlock, when we arrived at the mortuary at two o'clock that same day. A day that was proving to be far too long and was not yet over.

'This job's turning out to be full of surprises, Henry,' I said. 'And I suppose you've got another one for me.'

'You could say that.' Chuckling ominously, Mortlock led Dave and me across the white-walled room to where Clifford Gregory's naked body had been laid out on a stainless steel table. 'There are two superficial wounds to the skull, here and here,' he said, pointing with a pair of forceps. 'And although they were enough to have stunned him and produce a lot of blood that must've splashed on the killer, they weren't sufficient to have killed him. I would surmise that the blows were struck by a woman rather than a man. But I'm really only guessing.'

'So what did kill him, Henry?'

'Asphyxia.'

'Was he strangled?' I asked.

'No. The most likely method was suffocation. When I examined the body in situ, I noticed that although he was lying with his head on a bloodstained pillow, there was another one on the floor. That pillow had bloodstains on the underside, which probably means it was moved *after* the blows to the head were made. It might be as well if you got the scientific people to examine all the pillows in the room. Traces of saliva or mucus might be found on one of them. But whether such traces are found or not, there's no doubt in my mind that Gregory was suffocated, not bludgeoned to death. And there's one other thing that may interest you, Harry,' said Mortlock, peering at me over his rimless spectacles. 'Clifford Gregory had had a vasectomy.'

'Fascinating, but probably irrelevant,' I said. 'Incidentally, his wife said that he was drunk. She complained that he had a drink problem.'

'I doubt that somehow. His liver and other organs showed no signs of his having been a heavy drinker. And I found no trace of alcohol in his stomach, although there were traces of recently ingested cocoa. As I said at the time, there was a strong smell of alcohol surrounding the body, almost as if it had been sprinkled over him post-mortem.'

'That's interesting,' I said. 'When we examined the master bedroom there was no sign of a cup or a mug. And there were no washed-up cups or mugs on the draining board in the kitchen. And no dirty Scotch glasses either.'

'That's your problem rather than mine, Harry,' said Mortlock. 'However . . .' He paused and beamed, rather like a stage magician about to pull off an astonishing trick. 'I examined a sample of the victim's hair and it showed traces of the drug Rohypnol.'

'What, the date-rape drug?' I said.

'The very same,' said Mortlock. 'But in this case it was used to sedate the victim, thus making him defenceless against attack. And before you ask, Harry, Rohypnol's easily obtainable on the Internet if you know where to look.'

'It looks as though Mrs Gregory's story is beginning to unravel,' said Dave.

He was right. It was now becoming clear that Sharon's account of what had occurred had an increasing number of inconsistencies. I determined that she would be interviewed again, preferably at a police station, when I hoped she could be persuaded to reveal the name of her accomplice, because I was bloody sure there was one. But first, it was necessary to get Sidney Miller's detailed account of what had occurred.

FIVE

That afternoon, we drove back to West Drayton. This year's model of a Lexus IS was parked on Sidney Miller's drive, and Dave stopped briefly to admire it.

'This guy's not in the Job, that's for sure,' said Dave, running a hand over the bonnet of the car.

'Stop drooling, Dave,' I said as I rang the bell.

'Ah, I've been expecting you. You're the coppers dealing with Cliff's murder, aren't you?' said Miller, as he opened the door. He was a stocky, cheerful man, probably in his forties.

'Yes,' I said. 'I'm Detective Chief Inspector Brock and this is Detective Sergeant Poole.'

'Yes, of course. I met Sergeant Poole in the wee small hours. This is a dreadful business. You don't expect your next-door neighbour to be killed like that. Car accidents I can understand, but not murder. Of course, you hear about murders all the time these days, but you never think of them happening next door. It really turned my stomach seeing poor old Cliff lying there all covered in blood. God knows how it must've affected Sharon. Is she all right?'

'She seems to be holding up,' I said. In fact I thought she was holding up all too well.

'Come on in.' Miller led us into a large, pleasantly furnished sitting room with a couple of sofas, two or three armchairs, a long coffee table, an iPod player and a 40-inch television set. Dave looked around and nodded enviously.

'Make yourselves comfortable,' said Miller. 'I was just about to have some tea. D'you fancy some?'

'Thank you, yes,' I said. 'I hope we haven't kept you from your work, Mr Miller.'

'Kept me from my work?' Miller shot me a puzzled look and then chuckled. 'I'm a plumber, guv'nor, but I don't work on Sundays. Unlike you blokes.'

'Of course,' I said with a laugh. 'I'd quite forgotten that it was still Sunday.'

'I suppose it happens in your job,' said Miller. 'Hang on, and I'll get the missus to organize the tea.'

'A plumber!' exclaimed Dave, after Miller had left the room. 'I knew I'd made a wrong career choice, guv. I'd never be able to afford a car like his.'

'Didn't you notice it last night?'

'It was dark, *sir.*' Dave always called me 'sir' when I'd posed a fatuous question.

'Right, the tea will be here soon.' Miller returned, rubbing his hands together, and took a seat opposite us. 'Now then, gents, what d'you want to know?'

'Perhaps you could run through exactly what happened last night, Mr Miller. Right from when you heard the screaming that attracted your attention. Sergeant Poole will take down what you say in the form of a written statement, and then I'll ask you to sign it.'

'Yeah, sure. It must've been about a quarter to midnight. The missus had already gone to bed, but I'd stayed up late to watch some crap on the TV. I don't know why I bothered really. There's never anything worth watching these days, and it's mostly repeats. Anyway, I'd just turned off the telly and was about to shut the downstairs windows before going up to bed when I heard this screaming. It was really loud, but not the sort of screams you hear when a group of drunken tarts are making their way home after a night of binge drinking, if you know what I mean. And we get quite a lot of that, our road being a short cut from the nearest pub to a council estate.'

'Mrs Gregory told us about the pub,' I said.

'Well, at first that's what I thought it was, and so I—'

'Could you go a bit slower, Mr Miller,' said Dave, looking up from the statement form on which he was writing. 'I'm having a job keeping up with you.'

'Oh, sorry, yes. I forgot you chaps have to write everything down, even though Mr Brock just told me. As a matter of fact, I thought about joining your lot when I left school, but all that paperwork would do my head in. So I got an apprenticeship with a plumber. Best decision I ever made. And it pays better.'

'All right, Mr Miller, carry on,' said Dave. 'I've caught up with you now.'

'OK. So I went outside to see what it was all about, and realized straight away that it was coming from Cliff and Sharon's house. Their front door was open; well, not so much open as slightly ajar really. I went in and there was poor Sharon lying on the floor all tied up.'

At that point we were interrupted by the arrival of a well-endowed faux blonde bearing a tray of tea. She appeared to be quite a bit younger than her husband and I put her age at about thirty. Even so, the skirt she was wearing was too short and a bit too tight to suit her figure, and her make-up was definitely over the top; there was certainly an excessive amount of green eye shadow.

'Oh, this is the wife,' said Miller. 'These gents are from Scotland Yard dealing with poor Cliff's murder, doll.'

'Oh, that's nice,' said Miller's wife, seemingly unimpressed by our arrival or the reason for our being there. 'I'll leave you to do the honours, Sid.' She put the tray on a coffee table. 'Unless you want to ask me something about it,' she said, smiling at me.

'Do you know anything about what happened, Mrs Miller?' I asked.

'No, dear, I must've slept right through it all. I'm such a heavy sleeper that Sid always has a job waking me up in the morning. But it was the police sirens and all the noise outside that eventually brought me to life. I never knew nothing about it till Sid got back and told me what'd happened. Terrible, isn't it?' Miller's wife glanced at me and turned towards the door.

'Thanks, doll,' said Miller to his wife's departing back. 'Now then, gents, what's next?' he asked, as he poured the tea and handed it round.

'How exactly was Mrs Gregory tied up?' asked Dave.

'Now, let me see.' Miller took out a packet of cigarettes and offered it to Dave and me.

'No thanks, Mr Miller.' I'd been trying to give up for ages and managed to resist this latest temptation. Even my old schoolmaster's story of his brother's untimely death as a result of smoking-induced lung cancer had failed to have the required effect. But at least I wasn't smoking as many as I used to. I suppose that's progress of a sort.

'Thank you,' said Dave, accepting a cigarette. He'd given up giving up. 'You were about to tell us how Mrs Gregory was tied up.'

'Oh yes. She was lying on her side and her hands were tied behind her, round her wrists, and there was another piece of rope tying her ankles together.'

'How tightly was the rope tied, Mr Miller?' I asked, bearing in mind what Kate Ebdon had said about the lack of rope burns.

'Now that you mention it, not very tight,' said Miller thoughtfully. 'Not that I realized it at the time. The rope round her ankles was reasonably tight, but the rope round her wrists was not really tied at all. Sort of loose, if you know what I mean.'

'What exactly do you mean?' asked Dave.

'It was more like two loops that had been tied beforehand and slipped over her hands and on to her wrists. I was able to slide them off quite easily; I didn't have to undo the knots.'

'Are you quite sure about that, Mr Miller?' I asked. When we had examined the ropes, they had all been untied. If what Miller said was true, Mrs Gregory must've untied the wrist ropes between Miller finding her and our arrival on the scene. I made a mental note to ask Tom Watson about it.

'Positive,' said Miller.

'And what about the gag?' I asked. 'She told us that she'd managed to dislodge it, and that's when she'd started screaming.'

'I s'pose that's right. There was a bit of cloth on the floor near her head, so that's what must've happened. It looked like a piece of a tea towel.'

'What did she say after you'd freed her?' asked Dave.

'She wasn't making much sense, but she muttered something about a man breaking in and tying her up. She told me the man had gone, but I had a quick look round to make sure she was right.'

'And I presume he had?'

'Long since, I should think,' said Miller, 'but he hadn't half made a mess of the place.'

'And you're quite sure that she said the man had already left?' said Dave.

'Absolutely.'

'Changing the subject,' I said, 'what sort of couple were the Gregorys?'

'Normal, I s'pose,' said Miller. 'Kept themselves to themselves, if you know what I mean. Sharon's away a lot on account of her being an air hostess, and Cliff's an accountant, I think. He seems to do most of his work on a computer at home. And he certainly knows his stuff when it comes to computers. He fixed mine once when it went belly-up on me. Plumbers and computers don't always mix well. You can't fix a computer with a blowlamp. Give me water and pipes every time.'

'Did they get on, Cliff and Sharon?' It struck me that an air hostess and an accountant seemed a strange match. But it takes all sorts.

'As far as I know. Mind you, they were an odd couple. She's what I'd call a party girl. Loved getting around, so I've heard, but old Cliff was a bit of a stick-in-the-mud. He'd rather stay at home watching TV and making his model aeroplanes.'

'Did they have disagreements about their social life? Or lack of it.'

'I never heard them arguing, if that's what you mean. Mind you, Sharon spends a lot of time away on account of her job.'

'Sharon Gregory said that you and your wife were very good friends with her and her husband.'

'Really? I don't know where she got that idea from. We hardly ever spoke to them. We're just neighbourly, if you know what I mean. Pass the time of day whenever we see them. The usual sort of thing.'

'She also told us that her husband was a heavy drinker. Did you know anything about that?' I knew, from what Henry Mortlock had said, that this was unlikely, but I was interested to hear if Sharon had ever complained that her husband drank to excess.

'I find that hard to believe somehow. I asked Cliff if he fancied going for a drink down the local pub once, when Sharon was away, but he turned me down. He said he didn't drink much and didn't like pubs anyway. As a matter of fact, we invited him and Sharon in for a drink last Christmas Eve and Cliff only had the one glass of champagne. No, he's not a drinker in my book. Leastways, not unless he's one of those secret alcoholics. They're a bit devious from what I've heard. I knew a bloke once—'

'Can we get back to the point, Mr Miller?' Dave held up his hand. 'Sharon's a good-looking girl, isn't she?' he asked, intent on finding out whether she was not averse to the occasional affair.

'She certainly is,' said Miller warmly. 'And she's a bit of a flirt is Sharon.'

'What makes you think that, Mr Miller?' I asked.

'Well, when she's not in uniform, she always dresses in a way that's sure to get her noticed. And just to be on the safe side, I wouldn't take a chance on being alone with her if I could possibly avoid it. As a matter of fact, she rang me one morning about a month ago and said she couldn't turn off the shower and could I go round. She said Cliff was out and she didn't know what to do.'

'And did you go round?'

'No, I wasn't prepared to risk it. If she'd just got out of the shower there's no telling what I might've walked into, so to speak. I sent the missus instead; she's nearly as good at dealing with that sort of thing as I am. But on the whole, I'd say the Gregorys were an ideal couple. Mind you, it probably helps with them not being thrown together all day and every day.'

'Mrs Gregory told us that she was naked when you found her.'

'Yes, she was.' Miller gave a droll chuckle.

'But she said she couldn't remember whether she was still naked when she accompanied you around the house to see if the intruder was still there.'

'Oh yes, she definitely was. But I got the impression that she didn't care too much about that sort of thing. Of course it could've been the shock of what had just happened to her. She certainly didn't seem to know what she was doing. But there again, like I said, she *was* a bit of a flirt.'

'Didn't you suggest that she put some clothes on?' asked Dave.

Miller smiled wryly. 'No, of course not.'

'When you and she entered the main bedroom, Sharon said she fainted when she saw her husband's dead body.'

'I don't remember that,' said Miller. 'But I was a bit taken aback by seeing Cliff lying dead there, so my concentration was sort of on him. Like I said, I called 999 and when your blokes turned up they sent for an ambulance. Just following regulations, I suppose. But the paramedics said he was dead and they left it to the law.'

I decided that that was all we were going to get from Miller for the time being. Dave got him to sign his statement and we left.

'D'you want to have another word with Sharon Gregory, guv?' asked Dave. 'As we're right next door.'

'No, we'll leave it until tomorrow, Dave. That should give her time to get over her trauma. And it'll be interesting to hear if she still tells the same story. Or if she's prepared to tell us who the intruder really was, because I'm sure she knew him, despite what she said.'

I was not looking forward to Monday morning for a very good reason. And at one minute past ten precisely, my fears were confirmed when Colin Wilberforce appeared in my office.

'What is it, Colin?'

'The commander would like to see you, sir.'

'Thank you, Colin.' With a sigh, I walked the few yards down the corridor to the office of the chief.

'Ah, Mr Brock.' The commander looked up as though surprised to see me. I don't know why the hell he couldn't have just walked into my office like any other senior detective. Actually I did know: the commander wasn't a real detective. He'd been arbitrarily selected for what we in the trade call a 'sideways promotion', a term that Dave dismissed as an oxymoron. After a lifetime antagonizing football crowds and introducing new traffic schemes that merely resulted in further delaying drivers who were just trying to get to work, the commander had been sent to the CID. Obviously some dim-witted visionary in what is now called 'human resources' thought that we would benefit from his expertise. The outcome was that he thought he really was a detective. The truth, however, was that he'd been put out to grass until the age limit sent him home. For good. But none of that stopped him from viewing all our activities with deep-rooted mistrust. And constantly questioning what we were doing.

'You wanted me, sir?'

'Bring me up to date on this suspicious death you're dealing with, Mr Brock.' It was one of the commander's little foibles that he would never call a murder a murder in case it turned out to be manslaughter or suicide. Or even an accidental death. He hated to be wrong.

'It's a murder, sir,' I said firmly. 'No doubt about it.'

'Are you sure?'

'Quite definitely, sir.'

'Tell me about it.' The commander sighed and leaned back in his chair, peering at me over his half-moon spectacles. I doubted they contained corrective lenses; I think he wore them for effect.

I spent the next few minutes describing the case with which we were dealing, larding it with technical CID phrases that I knew he wouldn't understand but wouldn't query for fear of being found uninformed about the basics of crime investigation. I decided, however, not to voice my suspicions about Sharon Gregory's account of what had taken place at West Drayton. That would set him off theorizing. Anyway, we needed more than we had before we could justify arresting her.

'Yes, very well, Mr Brock. Keep me informed.' The commander carefully selected a file from his overflowing in-tray, placed it in the centre of his desk and caressed it lovingly.

I returned to my office. Dave was waiting for me.

'Give me an excuse to get out of here, Dave,' I said. 'Any excuse.'

'Will Heathrow Airport do, guv? I tracked down the security officer for the airline Sharon Gregory works for. His name's Ted Richie and he's an ex-CID officer. He was a DCI when he packed the Job in.'

'Thank God for that. When can he see us?'

'As soon as we can get there,' said Dave, 'but Charlie Flynn's got some information for you that you ought to know about before we go.'

DS Flynn came into my office carrying a sheaf of papers. 'I've checked through Mrs Gregory's credit card accounts, guv'nor. Turns out she was one careless lady.'

'How so, Charlie?'

'The window sash weight and the clothes line that Linda Mitchell found in the garage were purchased by Sharon Gregory from a DIY supermarket in Ruislip a week ago and paid for on her credit card.' Flynn thumbed through his pile of paper. 'She also paid an online pharmacy company in Mexico six weeks ago, but there's no indication what she bought.'

'Well, well,' I said. 'Why would an air hostess buy a window sash weight and a clothes line? The house is double glazed and there's a washer-drier in the utility room.' But the answer was obvious: she, or her accomplice, had murdered Clifford Gregory. And the pharmacy company in Mexico could have been the source of the Rohypnol that Dr Mortlock had found in Clifford Gregory's hair. But we had yet to discover a motive.

'That's not all, guv. The insurance policy that Sharon Gregory said her husband had taken out for twenty thousand pounds no longer exists. It was cashed in when the Gregorys bought their house five years ago. However . . .' Flynn paused, presumably for dramatic effect. 'Sharon took out a policy on her husband for one hundred thousand pounds.'

'When?' I asked.

'Would you believe one month ago, guv?' Flynn looked up and grinned.

'Thanks, Charlie. That's very helpful.'

'Miss Ebdon said it looked like a put-up job, guv,' said Dave, when Flynn had departed. 'So, what's next?'

'What's next, Dave, is that we go straight to West Drayton and nick Mrs Gregory on suspicion of murdering her husband. Not that she's going anywhere until Wednesday. At least that's when she said she was next on duty.'

It was only fifteen miles from ESB, as we had come to call the Empress State Building, to West Drayton. Even so, it took us nearly an hour, despite what Dave called 'positive motoring', an expertise that added another meaning to the term 'hard drive'. But when we arrived at the Gregorys' house, we found that our journey had been in vain.

The blue and white tapes were still in place across the front of the house, and a constable from the local station stood guard at the door.

'Are you looking for Mrs Gregory, sir?' asked the PC.

'Yes, I am.'

'She left about ten minutes ago in her Mini Cooper, sir,' said the PC.

'Did she say where she was going? Shopping, perhaps?'

'She said she was going on duty. She was in her airline uniform and was carrying a small suitcase.'

'I don't suppose you happened to take a note of the index mark of the Mini Cooper, did you?' I asked hopefully.

The PC opened his pocketbook and displayed a page. 'There you are, sir,' he said triumphantly.

'Well done,' I said. 'You should go far in the Job.' I'd often had that said to me when I was a young PC, but it hadn't seemed to have the desired effect. Quite a few of my contemporaries at the Metropolitan Police training school at Hendon were now chief superintendents and one was a commander, but they were in the Uniform Branch and I wondered, yet again, whether becoming a CID officer had been a wise choice. And another thing I'd learned is that a compliment of that sort only holds good until your next mistake.

I made a note of the details of Sharon's Mini Cooper, and Dave and I went inside and made for the sitting room. It was still in its state of chaos and Sharon had obviously made no attempt to clear up the mess. We had a final look round, but found nothing more to interest us.

'It looks as though she's changed her duties, Dave. She wasn't supposed to have been flying again until Wednesday,' I said. 'At least, that's what she told us, wasn't it?'

'To coin an apt phrase, guv,' said Dave, 'it looks as though the bird has flown.'

'Put details of her Mini Cooper on the Police National Computer, Dave. If it's found we might have some idea where she's gone. Ask for a check to be made on car parks, particularly at airports and railway stations. Then arrange for an all-ports warning. There's just a chance that she might've taken off for foreign parts,' I said. 'As a passenger.'

'I've already put her car's details on the PNC, sir. I made a note of the index mark when I saw it in the garage.'

'You could've told me that when I was talking to that PC, Dave.'

'What, and ruin his moment of glory, guv?' said Dave, and then offered me one of his pearls of wisdom. 'Miss Ebdon said she was a lying bitch. We should've nicked her when we had the chance.'

'On what grounds?'

'From reading her statement, it strikes me that her story doesn't hang together. But more importantly there are Doc Mortlock's findings that Cliff Gregory had been fed Rohypnol. Added to all of that, there's Charlie Flynn's information about her buying a sash weight and a clothes line in Ruislip. To say nothing of the new insurance policy for a hundred grand.'

'You have to remember that she was in shock when Miss Ebdon and I spoke to her, Dave,' I said, 'even though she seemed composed enough. And we didn't know that she'd bought the sash weight and the clothes line until recently. And we certainly don't know that she bought the Rohypnol.'

'What's next, then?' asked Dave, having made his point.

'There's nothing else we can do here,' I said. 'We'll see what Richie at the airport has to say about her.'

SIX

We found Ted Richie's office tucked away in Terminal Two at Heathrow Airport. There were maps and duty rosters adorning the walls, and his desk was cluttered with paperwork and a model of a passenger aircraft, several more of which were beside a kettle and a cafetière on a side table.

'DCI Harry Brock, from the Metropolitan Murder Investigation Team, Mr Richie, and this is DS Dave Poole.'

'Yeah, we spoke on the phone, Dave. The name's Ted, by the way. Come in, gents, and tell me how I can help you.' Richie was a large man with a bald pate, a North Country accent, a substantial moustache and a red face that seemed to indicate a fondness for alcohol. But he had been a CID officer and it's a hard life; at least that's always the excuse. 'I'm ex-Job myself. Did thirty years up North flogging my guts out getting a string of petty villains banged up, took my money and ran. Best decision I ever made. Take a pew, gents.'

I explained briefly about the murder of Sharon Gregory's husband.

'Yeah, I heard about that,' said Richie. 'Airline grapevine. People here seem to fall over themselves to tell me the latest scuttlebutt. Never happened in the Job. Mind you, I did have one or two good snouts.'

'Dave and I have just been to Sharon Gregory's house at West Drayton, Ted,' I continued, 'but I'm told that she left there less than an hour ago. According to the PC on duty at the house, Sharon was in uniform and she told him that she was going to work. But when we interviewed her on the night of the murder she told us that she wasn't rostered to fly until this coming Wednesday.'

Richie turned to one of the crew duty rotas on his wall and studied it for a moment or two. 'That's what it says here, Harry. According to the latest roster I've got, Sharon Gregory's not flying until Wednesday, LHR to MIA.' He paused and then explained. 'Heathrow to Miami International.'

'That's exactly what she told us,' I said. 'But is there anyone here who could tell us if that's been changed?'

'I could try the duty room. I don't know the girl personally, I'm afraid,' said Richie. 'We've got a lot of cabin crew working out of here, but to tell you the truth I don't have much to do with them. My job's more one of dealing with security on the ground: baggage that's been nicked, light-fingered baggage handlers, that sort of thing. Anything that's up in the air, to coin a phrase, is dealt with by the aircraft captain. That's the law; just like the captain of a ship. But occasionally I get involved, for theft on an aircraft in flight or thieving by the crew.'

'Must keep you busy, Ted,' said Dave, but I thought I detected a hint of sarcasm.

'You can say that again,' said Richie, 'and they always want me to use my contacts to short-circuit the system if someone's snuffed it in flight. You'd be surprised how many people die in transit; must be something to do with the cabin pressure. The powers-that-be want me to get in touch with the coroner's officer and smooth the wheels.' He sat down behind his desk. 'I had a word around and if it's of any interest, airport chit-chat suggests Sharon Gregory's got a bit of a reputation for sleeping around, usually in Miami. It pays to keep your ear to the ground in this job. But like I said, I don't know her personally.'

'We've heard that much, Ted. The people we've spoken to so far have suggested that she might not be averse to having a fling.'

'Anyway, to answer your question about her duties,' said Richie, 'first of all, I'll have a look through my memos to check that they haven't been changed. That's if they bothered to tell me. These girls sometimes do a mutual swap and the duty room doesn't always let me know.'

Having spent a few moments ploughing through the untidy pile of papers on his desk, he looked up. 'They haven't advised me of any change, Harry, not that that means a damned thing. As far as I know, what she told you still stands. The last I heard was that she should be flying out at fourteen thirty-three Zulu time this coming Wednesday bound for Miami. D'you want me to make a few enquiries?'

'Yes, please, Ted. And perhaps you could get someone to check if her car is in the staff car park.' Dave gave him the details of Sharon Gregory's Mini Cooper.

Ted Richie made a couple of calls, one to a member of his staff and another to the duty room. Twenty minutes later he got the first reply. 'The duty room guy said she hasn't shown up there, Harry, which is where she has to report for duty, and her schedule remains the same: fourteen thirty-three Zulu departure on Wednesday. What's more, no one in the duty room has seen her at any time today.'

The second reply came five minutes later.

'My guy says that her car's not where she usually parks it, Harry,' said Richie, switching off his mobile and tossing it on to the desk.

'Thanks, Ted. It looks like she's done a runner.'

'Anything else I can help you with, Harry?'

'No thanks. I'll get our port watch people to make some enquiries. Oh, there is one thing: where does Sharon Gregory usually stay in Miami?'

Richie delved into his pile of paperwork once again. 'The crew always spends stopovers at the Shannon Hotel on Miami Beach,' he said eventually.

'I don't know whether it'll help us,' said Dave, 'but I suppose there's an outside chance that she's gone there, even off duty. D'you have a phone number for the Shannon?'

'Sure.' Richie scribbled the details on a memo bearing the airline's crest and handed it to Dave. 'If the crew room's empty, and it should be, I could let you have a discreet look in her locker, Harry, if you think that would help?' he suggested. 'But for God's sake don't tell anyone that I let you have a gander without a warrant or I'll have the union on my back like a ton of bricks. The next thing that'd happen would be a strike, and I could do without that sort of aggro.'

'Thanks, Ted. A look in her locker might be useful.'

Richie picked up his personal radio, led us down a flight of stairs, along several passageways and through a door marked 'Private' until we reached the crew room. Fortunately it was deserted. Taking out a bunch of keys, the security chief opened a locker labelled 'Sharon Gregory'. 'Pays to have a skeleton key,' he said, with a laugh. 'Although if the shop steward found out he'd go ape.' It seemed that he was in constant fear of the trade union.

There was little in the locker to excite our interest: some clothing, including a spare uniform, a couple of packets of tights and a pair of high-heeled shoes.

'They wear high heels to greet the passengers,' said Richie, offering a piece of useless information, 'but they change into flats once they're airborne.'

'This might be useful, sir,' said Dave, picking up a mobile phone. 'I wonder why she didn't take it with her?' He picked up the phone and began to fiddle with it.

'What are you up to now, Dave?' I was always interested when Dave moved into his technical mode.

'Copying her contact list, sir,' said Dave, as he removed the SIM cards from his own phone and Sharon's. Placing her card into his phone, he copied her contact list, and then returned Sharon's card to her phone. 'And she'll never know we did it,' he said, as he replaced his own SIM card and put Sharon's phone back in her locker.

'D'you think she might've had something to do with topping her husband, Harry?' asked Richie, as we strolled back to his office. The suspicions of a career CID officer still remained.

'I very much doubt it, Ted,' I said, unwilling to disclose my concerns about the circumstances surrounding the murder of Clifford Gregory, even to an ex-copper. Loyalties tend to change with a change of career. 'But I'll keep you posted if anything interesting comes up. Oh, there's one other thing. D'you know if Sharon Gregory had a particular friend, one who is in the same crew maybe and might know what she gets up to when she's in Miami?'

'Leave it with me, Harry, I'll ask around. I'll give you a bell if I find out anything.' Richie glanced at his watch. 'You got time for a snifter?'

'Yes, why not? But Dave's driving, so he'll have an orange juice.'

Richie laughed. 'Rank hath its privileges,' he said, as Dave and I followed him into one of the many bars to be found in the Heathrow Airport complex.

*   *   *

Once back at ESB, I asked Dave to telephone the Shannon Hotel at Miami Beach and find out if Sharon was there.

Ten minutes later, he returned. 'She's not there, guv, and they aren't expecting the crew she's usually with until Wednesday.'

'That comes as no surprise,' I said, leaving Dave to list the contacts he had found on Sharon Gregory's mobile. I phoned Linda Mitchell in an attempt to clarify one or two points.

'How many mobile telephones did you come across at the Gregorys' house, Linda?'

'Two, Mr Brock,' said Linda promptly. 'One was in the study and the other was on the worktop in the kitchen. I'm about to examine them, but it's most likely that the one from the kitchen was Sharon's, and the one in the study belonged to her husband. I'll let you know.'

'A couple of other things. I'd be grateful if you'd have all the pillows that were in the master bedroom examined. Doctor Mortlock tells me that Clifford Gregory was suffocated, and he suspects it might've been one of the pillows that was used. So, a check for saliva or mucus would be useful, but you know better than me the sort of thing we're looking for. Also, the piece of material found in the hall that Sharon Gregory said the intruder used to gag her. See if there was any trace of her saliva on it.'

'Leave it with me,' said Linda. 'I'll get back to you as soon as I get a result.'

'How are you getting on, Dave?' I asked, returning to the incident room. 'Incidentally, Linda Mitchell told me that she found another mobile in the house that belonged to Sharon.'

'I'm not surprised, guv,' said Dave. 'The one we found at Heathrow has got all the usual girlie stuff on it, like hairdresser, manicurist, tanning studio, et cetera. But there are also six men's names and their telephone numbers. Four of them are in the UK, and the other two have numbers in the States.'

'And I'd put money on those men's names not being on the mobile that Linda found in the kitchen at West Drayton.'

Dave laughed. 'It's beginning to look as though our Sharon was the sort of girl who played the field, guv, and didn't want the late Clifford Gregory to come across the phone we found at the airport. Anyway, Colin Wilberforce is doing a subscriber check to find the addresses.'

'I just hope they're not too far away,' I said. I'd travelled long distances in the past to chase up promising leads, only to find that I'd wasted my time when I got there. 'Apart from going to Miami, I somehow doubt that Sharon would want to travel too far to get laid.'

'No, but the guys she was seeing might be prepared to,' said Dave cynically.

Linda Mitchell arrived in the incident room at two o'clock. She sat down and opened a file, resting it on her lap.

'I've got the initial results of the examination of the property, Mr Brock. And I'll start with the result I think will probably interest you the most: there was no trace of saliva on the gag that Sharon Gregory said had been stuffed in her mouth.'

'What do you conclude from that, Linda?' I asked. 'Scientifically speaking.'

'I would think that if she had been gagged and she'd eventually been able to dislodge it from her mouth, there should've been a trace. And in that case we'd almost certainly have been able to get a DNA sample from it. But there was nothing.'

'So, the chances are that her claim to have been gagged wasn't true.'

'That would be my view,' said Linda cautiously, and glanced at her notes again. 'We also found a tea towel in the kitchen with a piece torn from it. The gag that was found in the hall is a mechanical fit for the tea towel.'

'It looks as though the intruder tore the gag from that,' I conjectured.

'Or Sharon Gregory did,' said Dave.

'Moving on to the pillows,' continued Linda, 'there were traces of saliva and mucus on the pillow that we found on the floor beside the bed, and, of course, blood; the DNA on both pillows matches that of Clifford Gregory. It's scientifically certain, therefore, that it was that pillow that was used to suffocate the victim, as Doctor Mortlock suggested. The bloodstains on the pillow that was beneath the victim's head were also those of Clifford Gregory, but that was to be expected. His bloodstains were also on the sash weight I found in the garage, despite the fact that attempts had been made to wash them off.'

'That doesn't get me very far,' I said. 'We know that he was suffocated, rather than killed with the window sash weight. I suppose there was nothing else anywhere in the house that might indicate who the murderer was?' I knew instinctively that that was a vain hope. Not that it mattered. Now that we had the evidence that Sharon Gregory had purchased the sash weight and the clothes line, I was as certain as could be that she had killed her husband.

'Nothing that points directly to the killer, I'm afraid, but we made some interesting discoveries. We found traces of the victim's blood in the shower, although an attempt had been made to wash it away. If I can make a guess, I'd say that the murderer was naked and then showered. Furthermore, although the sash weight had been washed, we were still able to find traces of the victim's blood in the P-trap under the kitchen sink.'

'That fits with my theory that Sharon was the killer,' I said. 'And, of course, she was naked when Miller found her.'

'We also examined all the cupboards and drawers,' said Linda, 'and none of them was fitted with a lock. And, as you saw for yourself, there was no indication that the front door had been forced. No jemmy marks, no broken glass.'

'So,' I said thoughtfully, 'we now have traces of blood in the shower, the sink and on the sash weight, and Sharon appears to have been lying to us about the gag. Also, Doctor Mortlock found traces of Rohypnol in the victim's hair. All of which will give me something to question her further about. When we find her. What about fingerprints?'

'Early days yet, Mr Brock, although I can tell you that we couldn't find any identifiable prints on the jewellery. As you can imagine, there were a lot of dabs around the house and it'll take some time to sort them out and eliminate those of Clifford and Sharon Gregory. But I can tell you that although there were finger-prints on the whisky bottle we found in the dining room, they were *not* Clifford Gregory's. And there wasn't a dirty glass anywhere. It's made more difficult in that we don't yet know the identity of any friends who may have been frequent callers at the house. Or even Clifford Gregory's clients.'

'You could start by taking elimination prints from Sidney Miller, the neighbour who found her,' I suggested.

'I've got him on my list of things to do.' Linda looked up with a frown that implied that I shouldn't try to tell her how to do her job.

'Whoops! Sorry,' I said.

'However, there is one thing I'd like to say, Mr Brock. I've examined hundreds of crime scenes over the years and I've never come across a break-in where the burglar has created as much mess as is the case with this one.'

'Nor have I, Linda.'

'Now, about the two mobile phones in the house. They were as I suspected: the one in the kitchen was Sharon's and the other one belonged to her husband.'

'Give Linda the list you took from the mobile that was in Sharon's locker at the airport, Dave.' I gave Linda time to study the numbers, and then asked, 'Were any of those numbers on Sharon's house mobile, Linda?'

'Not one.' Having compared the list with her own notes, Linda handed it back. 'And no calls were made to any of those numbers from the mobile found at the house.'

'That confirms my original thought,' I said. 'That's a list of her fancy men. Will you let me know as soon as you have something on the prints?'

'Of course.' Linda closed her file, gave me a copy of her initial report and was about to leave when she paused. 'Incidentally, the rope with which Sharon Gregory was tied up was a mechanical fit to the clothes line we found in the garage.' And with that latest confirmation of our suspicions about the burglary and murder, she left to make her way back to Walworth.

Wilberforce glanced up as I walked into the incident room with Dave. 'I've got the results of the subscriber checks on the numbers on Sharon's phone, sir. The one Dave found at the airport.'

'Where do they live, Colin? Scotland, Wales, Cornwall, or none of the above?' I suggested cynically.

'As a matter of fact, we're in luck. One goes out to a Gordon Harrison in Glenn Road, Fulham; there's a Max Riley in Guildford; Frank Digby's at Chalfont St Giles; and a Julian Reed lives in Chelsea. I'm still waiting for Dave to get the details of the two in the United States.'

'At least that'll give us something to start with. Given that the subscribers probably all work, we'd better leave it until this evening.'

'Oh good!' exclaimed Dave. 'That's another evening taken care of.'

'Is Madeleine working, then?' Dave's wife was a principal dancer with the Royal Ballet and more often than not their hours of work conflicted rather than coincided.

'She's pretending to be a swan in *Swan Lake* at Covent Garden,' said Dave. 'For two whole weeks. I sometimes think that her job is worse than ours.'

I returned to my office and sent for DC Appleby.

'I've got a job for you, John.'

'Sir?' John Appleby was a young, smartly-dressed and very keen detective constable.

'Get on to the Driver and Vehicle Licensing Agency at Swansea and see if you can get details of any cars that might be owned by the names that Sergeant Poole found on Sharon Gregory's mobile phone. The British ones, of course.'

'Right, sir.' Appleby loved tasks like that and he set to work immediately.

I had no idea whether that information would be of any help to us, but in cases like the present one, I had to try everything. It was what Dave called clutching at non-existent straws.

It took Appleby half an hour to complete his check with the DVLA.

The list he handed me was interesting. Frank Digby of Chalfont St Giles boasted a Ford Galaxy; Julian Reed, who lived in Chelsea, owned a Mercedes; and Gordon Harrison, the man in Glenn Road, Fulham, owned a Jaguar XF. All expensive cars. But according to Swansea, Max Riley of Guildford was not registered as the keeper of a motor vehicle of any description.

'Well done, John. Give them to Sergeant Wilberforce and ask him to put them on the Police National Computer with the proviso that sightings are to be reported, but the driver is not to be questioned. Unless, of course,' I added, 'they've been stopped for a traffic offence. I wouldn't want to upset the Black Rats by preventing them from doing their job.'

Appleby looked rather pained. 'I can put them on the PNC, sir.'

'Sorry, John, of course you can. Go ahead, but tell DS Wilberforce what you've done.' I didn't want to upset our office genius either.

SEVEN

After leaving her home in West Drayton on Monday morning, Sharon Gregory had driven the four miles to the Chimes Shopping Centre at Uxbridge and spent half an hour looking around the shops. In one of them, a boutique that specialized in erotica, she selected a thong, a shelf bra and a pair of black hold-up stockings.

'That should get my man excited, don't you think?' Sharon asked the salesgirl.

'Without a doubt,' said the assistant. 'I've got a similar set and they work for me every time.'

'I should think you're lucky enough not to have to try very hard,' said Sharon, glancing enviously at the girl's décolletage, while paying for her purchases using her dead husband's credit card. The assistant didn't see the card and therefore wouldn't have noticed that it bore a man's name, but she wouldn't have cared anyway.

Her shopping finished, Sharon found an Italian restaurant and took a seat away from the window. It was not yet time for lunch, but she had skipped breakfast and was feeling a little hungry. She ordered an omelette, followed by a cup of coffee and a pastry. Twenty minutes later, she ordered a second cup of coffee, but dismissed the idea of another pastry. She did have her figure to worry about.

'Is there anything else you'd care for?' asked the handsome young waiter when Sharon asked for her bill.

'You never know,' she said, laying a hand on the waiter's arm. Perhaps no more than twenty, he was tall and slender and had a face that suggested Italian ancestry, although he spoke with a Cockney accent. He was certainly of the type that appealed to her. 'But I don't have the time right now. Maybe later?' She spoke in a contrived sultry voice and flashed the young man a beguiling smile. 'Why don't you give me your phone number?'

Agreeably surprised to have been propositioned by an attractive girl, the waiter scribbled his mobile number on a paper napkin and slid it surreptitiously across the table. 'I'm afraid I'm working until midnight tonight and tomorrow, but I'm off at six the day after,' he said.

'I'll call you,' said Sharon, putting the napkin into her handbag; she had to admit, if only to herself, that she could be a very deceitful temptress who enjoyed teasing handsome young men. However, she had other plans in which the waiter would play no part. Another time, perhaps?

Unsurprisingly, Sharon having flirted outrageously, the young waiter didn't notice that it was her dead husband's credit card that he put in the machine before handing it to her. Not that it would have worried him any more than it may have concerned the girl at the lingerie boutique, had she seen it.

It was one of the great advantages of the chip-and-pin method of payment.

Finally, Sharon found a mobile phone outlet and bought an untraceable pay-as-you-go throwaway for which she paid cash. She put ten-pounds'-worth of talk time on to it, for which she also paid cash.

And then it was time for what she hoped would be a 'fun' afternoon.

Arriving at the Dickin Hotel on the fringes of Heathrow Airport at midday, Sharon checked in and took the lift to the second floor. Ten minutes later, recalling the number from memory, she made a telephone call on her new mobile.

'I'm ready and waiting for you, darling,' she said, when the man answered.

'Are you at our usual hotel?' asked the man, his excitement mounting.

'Of course, darling. I'm in room 219 this time.'

There was a pause while the man jotted down the room number on the pad by the telephone and calculated how long it would take him to get there. 'I'll be as quick as I can, darling,' he said, having told Sharon when he expected to arrive.

'Drive carefully,' cautioned Sharon. She terminated the call and deleted the number from the phone.

She undressed and hung her uniform in the clothes closet. Crossing the room to her suitcase, she put in the underwear and tights in which she had arrived. During the time she had to wait until the man arrived, she took a much-needed shower. The weather was still in the low eighties Fahrenheit and even the air conditioning in the hotel was struggling to alleviate the humidity.

Emerging from the shower room, she dried herself, brushed her long, honey blonde hair and skilfully applied her make-up. And from her selection of perfumes, she applied the one that had been given to her by the man she was expecting. Next she donned the tiny red thong, matching shelf bra and a pair of sheer black hold-up stockings, all of which she had purchased in Uxbridge. Having slipped into a cream satin robe, she pushed her feet into a pair of black stilettos.

Pouring herself a gin and tonic from the minibar, she sat down in an armchair to await the arrival of her lover.

When the expected knock came, she crossed the room and peered through the peephole. Disconnecting the security chain, she opened the door.

Her lover, attired in a sports shirt and slacks, hastened into the room, pausing only to hang a 'Do Not Disturb' sign on the outside handle. He closed the door behind him, locked it and reconnected the security chain.

Sharon slipped off her robe and tossed it on to a chair; it hung there briefly before slithering to the floor. For a moment or two the man stood admiring the girl's trim and exciting figure. She in turn studied his firm body.

The next twenty seconds were filled with a frenzy of lust as his clothing was strewn about the room and he divested Sharon of her minimal attire, apart from her stockings. Effortlessly lifting her in his arms, he placed her on the bed.

An hour later they lay on top of the duvet, satiated and perspiring. Sharon turned and nestled closer to her lover. 'I've something wonderful to tell you, darling, something that means we can now be together forever,' she said, moving her hand enticingly down his torso.

Purely on the basis that Fulham was closer to our Empress State Building office than the other names on Sharon's list, I decided that Dave and I would interview Gordon Harrison first.

It was half past five when we arrived at Glenn Road. Harrison's

terraced house was one of several in the road that had been 'gentri-
fied'. According to the electoral roll, he lived there by himself.
I'd taken a chance on him being at home, and I was lucky.

'Hi!' The man who answered the door was attired in shorts,
tee-shirt and a pair of flip-flops. He looked to be in his mid-thirties,
had a shock of unruly blond hair and was suntanned.

'Mr Harrison?' I asked.

'Yes, I'm Gordon Harrison.' He looked slightly concerned to
be confronted by two strangers on his doorstep, one of whom was
six foot tall, well-built and black. 'You're not Bible bashers, are
you?'

'No, Mr Harrison, we're police officers.' I produced my warrant
card to allay any suspicion that we might be undercover evangelists.
'I'm Detective Chief Inspector Brock of Scotland Yard and this is
Detective Sergeant Poole.'

'Are you sure you've got the right Gordon Harrison? I mean,
what could the police possibly want with me?' Harrison's face
took on a shifty expression.

'I think so,' said Dave. 'We understand that you're acquainted
with Sharon Gregory.'

'Oh, Sharon, yah!' said Harrison, with an air of relief. 'What's
that sexy blonde bombshell been up to now?' He stepped forward
and shot a glance at the front door that was immediately next to
his own, as if fearful that a neighbour might be lurking behind
it, listening. 'You'd better come in and make yourselves
comfortable.'

Now that Harrison had said more than a few words, I detected
a possibly contrived mid-Atlantic accent. We followed him into
his sitting room which, like the hall, had woodblock flooring. I
was conscious of the noise my shoes made as we crossed to the
only two armchairs in the room.

'What's this about Sharon, then? Has something happened to
the gorgeous creature? She hasn't crashed that Mini Cooper of
hers, has she?' Harrison opened the Venetian blinds, moved the
chair from his computer workstation, and swung it round so that
he could sit down opposite us.

I heard a door closing upstairs somewhere and Harrison cast a
nervous glance across the room.

'She was the victim of a rather brutal burglary last Saturday evening,' I said, 'during the course of which her husband was murdered.'

'Her *husband*!' Harrison's face registered shock. Although whether it was shock at the news of Clifford Gregory's murder or the fact that Sharon was married was not immediately apparent.

'I take it you didn't know she was married, Mr Harrison,' said Dave, rightly assuming the latter to be the case.

'Christ, no! I certainly didn't. How long had she been married?'

'About seven years,' said Dave.

'Ye Gods!' exclaimed Harrison. 'Well, the deceitful little bitch. She never mentioned a husband.'

'How did you meet her?' I asked.

'On a flight to Miami. I go there quite often. She's an air hostess, you know.'

'Yes, we know. Were you travelling to Miami on business?'

'Sure. I fly to the States quite a lot. I arrange bespoke holidays for rich executives.'

That explained the accent I'd noticed earlier. Maybe.

'What on earth are bespoke holidays for rich executives?' asked Dave.

Harrison gave a boyish grin. 'Between you and me, it's for guys who've got more money than they know what to do with. Often they're the sort who work in the financial sector and get a bigger bonus than I make in a year, and that's saying something. They come to me to arrange a custom-built holiday at virtually any place of their choosing. Money no object. And I arrange all the bookings on the Internet, so it keeps my overheads down.' He half turned to wave at his computer. 'But I still have to go to these places and check them out. More often than not, they want a discreet hideaway so they can take their latest squeeze for a dirty weekend. Or even a week. I suppose they tell their wives or current live-ins that they're away on business, but should I worry?'

'How very deceitful,' murmured Dave.

'Yeah, it is, isn't it?' said Harrison with a laugh. 'But I make a handsome profit out of it.'

'Is Miami always the venue for these getaways?' I asked, thinking that the story he'd just told was too good to be true.

'Not always, although that's one of the more popular destinations. Well, Florida and California are the two favourites, but I travel all over the world. I even arranged one for a guy who wanted to spend a week at a monastery in the Himalayas. And before you ask, no, he didn't take his bird with him. As a matter of fact, I think he finished up staying there for good. Still, it takes all sorts, I suppose.'

'When did you last see Sharon Gregory?' I asked, steering Harrison away from verbally downloading his holiday brochure.

Harrison pondered the question. 'About a month ago, I suppose,' he said eventually. 'We spent a happy forty-eight hours in a hotel room overlooking Miami Beach. And that wasn't the first time, either. Mind you, I don't think I was the only guy in her life. But I didn't know she was married; she wasn't wearing a ring or anything.' He forced a laugh. 'In fact, she wasn't wearing anything at all most of the time,' he added, and lapsed momentarily into silence. 'D'you reckon it was one of those other guys who murdered her husband?'

'We've no idea,' I said. 'Was it you?' Sometimes the occasional direct question produces an unexpected admission. But not this time.

'Christ, no! As I said, I didn't even know she was married.'

'I presume you met on a flight when she was on duty?' said Dave.

'That's right. That must've been about a year or so ago, I suppose. Nine hours is quite a long time to get to know someone, and she made a point of giving me the address of the stopover hotel where she'd be staying with the crew. Three times! And finished up by jotting it down on one of those little paper mats they put the drinks on. I guessed I was on a promise, so I changed my hotel reservation and spent a pleasant couple of nights in the sack with her.'

'Has she been in touch with you recently, say, in the last twenty-four hours?' I was hoping that Sharon had contacted him and told him where she was. But again I was disappointed.

'No. I gave her my mobile number ages ago so she could tell me when she'd next be going to Miami, but I haven't heard from her since the last time we were there. I suppose we must've arranged meetings at her hotel in Miami at least four or five times over the past year. I even thought about getting serious over her, though I guessed she was seeing other guys. But now you tell me she's married.'

'Not any more she isn't,' said Dave.

'I might call her, then,' said Harrison.

'If you do find her, perhaps you'd let me know,' I said, as we rose to leave. I handed Harrison one of my cards. 'We're rather anxious to have a word with her. Just to tidy up a few loose ends.'

'Yeah, sure.' Harrison tucked the card into a pocket of his shorts, and escorted us to the front door.

'Who was that, darling?' A coffee-skinned Jamaican girl wearing only a pair of denim shorts entered the living room once she was satisfied that the front door was closed.

'The police, Shona, my love,' said Harrison.

'The police! What did they want?'

'It was something to do with the car, but they got the wrong car and the wrong Gordon Harrison.'

'That's all right, then. I thought for one horrible moment it might've been your wife. Or worse still that they were on to you about your other business.'

'No chance of that, sweetie. And as for Krisztina, she's in Botoşani visiting her parents.' Harrison told the lie smoothly; it didn't do for the two women in his enterprise to know too much about each other.

'Good.' Shona moved closer and put her arms around Harrison's neck. 'Now, where were we when we were so rudely interrupted?'

'One down and five to go,' I said, as we drove away from Fulham.

'And two of those are in the States,' said Dave hopefully. 'D'you think . . .?'

'No, Dave. Don't get too excited,' I said. 'The commander would have a blue fit if I suggested we flew there in pursuit of our enquiries.' I glanced at my watch. 'Drop me at Waterloo Station and then go home.'

I caught the train to Surbiton with minutes to spare and immediately called Gail on my mobile, resisting the temptation to use that hackneyed phrase that one hears so often: 'I'm on a train.'

'Hello, stranger,' said Gail. 'Is there any danger of my seeing you in the near future?' In the course of our relationship, Gail Sutton had become somewhat blasé about my job and the antisocial hours that went with it.

'I'm on my way, darling,' I said. 'I should be with you in about half an hour. And I'm hungry.'

'Hungry for what?' asked Gail.

I'd met Gail some years ago while investigating the murder of her friend Patricia Hunter. They had both been appearing in the chorus line of a second-rate revue called *Scatterbrain* at London's Granville Theatre.

There is a story behind Gail's demotion from actress to chorus girl. A year or so prior to that, she'd been appearing in the lead female role of Amanda Prynne in a revival of Sir Noël Coward's *Private Lives* at the Richmond Theatre. Feeling unwell, she'd handed over the part to her understudy and returned home unexpectedly to find her husband, Gerald Andrews, in the marital bed with a nude dancer who, according to Gail, was still performing in character. That was the final indignity to be visited upon Gail by her philandering husband and signalled the end of a marriage that had fast been unravelling anyway. After the divorce Gail had reverted to using her maiden name of Sutton.

However, in a chauvinistically unreasonable act of spite, Andrews, a theatrical director, had done his best to prevent Gail from getting any decent parts thereafter. Hence her appearance in the chorus line at the Granville. Or as she described it: 'Kicking the air for a living.'

Not that Gail had to worry about earning a living. Her father, George, was a multimillionaire property developer whose home and business were in Nottingham, and he gave his only daughter a generous allowance. George's only apparent vice was a tendency to talk non-stop about the land speed record and Formula One motor racing until his wife, Sally, an effervescent former dancer, told him to shut up. But I could put up with non-stop lectures about such historical luminaries as Sir Malcolm Campbell, Sir Henry Segrave, Tazio Nuvolari, Hans Stück and their contemporaries on the odd occasion that I was in George's company.

Alighting from the train at Surbiton, I bought a bottle of chilled champagne from a local wine shop and took a taxi to Kingston.

Gail's neo-Georgian townhouse – a euphemism for a modern three-storied terraced house – was only a mile or so from my flat on the other side of Surbiton railway station. But these days I tended to spend more time at Gail's house, and in her bed, than at my own pad.

I let myself in with the key that Gail had given me a few months ago. In return, I'd given her a key to my flat. It was a sort of compromise; we had discussed my moving in with her, but had eventually reached a mutual agreement that our relationship might become less harmonious if we lived with each other on a permanent basis. This was especially true given the odd hours at which I was called back to duty.

'Where are you?' I shouted.

'In here,' Gail replied unhelpfully.

I took a guess and walked through to the dining room on the ground floor. Gail was busy setting out some exotic cold supper. Barefooted, she was attired in a pair of short denim shorts that were almost hidden by one of my casual shirts. I'd often wondered where that shirt had gone.

'Ah, the wanderer returns,' she said. 'I haven't seen you for ages, darling. What's kept you away? Another dead body?'

'You guessed,' I said, as I opened the champagne and took a couple of flutes from the sideboard.

'I'm just about finished here. Let's go upstairs and have our drink.'

I gave her a hug and a kiss, and ran my forefinger up her spine, but she smacked my hand away. 'First things first,' she said playfully.

'Just what I was thinking,' I said. I picked up the two glasses and the bottle and followed her upstairs to the sitting room.

The meal was superb, as usual – Gail's a brilliant cook – and I drank too much wine. Declaring myself unfit to walk home, and having no hope of finding a taxi, I stayed the night. Again.

I arrived at work about nine o'clock on Tuesday morning, feeling tired and reminding myself not to spend the night with Gail when I'm working on a case. And not to drink too much.

I'd just settled in my office with a strong cup of coffee and a couple of paracetamol tablets when Colin Wilberforce appeared on the scene.

'What is it, Colin?'

'An interesting development, sir. I did the usual routine check

of criminal records on all the names that have come up so far in
the enquiry. The only one to have previous convictions is Sidney
Miller, Sharon Gregory's neighbour.'

'Oh?' I took a sip of my coffee, but decided I didn't need the
paracetamol after all. There's nothing quite like that sort of revelation to bring me back to life. 'What's his form, Colin?'

'One for burglary when he was seventeen, sir . . .' Wilberforce
smiled knowingly. 'And one for rape when he was thirty years
of age. He was sent down for a seven-year stretch, but was
released on licence after he'd served three and a half years. He
was placed on the Sex Offenders' Register for twenty years.
He's got another five to go before he's clear.'

'What did he get for the burglary?'

'Probation, sir. It seemed there were extenuating circumstances.'

'Is that it, Colin?'

'Yes, sir.' Wilberforce handed me a printout. 'Apart from the
rape, he's not been convicted of any offence since the burglary.'

'You mean he hasn't been caught. Thank you, Colin.'

For the next ten minutes I mulled over the implications of a
convicted housebreaker living next door to a recently burgled
house. Especially one where the householder had been murdered.

I sent for Kate Ebdon. 'I've heard, guv,' she said, when I began
to tell her about Miller's past. 'What d'you intend to do about it?'

'I've thought all along that Sharon Gregory's burglar was an
accomplice, rather than an unknown intruder, Kate. I want you
and Dave to go out to West Drayton and feel Miller's collar on
suspicion of aggravated burglary. That'll do for a start, but we
might be able to up it to murder if we're lucky.'

'Shall I take him to Uxbridge nick? I think that's the nearest.'

'To hell with that,' I said. 'Bring him up to Fulham. And give
me a ring when you're there. Of course, he might be out plumbing,
but his bosomy wife will probably know where he can be found.'

It was midday before I heard from Kate. 'I've got him banged
up in Fulham, guv, and he's not happy.'

'I didn't expect him to be, Kate. I'll be with you shortly. Has
he said anything, apart from complaining?'

'Nothing relevant, guv.'

EIGHT

'What's this all about, Mr Brock? I ain't done nothing wrong,' whined Miller plaintively, the moment that Dave and I entered the interview room at Fulham police station in Heckfield Road. It was apparent that the confident, almost cocky plumber we'd interviewed at his home in West Drayton had reverted to type, replaced by the obsequious ex-con.

Dave turned on the recording machine and announced who was present.

'Twenty-eight years ago you were convicted of a burglary at a dwelling house in Harwich, Mr Miller,' I began.

'It was a mistake,' said Miller.

'They always say that,' murmured Dave.

'But it's true,' protested Miller. 'It was my mate's fault, see. It was just after midnight and we'd been out clubbing. My mate reckoned as how he'd lost his key and he asked me to help him get into his house without waking up his parents. I'd just got through a ground floor window round the back when I was grabbed by the bloke who lived there. Far from being in bed, him and his missus had been watching telly. Well, you could've knocked me down with a feather. His wife must've got straight on the blower because the next thing I knew was the law turning up. By that time, my mate had scarpered and I got nicked. Turned out it wasn't his house at all, but a drum he'd fancied screwing. I still got done for it, though.'

'Didn't you know where your mate lived, then?' Dave was obviously having a problem swallowing this tale.

'Of course not,' said Miller. 'I wouldn't've got talked into it if I'd known it wasn't his house. It was only later I learned he'd been done for burglary before. Some mate he turned out to be.'

'And the rape of a fifteen-year-old girl called Janet Smith?' I asked. I didn't believe Miller's tale about the burglary, but I intended to return to it later.

'That wasn't rape. I was stitched up.' Miller leaned forward and placed his arms on the table, implying that he was about to impart a confidence. 'We'd met at a nightclub down Harwich—'

'That's where you were living at the time, was it?' asked Dave.

'Yeah, I was born and bred there. Can't you hear my Essex accent?' said Miller, with a twisted grin. 'Anyway, me and Janet had been going steady for about six months and we'd just got engaged. We was in love, see. And it was her what suggested having sex. She said it was OK, now we was going to get spliced, and we took precautions an' all. But after, when she got home, her mum cottoned on straight off what she'd been up to. That's the trouble with mothers, they can always tell. Anyhow, Janet got the third degree from her parents and they threatened to throw her out on the street if she didn't say I'd raped her.'

'And I suppose it was her parents who called the police?' I said.

'*Called* 'em?' Miller scoffed heatedly. 'They marched her straight down to the bloody nick, didn't they? Well, it turned out she was only fifteen. She'd told me she was nineteen, coming up twenty. Anyway, the next thing I know is I'm nicked and I went down for seven years. The prosecuting brief had her tied up in knots in the box. The poor little bitch was in tears by the time he'd finished with her, and she eventually admitted that she was only fifteen and the brief conned her into saying that I'd forced her into having sex.'

'And did you?' asked Dave. 'Force her, I mean.'

'Of course I never. She was willing enough, but it was all down to her bloody parents. They'd told her that she wasn't old enough to give her consent and that meant it was automatically rape, whether she'd agreed or not. But that was all bullshit because after I got banged up I shared a cell with a bent solicitor and he told me what the law was. I thought about appealing, but he said I'd got no chance. And he said that if Janet changed her statement now, then she'd get done for perjury and she'd finish up in the nick an' all.'

'Did you ever see this girl again?' I asked.

'Of course I did, and you've met her an' all, Mr Brock. I'm married to her. She waited till I got out and we was wed eleven years ago. And I've been going straight ever since.'

'Let's get back to the night that Clifford Gregory was murdered, Sid.'

'What d'you want to know that I ain't told you already, Mr Brock?'

'Just run through what you said to us before.'

Miller recounted, word for word, what he had told us the previous Sunday afternoon. When he finished, I glanced at Dave, who had been following Miller's account against a copy of his statement. He nodded.

Nevertheless, I deemed it politic to caution Miller at this stage of the interview.

'You're a convicted burglar, Sid, so think carefully before you answer my next question,' I said. 'Did you have anything to do with the burglary at the Gregorys' house or the death of Clifford Gregory?'

'No, I bloody didn't,' said Miller vehemently. 'When I came out of the nick, I swore I'd never go back again, Mr Brock, and that's the God's honest truth,' he said. 'It's no joke being banged up for rape, especially when you ain't done it. You get sick of everyone calling you a nonce. Even the screws would have a sly dig every chance they got.'

'Were you having an affair with Sharon Gregory?'

'No, I wasn't. D'you think I'm mad, Mr Brock? You don't do it on your own doorstep. Anyway, I wouldn't do a thing like that to my Janet. I'd never cheat on her.'

'Very well. I shall admit you to police bail to report to Uxbridge police station one month from now. If your attendance is not required, I'll let you know.'

'That's bloody rich, that is,' said Miller disgustedly. 'I go and help the girl next door in her hour of need and this is all the thanks I get for it.'

'What's next, guv?' asked Dave, once Miller had departed, still muttering to himself about the injustice of the world.

'We go back to the factory and see if Sharon Gregory's turned up yet. But I don't suppose she has. I've got a nasty feeling that she could be anywhere in the world by now and doesn't want to be found.'

It wasn't until later that day that we discovered Sharon Gregory wasn't missing any more.

DI Len Driscoll was waiting for me when Dave and I got back to the office.

'I've got all the results from the house-to-house enquiries, guv.'

'Did you find anything useful, Len?'

'It was the usual blow out,' said Driscoll. 'Nobody saw anything. No one saw any unusual cars. Nobody saw anybody hanging around. Mind you, it was late on a Saturday evening and apparently Tarhill Road is a cut-through from a pub to a council estate.'

'Yes, Miller told us that. So did Sharon.'

'One or two near neighbours heard screaming, but put it down to kids coming back from the pub,' continued Driscoll. 'Even so, one of 'em did actually *think* about calling the police.' That statement was followed by a cynical laugh. 'But then the screaming stopped, so they all went to bed.'

'Did any of them know the Gregorys, Len?'

'Only in passing. I got the impression that they're all at pains to keep themselves to themselves. It was the usual "don't want to get involved" attitude. A lot of them work at Heathrow, of course, and that means that many of them are on shift work. Those who knew Sharon knew she was a flight attendant – they'd seen her going to work in uniform – but didn't suggest that that made her flighty.' Driscoll chuckled at his little joke. 'But as for visitors, or any suggestion that she put herself about, zilch! Mind you, guv, they probably knew, but weren't prepared to say. And I wouldn't have put it past some of them to have got across her themselves.'

'All of which is more or less what I expected, Len. Thanks, and thank the team for their efforts.'

'By the way, the Gregorys haven't come to the notice of the local police either. No domestics or anything like that,' said Driscoll. 'But there was one other thing, although I don't think it means much. We spoke to the customers at the local pub and one of them, a lad of about nineteen, said he was passing the Gregorys' house at just after ten on Saturday night when he caught sight of a naked girl at the window. He stopped to have a good look and whistled, but the girl quickly drew the curtains.'

'That fits in with her story,' I said. 'She must've gone up to bed just after that, and then come down again later when she heard this noise she claimed disturbed her.'

As a result of my interview with Sidney Miller at Fulham nick, I'd missed lunch, but I'd had the foresight to pick up a packet of sandwiches from the local Starbucks. I'd just settled in my office with the door firmly shut and was stirring my cup of coffee when Colin Wilberforce appeared again.

'What is it now, Colin?' I had to admit to being a little irritated at having my scratch lunch interrupted.

'Sharon Gregory's been found, sir. She's dead.'

'Where and when was this?' Don't ask me why, but I'd somehow expected this. Call it 'copper's nose', if you like.

'Just after midday at the Dickin Hotel at Heathrow Airport, sir. According to the DI on the Homicide Assessment Team, it looked as though she'd been strangled.'

Believe it or not, Homicide and Serious Crime Command West is responsible for investigating homicide and serious crime in the west of London. And there aren't many units left with a title that tells you exactly what they do. Our remit, as the hierarchy is fond of saying, stretches from Westminster to Hillingdon on the edge of the Metropolitan Police District and encompasses all the heavy-duty villainy that takes place in between. Unfortunately, that area also includes Heathrow Airport. Not that it would have made any difference in this particular case; anything to do with Sharon Gregory, wherever she'd been found – in the London area, of course – was down to me.

'What's the SP, Colin?'

'According to the HAT DI, sir, Sharon Gregory checked in at about twelve o'clock midday yesterday for one night only and was allocated room 219. The room was booked until twelve noon today, but she hadn't checked out by then, and a "Do Not Disturb" sign was still on the door of her room. The chambermaid knocked several times, but got no answer. Rather than go in, she called the duty manager, and when they entered the room they found Sharon Gregory's dead body naked on the bed.'

'Was her Mini Cooper at the hotel?'

'Yes, sir. In the car park.'

'Now you know why I joined the Job, Colin,' I said, reluctantly dropping the remains of my sandwich into the waste paper basket. 'It's the excitement of it all.'

The moment Dave and I stepped through the doors of the Dickin Hotel we were confronted by an agitated, fussy little man hovering in the foyer.

'Are you in charge?' he demanded, peering through rimless spectacles and stepping towards me as if to prevent me from going any further.

'And who might you be?' asked Dave.

'My name's Mr Sharp and I am the general manager. And I'd like to know how much longer your people are likely to be here. It's not good for the image of the hotel having the police running about all over the place.'

'It doesn't do much for its image if you allow your guests to be murdered, either,' observed Dave drily. 'But to answer your question, as long as it takes. What you've got on the second floor is a crime scene, and until my chief inspector here says otherwise, it'll remain a crime scene.'

'Oh my God!' The anguished Mr Sharp spent a moment or two wringing his hands. 'The board of directors will be furious.'

'Very likely,' said Dave unsympathetically.

'I'm Detective Chief Inspector Brock, Mr Sharp,' I said. 'Now that we've got you here, perhaps you can tell me at what time Mrs Gregory checked in.' I knew what Wilberforce had said, but I always like to verify information I've received second-hand.

Sharp turned to the young woman behind the counter, flicked his fingers and repeated my question.

The receptionist, whose badge bore the name Kirsty, scrolled through the computer. 'Ms Gregory checked in at twelve-oh-two yesterday afternoon, Mr Sharp,' she said.

'Was anyone with her?' asked Dave, bypassing the manager and speaking directly to Kirsty.

'I can't tell from the entry on the computer. We don't record both names if it happens to be a couple, just the name of the person making the booking. She did ask specifically for a double room with a double bed, though.' Kirsty smiled at Dave, but most young women do. Even some of the more mature ones have been known to cast an appraising eye over him.

'Could you let me have a printout, Kirsty?' asked Dave, returning the girl's smile.

'Did she have any visitors that you know of, Kirsty?' I asked, once she had given Dave the printout. 'Did anyone call at the desk asking for her room number?'

'I don't know. I wasn't on duty when Ms Gregory checked in.'

'Who was, Mr Sharp?' Dave turned back to the manager.

Sharp walked round the counter to consult a duty roster. 'Natalie Lester,' he said. 'She'll be on at four o'clock.'

'She'll need to be interviewed when she arrives,' I said.

The manager tutted. 'This is all very inconvenient,' he said.

'It was for Mrs Gregory, too,' said Dave.

We took the lift to the second floor, gave our details to the incident officer at the tapes and made our way along the corridor.

Linda Mitchell met us at the door to room 219. Kate Ebdon was with her.

'Kate, there's a receptionist named Natalie Lester who's due on duty at four o'clock. It's a long shot, I know, but ask her if during her tour of duty anyone enquired for Sharon Gregory. And would you also ask if there was anyone with her when she checked in.'

'Leave it with me,' said Kate, and made her way downstairs.

'We've finished here, Mr Brock,' said Linda. 'It didn't take long, being only the one room. I gathered a few hairs from the pillows and the bed that might give us a DNA that we can profile. And there are fingerprints all over the place, so I doubt we'll be able to get any immediate idents, but we might be lucky. I guess the chambermaids don't do too much in the way of cleaning. At least, not every day.'

'I'd better have a serious word with the manager about that,' said Dave. 'Definitely not what one would expect of a hotel of this standard.'

'By the way . . .' Linda gave me a wry smile. 'You might care to have a look at her underwear. It's on the floor, what there is of it, but I wouldn't think it's the sort that the airline would approve of its staff wearing. There's a uniform hanging in the closet, but I've not opened the suitcase or her handbag. If there are any items in them that you want examined, let me know.'

Inside the room, Dr Mortlock was in the act of packing away his thermometers and the other tools of his trade. The body of Sharon Gregory lay spreadeagled on the bed, her sightless eyes staring at the ceiling. She was naked save for a pair of sheer black hold-up stockings. A cream satin robe had been thrown carelessly on the floor near a chair. Beside the chair was a small suitcase on a luggage rack. Scattered about the room, as though they'd been cast aside in a hurry, were a pair of high-heeled shoes, a scarlet thong and what I recognized as a shelf bra. Gail keeps me up to date about these things; in fact, she often wore them herself.

All of which told me that Sharon had undressed – or had been undressed – hurriedly after her attacker arrived. Everything pointed to her having known him, and it looked very much like an assignation that for some reason had gone fatally wrong.

'You seem to be making a habit of providing me with dead bodies just recently, Harry,' said Mortlock, by way of a greeting.

'It's the trade I'm in, Henry. What can you tell me?'

'Manual strangulation. By the look of it, I'd say that her killer used both hands. Someone with a pretty powerful grip, I'd think. I might be able to tell you more when I carve her up, but I doubt it.'

'Any idea of the time of death?' I asked.

'A bit tricky given the weather, the open windows and the air conditioning, Harry, but I'd hazard a guess at sometime after six o'clock last night. I can't pin it down any nearer than that. I might know a bit more when I've analysed her stomach contents.'

'Have you finished with the body, Henry?'

'Yes. You can shift it to the mortuary as soon as you like.'

The laboratory liaison officer had been waiting in the wings. His job was to preserve continuity of evidence by taking charge of the mortal remains of Sharon Gregory and making the necessary phone calls. It was an important function; the last thing we wanted was some smart-arse barrister suggesting that the cadaver Henry had carved up at the mortuary was not the one found in room 219 of the Dickin Hotel. It had been known in the past for prosecutions to founder on minor technicalities, such as a detective omitting to put a signature on the right form at the right time, thus breaking the chain of evidence.

I opened the suitcase. It contained, among other necessaries, two summer dresses, a linen trouser suit, changes of sensible underwear, spare tights, a somewhat risqué bikini, and a make-up bag. There was also a small leather bag containing a variety of perfumes. It looked as though she'd intended staying away from West Drayton for some time. One thing was for sure: she'd never be going back there now.

Sharon's handbag was on a bedside table. It was a black satchel bag from Aspinal of London, and I knew from my occasional enforced shopping trips with Gail that it retailed for not much less than £500. Inside, apart from what one would expect to find in a woman's handbag, I found a small wallet containing credit cards, one of which was in the name of Clifford Gregory. According to the partial number on the receipts, that card had been used at a retail outlet and a restaurant at the Chimes Shopping Centre, Uxbridge. There was also a paper napkin bearing a mobile telephone number.

'Give the credit cards and the receipts to Charlie Flynn, Dave. He might be able to tell us if there's anything interesting on the various accounts. And check out the number on this napkin.'

'There's this mobile on the bedside cabinet, guv.' Dave picked up the phone with latex-gloved hands and scrolled through to the record of sent messages. 'There's nothing on it,' he said. 'I suspect it's a pay-as-you-go throwaway job.'

'Is there anything to say whether it's Sharon's?' I asked. 'There is a receipt dated yesterday in her handbag for a mobile purchased in Uxbridge. Oddly enough it was a cash purchase, but she paid for the other items with a card.'

'Looks as though she didn't want it to be traced,' said Dave. 'I'll check it out, but I doubt I'll be able to confirm it. It's probably one that she used to arrange a meeting with her lover and wiped clean after she made the call. Either that or it hasn't been used at all.'

'It's not the one we found at the airport, then?'

'No, it's not,' said Dave, 'but we're fairly sure she didn't go back there, so that one's probably still in her locker. Which is why she had to buy another one.'

'I suppose she might've used the hotel phone from this room.'

'I'll have a word with the receptionist,' said Dave. 'She'll be able to tell me. Guests get billed for calls. Usually quite heavily.'

'I know,' I said, recalling the commander's horror when he'd discovered the cost of the calls we'd made to London while in Bermuda on an enquiry a few years ago.

Dave and I returned to the ground floor to be met by Kate Ebdon.

'I've spoken to Natalie Lester, the receptionist who was on duty at the desk yesterday afternoon and evening, guv.' Kate indicated a smiling Eurasian girl who was dealing with a couple of casually-dressed middle-aged Americans. Half a dozen other people were vying impatiently for the girl's attention. 'She said that they were extremely busy during that time and she doesn't recall anyone asking for the Gregory woman. She also said that a visitor could've asked any member of staff who happened to be helping out on reception. And she confirmed that no one was with Sharon when she checked in.'

'That's what I expected,' I said.

'But she pointed out that if a visitor knew which room Sharon was staying in, there'd be nothing to stop him or her going straight up,' continued Kate. 'There are so many guests milling about that they never know who's who. Incidentally, she mentioned that Sharon Gregory had stayed here before. At least four or five times during the past year, and she always asked for a double room with a double bed.'

'Did anybody see an agitated man leaving during the afternoon or early evening?' I knew that it was a hopeless query, but sometimes a piece of vital evidence resulted.

'You must be joking, guv.' Kate laughed outright at such a preposterous idea. 'There are always crowds of people in the hotel. And if any of yesterday's guests saw anything, you can bet that they're on the other side of the world by now. Most of the people who stay here are transiting airline passengers who book in for just the one night.'

'Thanks, Kate. I'd guessed that the killer wouldn't have made himself known to the receptionist. Judging by the saucy underwear in Sharon Gregory's room, I think she knew the guy and had probably arranged to meet him here for a quick tumble. And told him the room number where he'd find her. What we don't know is why it went so disastrously wrong.'

'Of course, we're assuming that it was lover boy who topped her,' said Dave, injecting his customary valid scepticism into the discussion. 'On the other hand, it might've been a passing floor waiter who happened to walk in and find Sharon prancing about in a thong.'

'That's in hand,' said Kate. 'I've got a team interviewing all the staff. And we'll have to carry on tomorrow because not all yesterday's people are on duty today.'

'The receptionist confirmed that Sharon didn't use the hotel phone, guv,' said Dave, 'but as I said earlier, she probably used the mobile we found and then deleted the call from the sent calls list.'

'I wonder why?' I asked, half to myself.

'There again, her killer might've been a careful bastard and deleted the calls himself before taking off.'

'Maybe,' I said, 'but why not take the damned phone with him? He could've chucked it in the river rather than leaving it here for us to find.'

Leaving those imponderables for the time being, we returned to Sharon Gregory's hotel room for another search, primarily to make sure that we hadn't overlooked anything of importance. But we found nothing more that would help to tell us who'd killed her.

Back downstairs, we questioned members of staff who might've seen anything, but they were of no assistance at all. Finally we gave Sharon Gregory's room back to Mr Sharp, the general manager.

'However, Mr Sharp,' I said, 'other officers will be here tomorrow to question those members of staff who are not here today.'

'I hope this doesn't get into the papers,' said Sharp, his shoulders slumping as he sighed.

'What, with an airport full of freelance journalists and paparazzi?' scoffed Dave. 'You must be joking.' He glanced across the lobby at a Japanese tourist with an expensive camera slung around his neck. 'I think he might be one of them,' he added.

The manager beetled off to intercept the innocent guest, but then stopped abruptly at the sight of a wheeled stretcher being pushed across the foyer. On it was a body bag containing Sharon's corpse. 'Oh my Godfathers!' he exclaimed.

NINE

We got back to our office at ESB at about nine o'clock that evening, and I decided we'd done enough for one day. I sent the team home and told them to return early next morning. There was much to do.

In the interests of remaining alert the following day, I considered it inadvisable to spend another night with Gail and went home to the flat in Surbiton I'd bought after my divorce from Helga.

When I was a young uniformed PC, I'd met and married a German girl. Originally from Cologne, Helga Büchner had been a physiotherapist at Westminster Hospital and had pummelled my wrenched shoulder back into place following a confrontation with some youths I'd arrested in Whitehall.

I took her out to dinner that same night, and to a police dance at Caxton Hall on the following Saturday. After a whirlwind romance we were married two months later and began our shared life in an insalubrious flat in Earlsfield, South London. The marriage had lasted sixteen years, which was about fifteen and a half years longer than the predictions of my colleagues, mainly the female ones.

Over the years, and thanks mainly to my job, we had slowly drifted apart, but the last straw came when Helga left our four-year-old son Robert with a neighbour while she went to work. The boy fell into an ornamental pond and drowned. I didn't blame the neighbour; I blamed Helga. I might be old-fashioned, but I thought that Helga should've put her career on hold, at least until Robert had started school.

On the day of the tragedy the superintendent called me into his office to break the news. It's a day that is forever etched in my memory.

'Sit down, Harry,' he had said. 'I'm sorry to have to tell you your son has been drowned.' Just like that.

Typically, the guv'nor hadn't waltzed around the subject, but had got straight to the point. That, of course, is the CID way.

'Take whatever time you need,' he'd said, after filling me in with the brief details. 'I'll square it with the commander. The duty inspector at Wandsworth nick dealt with it, if you want to have a word.'

That awful event had finally torn apart the tattered remains of a marriage that had been full of arguments, accusations and counter-accusations. It hadn't been helped by adultery on both sides, and ultimately Helga's decision to leave me for a doctor with whom, unbeknown to me, she'd been having an affair for the previous six months.

The only lasting benefit I derived from the marriage was the ability to speak fluent German. On balance it might've been cheaper to have gone to night school.

Gladys Gurney, my 'lady-who-does', had been working miracles on my flat. She really is a gem, and Gail had repeatedly tried to filch her from me. The whole place had been tidied, polished and hoovered from top to bottom. Even the windows had been cleaned, at least on the inside. My shirts had been washed, ironed and put away in the wardrobe. The bed had been changed and the dirty sheets and pillow slips laundered and placed tidily in the appropriate drawers. The detritus I'd left after my last stay had miraculously disappeared. And there was one of Gladys's charming little notes on the kitchen worktop.

> *Dear Mr Brock*
> *I found a pair of Miss Sutton's shoes the ones with high heels what seemed to somehow have got under your bed. I've give them a polish and left them in the wardrobe. I hope she never hurt her feet getting home without no shoes on.*
> *Yours faithfully*
> *Gladys Gurney (Mrs)*
> *P.S. Your microwave has broke down.*

As I said, Gladys is an absolute gem. I left her wages on the kitchen worktop and added an extra five pounds and a note of thanks. She's worth every penny.

I was in the office at eight o'clock the next morning, thus giving me two hours before the commander arrived at the stroke of ten.

He was never at work earlier than that and I suspected he had been warned not to overdo it by Mrs Commander, a harridan of a woman if the photograph that adorned her husband's desk was anything to go by.

My team had been busy. At nine o'clock, DS Flynn came into my office.

'I've been checking on the credit cards found at the murder scene, guv. Clifford Gregory's card was used twice at the Chimes Shopping Centre at Uxbridge the day before yesterday. The receipts show that it was first used for the purchase of underwear at ten-sixteen, and again for an omelette, a pastry and two coffees at ten-thirty-seven at an Italian restaurant at the shopping centre.' Flynn closed his daybook. 'I've got Sheila Armitage checking it out at the shopping centre; she might turn up something useful. And the hotel told me that Clifford Gregory's card was swiped by the receptionist Natalie Lester at the Dickin Hotel at twelve-oh-two. But we knew what time she'd booked in, of course.'

Dave appeared with cups of coffee. 'Not much joy so far, then, guv,' he said, when I'd brought him up to date.

'I think there's no doubt that Sharon Gregory murdered her husband, Dave. The purchase of the window sash weight and the clothes line is down to her, and the online transaction with the Mexican pharmaceutical company was almost certainly for the Rohypnol. As well as the evidence of Clifford Gregory's blood in the shower tray and on the sash weight.'

'I can't see this ghostly intruder bothering to take a shower,' said Dave, 'unless he hadn't got any clothes on either. And that would create a whole new ball game. Frankly, I don't think he exists.'

'Perhaps not an intruder as such, Dave,' I said. 'Even so, it might be a good idea to examine the computer at the Gregorys' house to see if it turns up any other names. And Charlie Flynn has confirmed that she used her husband's credit card on two occasions in Uxbridge, and to check in at the hotel.'

'And they haven't got a hope in hell of getting their money. What a terrible shame!' commented Dave, who had jousted with credit card companies in the past.

'The only question,' I continued, 'was whether she had any help to murder her husband. Was this mysterious intruder known to her and was he an accomplice in the murder? Or perhaps he didn't exist at all.'

'I just said that . . . *sir*,' said Dave.

At two o'clock that afternoon, we were back at Henry Mortlock's mortuary.

The naked body of Sharon Gregory, sewn roughly together after Mortlock's probing, lay on a table.

'As I said at the scene, Harry, the cause of death was manual strangulation.' Mortlock finished washing his hands and turned to face us. 'Petechiae, cyanosis and congestion all indicate pressure on the jugular veins. There was also heavy bruising in that area – probably caused by the killer's thumbs – which, as I suggested previously, implies that he had some strength in his hands.'

'Like a surgeon, Doc?' queried Dave, with feigned innocence. 'They've got strong hands, haven't they?'

'Very funny, Sergeant Poole.' Mortlock put on his jacket. 'There's something else that may interest you, Harry. Sharon Gregory was two months pregnant. In view of the fact that her husband had had a vasectomy, it might give you something to think about.'

'From what we've learned about her, Henry, I'm not at all surprised. Is it possible to get a DNA sample from the fetus?'

'Already done,' said Mortlock. 'It's on its way to the forensic science lab. But that'll only help you if the father's DNA is on record.'

'It will be, by the time I've finished,' I said. It was more a pious hope than a certainty, although the father of Sharon Gregory's unborn child was not necessarily the murderer. And from what I'd learned so far, the father could be any one of a dozen men that she had known.

'Incidentally,' continued Mortlock, 'she'd recently had unprotected sex. It's possible that the DNA of the sperm will match any that's found in the fetus.'

'This job's turning into a nightmare,' I said.

'It gets better,' said Mortlock. 'There were two different traces of vaginal fluid on Sharon Gregory's body. One was hers, but the other has yet to be identified.'

'Great!' I exclaimed. 'So now we've got another woman in the equation. Thanks a bundle, Henry.'

'Don't shoot the messenger,' commented Mortlock drily.

When Dave and I returned to ESB, I was still thinking about the identity of Sharon's murderer, and the added complication of another woman having been at the murder scene. Sidney Miller kept coming into mind. He was on the scene of Clifford Gregory's murder very quickly – much too quickly, perhaps – and I wondered whether he had been involved in it. Sharon's belated admission that she was naked when she'd wandered around the house with Miller, and his ready confirmation that she was, led me to believe that there might've been a greater degree of intimacy between the two than either of them had been prepared to admit. More to the point, Miller had instantly and vehemently denied any such relationship: 'You don't do it on your own doorstep,' he had claimed. I'd thought at the time that the denial was just a little too instant and a little too emphatic to be true. But CID officers are, by the very nature of their calling, cynical and disbelieving.

Set against that was the evidence that had come to light that Sharon Gregory was promiscuous. Miller had said she was a flirt, and Gordon Harrison admitted to having had sexual intercourse with her whenever they were both in Miami. But now, it seemed, she was also bisexual.

Gordon Harrison's name had, of course, been only one of those on the mobile that Sharon had kept at the airport, well away from where her husband might've found it. There were three others who we had yet to see.

And that reminded me . . .

'How are you getting on with tracking down the two Florida telephone numbers, Dave?' I asked.

'I've been on to the Miami-Dade Police, guv, and they were able to give me details of the subscribers. Both were cellphones, as the Americans call them. One went out to a Lance Kramer, a theatrical designer, and the other to a Miles Donahue, described as an entrepreneur.' Dave laughed. 'And that's a job description that covers a multitude of sins. Both these guys are resident in the Miami Beach area within a ten-mile radius of the Shannon Hotel.'

'I think we need to ask the Miami-Dade Police to interview

them and find out how well they knew Sharon. And where they were on the night of her murder.'

'It's the Miami Beach Police we need to talk to, sir,' said Dave. 'Apparently, that's the force that covers that area.'

'On second thoughts, Dave, I don't think so. This enquiry is beginning to get complicated. We'll have a word with Ben Donaldson.' Donaldson was the resident FBI agent at the United States Embassy in London and masqueraded as their legal attaché. 'He'll know the best people to get in touch with in Florida, and while he's at it, we'll ask for enquiries to be made at the Shannon Hotel. We know Sharon was visited there by Gordon Harrison, but I'm interested in any other visitors she might've had while she was staying there on a stopover. And see if you can get a decent photograph of her that we can take with us to the embassy.'

'We've got the post-mortem photograph that was taken at the scene, guv. Will that do?'

'It'll have to, Dave. I don't want to delay this investigation any more than is necessary.'

'Surely you don't think that one of these guys might've come over to Heathrow for one night just to strangle Sharon Gregory, do you, guv?' There was doubt combined with cynicism in Dave's voice.

'Funnier things have happened,' I said. 'Get a car and we'll make our way to the embassy.'

'By the way, guv, Ted Richie rang back. He's made a few enquiries and he's come up with a name.'

'What name?'

'D'you remember asking him if Sharon had a special friend among the crew. Richie reckons that a girl called Cindy Patterson and Sharon were as thick as thieves. She might be able to shed some light on what Sharon got up to in Miami.'

'We'll make a point of seeing her at some time,' I said. 'Remind me.'

'Got a minute, sir?' asked DC Sheila Armitage, appearing in my office.

'What is it, Sheila?'

'I went out to Uxbridge, sir, and followed up on the purchases that were made on Clifford Gregory's credit card.'

'And?'

'Sharon Gregory was identified by the shop assistant who sold her the kinky underwear. At least, she said it was a woman in airline uniform and the time and the description fitted. Apparently they had a discussion about the erotic underwear Sharon purchased. I also spoke to the waiter who served her in the Italian restaurant. He remembered her very clearly.'

'Was he sure?'

'Definitely, sir. He said she flirted with him outrageously. So much so, that when he put her credit card in his machine he didn't notice that it was in a man's name. What's more, Sharon propositioned him, and he scribbled his phone number on a napkin and gave it to her.' Armitage turned over a page in her pocketbook. 'It's the number found on the napkin that was in her handbag at the hotel. And before you ask,' she added with a smile, 'the waiter was on duty until midnight that evening, and the following evening. And that checks out. He said he hadn't heard from her again.'

'Anything about the mobile phone we found at the scene, Sheila?'

'Ah, the mobile. Yes, sir. A mobile phone was certainly purchased by Sharon Gregory at an outlet in the Chimes Centre. But according to the cash receipt you found in her handbag, it wasn't the phone found in her room at the Dickin Hotel. I checked the serial number with Linda Mitchell.'

'Interesting,' I said. 'I wonder what happened to it? More to the point, where did the one we found come from?'

'I doubt we'll be able to find out, sir,' said Sheila. 'Mobile phones are difficult to track down.'

I'd not met Ben Donaldson before, but he'd taken over the legal attaché's post when Joe Daly had returned to New York on retirement after twenty-four years with the Bureau.

Ben was a big man who originated from Montgomery, Alabama. Although he later told me that he'd spent many years in Washington and New York, with spells in Ottawa and Paris, his accent and Southern bonhomie hadn't left him. He almost leaped across the office as we entered.

'How ya doin', Harry?' he said, as though he'd known me all my life.

'Pleased to meet you at last, Ben,' I said. 'This is Dave Poole, my sergeant.'

Donaldson seized each of our hands in turn and pumped them vigorously. 'Guess you know Darlene,' he said, as his secretary came into the room bearing a tray of coffee. 'Joe left her behind when he went back to the States.'

'Yes, we've met,' I said, smiling. That Darlene was still here rather surprised me; I thought that she and Joe had had a 'thing' going. She was a beautifully packaged American redhead who looked as though she belonged in a Hollywood movie rather than in a London office. And she had the happy knack of producing coffee the minute we arrived at Grosvenor Square. And for anyone else who arrived, I imagined.

'Take a seat, fellers.' Donaldson swept his hand magnanimously towards the bank of armchairs in one corner of his impressive office. 'What can I do for y'all?'

I explained about the murder of Sharon Gregory and the events that led up to it, including our certainty that she'd murdered her husband. Both Ben and I were law enforcement officers and, even though this was our first meeting, I trusted him implicitly to keep my theories to himself.

'Dave has discovered that the phone numbers of two men, Lance Kramer and Miles Donahue, were on our murder victim's mobile—'

'What's a mobile?' asked Donaldson, feigning innocence.

'It's what you call a cellphone in America, Ben.'

'Oh, I thought you were talking about one of those gadgets you hang over a baby's crib.' Donaldson laughed. 'I've only been here about three weeks, but I guess I'll come to grips with your language if I stay long enough.' He paused. 'Only kidding, Harry.'

'Both these men live in the Miami Beach area of Florida.' I turned to Dave. 'Tell Ben your problem,' I said.

'We don't know whether to contact Miami-Dade Police Department, or the Miami Beach Police, which seems the more obvious,' said Dave. 'Or even the Florida State Police.'

Donaldson took a mouthful of coffee and set down his cup before replying. 'The set-up of the American police is a minefield, Dave,' he said. 'Half the guys in it don't even understand who to talk with about interstate enquiries, let alone how to deal with international ones. But you've come to the right place. When in doubt, contact the FBI. As it happens, we have a Bureau office on Second Avenue at North Miami Beach, and I'll contact the special agent in charge ASAP.'

'Excellent,' said Dave.

'Yeah, excellent.' Donaldson savoured the word and grinned. 'I like that,' he said, and shouted for Darlene. 'Dave here will give you the details, Darlene. Perhaps you'd send a request to the Florida office and ask them to make enquiries.'

Darlene sat down in the armchair next to Dave and spent the next few minutes noting down the sparse details of the relevant dates, and what we knew about Kramer and Donahue.

'I'll call you as soon as they come back with the information, Harry.'

'Thanks, Ben,' I said. 'We must have a drink sometime.'

'Sure, I'd like that.' Donaldson paused. 'D'you happen to know an English pub that doesn't serve warm beer?'

'You'll get used to it,' said Dave.

'Excellent!' Donaldson laughed, stood up and shook hands again. 'Like I said, Harry, I'll call you.'

TEN

I t was past five o'clock when we left the embassy, and I decided it was time to start talking to the other subscribers to the British telephone numbers that Dave had found on Sharon's airport mobile.

'Where d'you want to go first, guv?'

'We'll try this Julian Reed in Chelsea for a kick off. It's not far from here.'

The house in Chelsea where Reed lived would undoubtedly have attracted a price tag of several millions in today's property market.

The woman who answered the door was about thirty, maybe thirty-five. She had long titian hair and was expensively dressed. But given the value of the house in which she lived, her designer white-linen trouser suit came as no surprise. Neither did the expensive jewellery she was wearing.

'Can I help you?' She cast an enquiring, superior gaze over us.

'We're police officers, madam,' I said. 'I was hoping to have a word with Mr Julian Reed. I am given to understand he lives here.' This was going to be a difficult interview if this was Reed's wife.

'I'm Muriel Reed, his wife,' said the woman, confirming what I'd feared to be the case. 'I think Julian's in the study. If you'd like to come in, I'll get him for you. Just as soon as I can find him.'

In my experience, a woman usually expressed surprise when the police came to her door asking to speak to her husband, and demanded to know why. But this woman didn't seem in the slightest bit curious about our arrival. *Perhaps she knew what we wanted.*

We followed the woman upstairs and were shown into a large airy room that was predominately white in décor: white walls, white carpet, and matching white sofas and armchairs that had the appearance of having been selected for their style rather than their comfort. A few original abstract paintings adorned the walls. The white marble fireplace contained a gas-operated fake log fire, and the mantelshelf was crowded with white candlesticks of varying sizes. In the centre of this Arctic-style room was a wrought-iron glass-topped table upon which was the usual pile of coffee-table books. Against this snowy background the white-suited Muriel Reed all but disappeared.

As Dave commented later, the room looked like a large igloo inhabited by a rich Eskimo.

'Do please take a seat, gentlemen,' said Muriel Reed. 'May I offer you a drink? Tea or coffee? Something stronger, perhaps?'

'No thank you, Mrs Reed,' I said.

'I'll go and see if I can find my husband, then.' The woman still didn't enquire why we wished to see him, and walked gracefully from the room.

When she returned, she was accompanied by a man, probably between thirty-five and forty, who was scruffily dressed in khaki shorts that were too long to be fashionable, a casual shirt and sandals. He wore heavily-framed spectacles and an innocent expression on his face that, together with his untrimmed auburn hair, lent him the overall appearance of an ageing Boy Scout. He did appear to be quite well-built, though.

'I'm Julian Reed, gentlemen. My wife tells me you wanted to speak to me.' He gazed at us quizzically with his head on one side.

'I'm Detective Chief Inspector Brock and this is Detective Sergeant Poole, Mr Reed. We're investigating a murder that occurred on Monday, the twenty-ninth of July.'

'Really?' Julian Reed blinked at us through his finger-marked spectacles, his reaction one of bland acceptance that such things were commonplace these days.

'Good gracious!' Muriel Reed's response was much the same, but her tone indicated interest rather than shock. 'Was this locally?' she asked.

'No, at Heathrow Airport. Well, in one of the hotels near there, to be precise.'

'How d'you think that I can help?' Leaning forward, Reed seemed genuinely interested that we thought he may be able to assist us.

'The murder victim was a stewardess who regularly flew on the service from Heathrow to Miami in Florida,' I said hesitantly.

Muriel Reed laughed. 'And you want to know if Julian was having an affair with her, I suppose?'

The woman's candour stunned me for a moment, as did her husband's lack of protest at his wife's comment. 'I was certainly wondering if you'd met her, Mr Reed,' I said eventually, unable to think of anything else to say. I was not yet prepared to mention that his phone number had been found on Sharon's airport mobile, at least not while his wife was there.

'Was she a tart, in her twenties and willing to open her legs at the drop of a hat?' Muriel's coarse language seemed strangely at odds with her rounded upper-class tones.

'Well, I—'

'Oh, come on, Chief Inspector, don't beat about the bush,' said Muriel, throwing back her head and laughing. 'Julian might've had a fling with this woman, but he wouldn't't've murdered her. To be quite frank, he hasn't got the guts for that sort of thing. Have you, darling?' she added, shooting a mischievous glance in her husband's direction.

'Are you in the habit of having casual affairs, Mr Reed?' Dave was much less inhibited with his questions than I was, and got straight to the crux of the matter.

'All the time, Sergeant Poole.' It was Muriel Reed who replied, at the same time raising her eyebrows in surprise at Dave's educated and well-modulated English accent. Perhaps she was expecting a stereotypical Jamaican sing-song delivery. 'I think the term is screwing around, and my husband's very good at it.'

This woman was quite obviously quick to grasp people's names and to remember them. And she didn't mind telling us that her husband was a philanderer, even in his presence. She was so composed and overbearing that it seemed to me that Julian Reed was completely dominated by her.

As if to confirm it, he didn't react to his wife's statement and gazed into the middle distance with a blank expression on his face.

'Do you ever go to Miami, Mr Reed,' I asked, hoping to get a response from this largely unresponsive man.

'I go fairly regularly, as a matter of fact, Chief Inspector.'

'On holiday, or do you have business interests there?'

'I'm an international property developer,' said Reed. 'So, yes, on business . . .'

Julian Reed seemed to be about to say something more, but before he could continue, Muriel Reed intervened yet again. 'My late father took Julian into partnership when Julian and I were married eight years ago, Chief Inspector, and when my father died, he left Julian the business. And my father left me this house and a large sum of money.' She raised her chin slightly. 'Is there anything else you want to know about our private life, Chief Inspector?' It was an enquiry laden with sarcasm. 'I don't really know what you want of my husband. He obviously doesn't know this woman who was murdered.'

'Were you here the day before yesterday, Mr Reed?' I ignored the woman's petty attempt to defend her husband and decided to take her advice to get straight to the point.

'Yes, I was.'

'All day?'

'No, I was out during the afternoon.'

'And the evening?'

'I was here all evening.'

'That's quite right, but God knows where he was that afternoon. Most likely stuffing five-pound notes into a stripper's garter at some sleazy Soho club; that's the usual way he fills his otherwise empty days,' said Muriel, continuing to speak as though her husband was not there. 'Isn't that so, darling? Didn't you say something about having been to the Dizzy Club?'

'Er, yes. As a matter of fact, I spent all afternoon there,' said Reed hesitantly, before shooting a guilty glance in his wife's direction. 'But why d'you want to know, Chief Inspector?' I got the impression that he had lied when confirming his whereabouts.

Not only did Muriel Reed ignore her husband's sheepish admission, but she continued to talk as though he hadn't spoken or wasn't even in the room. 'We tend to live separate lives, you see, Mr Brock, and before you ask, no, we're not getting divorced.' She laughed again. 'Despite his waywardness, Julian's fun to be with and I rather like having him around. Apart from which, he couldn't afford to leave me.' Reed's wife stood up. 'I'll show you out.'

With that final enigmatic statement, it was obvious that Muriel Reed had decided the interview was over. But I hadn't finished yet.

'Did you ever meet a stewardess on the Heathrow to Miami flight by the name of Sharon Gregory, Mr Reed?'

So far Julian Reed had said very little of consequence, but at the mention of the victim's name he suddenly gripped the arms of the chair in which he was sitting and the colour drained from his face. 'Was she the girl who was murdered?' he asked, his voice barely above a whisper.

'Yes, she was. As I said, at a hotel near Heathrow Airport. Have you ever stayed at the Dickin Hotel, Mr Reed?'

'Oh my God! I don't believe it. What happened?'

'So you did know her, Mr Reed. How well?'

'I don't think you should say any more, Julian,' said his wife authoritatively, 'not without Brian being here.'

'Who is Brian?' asked Dave.

'Our solicitor,' said Muriel.

'Where were you on the twenty-ninth of this month, Mr Reed?' I asked. 'That was the day before yesterday.'

'My husband's already told you that, Chief Inspector,' snapped Muriel. 'He was at the Dizzy Club in Soho in the afternoon and he was here with me all evening.'

'I presume there's someone at the Dizzy Club who can vouch for your presence there, Mr Reed?'

'Of course there is,' said Muriel, before Reed could reply. 'Half a dozen of their resident trollops, I should imagine.'

'I think my wife's right, Mr Brock,' said Reed. 'I think I need to speak to my solicitor.'

'I'll see the gentlemen out, Julian,' said his wife, crossing swiftly to the sitting room door before her husband could move.

Once outside the sitting room and with the door firmly closed, Muriel continued the conversation at the top of the stairs. 'He might've been at the Dizzy Club in the afternoon,' she said, 'but it's not true that we were at home during the evening. This is where we were the evening before last.' She put a hand in her jacket pocket and handed me a printed card upon which was an address in Dorking. 'In fact, we were there most of the night.'

'What happens there?' asked Dave. He took the card from me and wrote the details in his pocketbook. 'It appears to be a private address. Are they friends of yours, the people who live there?'

'Not exactly,' Muriel responded guiltily. 'It's a sort of private

club. My husband didn't tell you because he's embarrassed that
we go there. But he enjoys what goes on and so do I.'

'And what does go on there, Mrs Reed?'

Muriel paused only momentarily. 'Oh, it's a sort of intimate
social club, Sergeant Poole,' she said. 'An opportunity to meet
other people of our persuasion. It's very select,' she added, implying
that mere policemen wouldn't be welcome. 'You can check if you
like.'

'Oh, I don't think that'll be necessary,' said Dave, closing his
pocketbook and putting it away.

'But I'd be grateful if you didn't mention to my husband that
I told you. He doesn't like it to be known that he goes there.'

'Your secret's safe with us, Mrs Reed,' said Dave. But I could
always tell when he was lying.

'Why did you tell them that we weren't getting divorced, Muriel?'
asked Reed, when his wife returned to the sitting room. 'You know
damned well that I can't wait to be separated from you.'

'Just because you think you're going to leave me, Julian, our
domestic affairs are really nothing to do with the damned police.
But apart from anything else, it's obvious they think you murdered
this Sharon Gregory. And once they start poking about, there's no
telling what they might come up with. And the more you say, the
more they'll twist it. It wouldn't be the first time an innocent man
has been sent to prison. You must speak to Brian before they ask
you any more questions. I'll ring him straight away.' Muriel paused
in the doorway. 'I suppose you didn't murder her, did you?'

'Of course not, and you know why,' said Reed. 'But why did
you tell them that our money was all yours? You know full well
it's mine. And your father didn't take me into any sort of partnership; he was a bloody estate agent who went bankrupt. And that
takes some doing for an estate agent.'

'For the same reason: it muddies the waters. The police are
naturally nosy, it's what they do. And just because you were
screwing this Sharon Gregory person doesn't mean you have to
tell them about it. And I repeat: they'll think you murdered her.
They'll put two and two together and before you know it you'll
be in the dock at the Old Bailey. And don't run away with the
idea that you were the only one who was shafting the little slut;

there's bound to have been dozens of others.' And with that parting sally, Muriel Reed swept from the room. 'I'm going for a swim,' she said, over her shoulder.

'What d'you think, Dave?' I asked, as we made our way back to the car.

'He's a wimp, guv, and firmly under his wife's thumb. I think he knows more than he's telling, but he didn't dare say another word while she was there. As Muriel Reed said, I doubt he's got the guts to murder anyone. Except possibly his own wife. And I reckon that's a non-starter. From what she said, I suspect he's living on her money. And it wasn't a coincidence that she was able to produce that card with the Dorking address on it so quickly.'

'I'll get Charlie Flynn to have a look at his company's records,' I said. 'Might turn up something useful. And tomorrow we'll visit the address Mrs Reed gave us to check on his alibi. But for now we'll have a word with the Dizzy Club.'

I rang the office on my mobile and told Colin Wilberforce what we'd learned from our visit to the Reeds, and asked him to get Flynn to make the necessary enquiries.

We drove straight from Chelsea to Regent Street, a distance of about three miles. For security reasons we parked the car at West End Central police station and took a taxi the rest of the way. Villains have even been known to steal police cars these days.

The Dizzy Club was one of many similar establishments that abound in the sleazy streets of Soho. The entrance to this one was next to a shop specializing in pornographic DVDs.

'Good evening, gents.' A shaven-headed, blue-chinned bouncer in an ill-fitting dinner jacket guarded the entrance. 'Membership fee is twenty-five pounds each.'

'We're members,' said Dave, and produced his warrant card.

'Oh!' The bouncer moved towards a telephone on the wall near the door.

'If you're calling the manager, tell him we want to see him right now, right here,' said Dave.

It was all of thirty seconds after the bouncer finished making the call that a short, squat, bald-headed individual rushed into the entrance hall. He was sweating and had greasy skin, with little rolls of fat perched on the back of his collar.

'Welcome, gentlemen.' The manager, speaking with a vaguely mid-European accent, wrung his hands in a manner of supplication. 'Do come in and see the show. We wouldn't charge you, of course.'

'I can't promise to reciprocate that courtesy,' commented Dave quietly, a barb that was clearly not misunderstood by the manager.

'Everything's quite proper here, Superintendent,' said the manager, doing a bit more nervous hand-wringing. 'We often have a visit from your Vice Squad. Just to check up, like.'

'I'll bet you do,' said Dave. 'And I'm a detective sergeant, not a superintendent.'

The manager opened his hands and shrugged. 'Only a matter of time, Officer,' he said.

'I'm Detective Chief Inspector Brock of New Scotland Yard,' I said, cutting across this verbal sparring match, 'and I'm investigating a murder.' It was an announcement that did nothing to restore the manager's peace of mind.

'Not here, surely? I can tell you that no murders have happened here.'

'And now I want to see your list of members,' I continued, ignoring his pointless protest.

'Of course, of course. This way, gentlemen, please.'

Following this oleaginous individual down a flight of stairs, we found ourselves in a gloomy, cavernous basement. In the centre of a brightly illuminated circular stage, a naked girl was doing her artistic best to make love to a chromium pole. It was a lacklustre performance.

Surrounding this tiny stage, tables were tightly packed together and crowded with a mainly male clientele. I did, however, spot one or two women among this gullible audience, but God knows what they saw to entertain them. I suspected that most of the club's customers were from out of town, and had fetched up in the Dizzy Club doubtless believing that they were experiencing something terribly risqué.

The reality was that they would finish up being ripped off.

The manager closed the door of his microscopic office and handed me a book from the top of a rusting filing cabinet.

'This Julian Reed,' I said, having found the entry. 'Was he here on the twenty-ninth of July?'

The manager took back the book and glanced at the entry. 'He might've been,' he said, shrugging. 'We don't keep a record of when our members come here. They just show their membership card to the doorman.'

'Is he well known to your girls?' asked Dave.

'Possibly.' The manager smiled nervously. 'But only if he's generous.'

'Is there any one girl that he seems to like more than the others?'

'I don't know. You'd have to ask them.'

'Then we will. How many girls work here?' Dave was beginning to get annoyed.

'Only five.'

'Are they all here at the moment?'

'Of course. But one of them is on stage right now.'

'Very well,' said Dave, 'then we'll speak to the other four for a start.'

With a sigh of resignation, the manager led us next door to the women's dressing room. Some optimist had put a star on the door. Without knocking, he barged straight in.

Four girls were sitting around in various stages of undress. They all appeared to be in their late teens or early twenties. One wore a cotton wrap, the other a thong and a bra, and another was wearing just a thong. A fourth girl, sitting on a stool in front of a mirror, was completely naked apart from a garter. Three of them were reading magazines, while the naked girl was generously applying oil to her upper body. They each glanced briefly at us, but apart from that glazed look there was no reaction to the arrival of the manager and two strange men.

'These gentlemen are from the police,' announced the manager. 'They're investigating a murder.'

Still there was no reaction, but that was not unusual from my knowledge of the girls who worked in the sex industry. I guessed that these young strippers, who probably doubled as prostitutes, had become so jaundiced after experiencing more of the seamier side of life than most women see in their entire lives that nothing would surprise them any more.

'Do any of you know a customer called Julian Reed?' I asked.

'What's he look like?' It was the bra-and-thong girl who spoke.

Dave described Julian Reed in some detail.

'Oh, Jolly Jules, we call him. Yeah, I know him.' The nude who had been oiling herself swung round on her stool. 'But I never knew his other name. We don't go in for real names much.' She spoke with a rich Cockney accent. 'He's always good for a few tenners in the garter, though. Know what I mean?'

'What's your name?' I asked.

'Estelle La Blanche.'

'No, your real name.'

There was a pause before Estelle answered. 'Rose Mooney,' she said.

'Was Jolly Jules in here last Monday?'

'No,' said Rose.

'Are you certain?'

'Course I am. You don't forget a bloke who drops you a century just for watching you get up close and personal to a bloody pole.' Rose sniffed. 'I'm paid to do it anyway, whether he's here or not.'

We left the Dizzy Club and walked back to the police station.

'So where was Reed that afternoon, Dave?' I asked. But it was a rhetorical question.

The following day was the first of August and it seemed as though the weather was aware of the change of month. The temperature had fallen to seventy-two degrees Fahrenheit and the humidity had given way to a balmy breeze.

I began the morning by reviewing the evidence that had been gleaned in the Sharon Gregory murder investigation, and going through the statements that had been taken so far. I held a brief conference with my team and brought them up to date.

At one minute past ten, Colin Wilberforce appeared and told me that the commander wished to see me. I made my way to his office, all of two yards down the corridor.

For a few seconds, the commander continued to read a bulky file, skimming back and forth through the pages. But then he looked up, as though surprised to see me standing there.

'Ah, Mr Brock.'

'You wanted to see me, sir?'

'So I did,' said the commander, closing the file with obvious reluctance. 'About this second suspicious death you're dealing with . . .'

'It's a sight more than suspicious, sir. It's a murder. The woman died as a result of manual strangulation. In the Dickin Hotel near Heathrow Airport.'

'Are you sure?'

'Oh yes, it was definitely the Dickin Hotel, sir,' I said, taking a risk on matching his pedantry.

'Yes, yes. I meant, are you sure she was strangled?'

'Doctor Mortlock, the Home Office pathologist, is adamant, sir.'

'I see.' The commander had great respect for anyone with letters after their name that denoted a professional qualification and was ill disposed to question their findings. 'Do we know the identity of her assailant?' he asked, still avoiding committing himself by referring to Sharon Gregory's killer as a 'murderer'. At least, not until the jury came in with a guilty verdict, and probably not until the appeal stage had confirmed that verdict.

'Not yet, sir.'

'Two murders, of a husband and wife on different dates in different places, but no arrests. Have I got that right?' Slipping into his censorious mode, the commander raised his eyebrows.

'You have indeed, sir.' I said nothing further and waited for some magisterial advice.

'No arrests? The DAC was enquiring. He's very interested in the outcome.'

'No, sir, no arrests.' I could visualize the consternation that had ensued when the deputy assistant commissioner had posed a question to which the commander had no answer, if in fact the DAC had posed it at all. It was one of the commander's traits that he tried to shift responsibility for asking a question by implying that the query had come from higher up the food chain. But I decided to put him out of his misery. 'But such evidence that we have gathered so far suggests that Clifford Gregory was murdered by Sharon Gregory, his wife.'

'She murdered her own *husband*? Good gracious me.' For a moment or two, the commander gazed at me, slack-jawed. And then he glanced at the photograph of his battleaxe of a wife. Perhaps he was wondering if he might one day fall victim to a spousal attack.

'But of course we can't arrest her now because she too is dead.'

'Quite so, quite so,' murmured the commander, apparently still stunned by the realization that a woman could actually murder her husband. 'Keep me informed, Mr Brock.'

'Of course, sir,' I said smoothly, and hastened away to get on with the job in hand before the boss could think of another question.

At ten-thirty a call came in from the police in Essex to say that earlier that morning they had at last managed to contact Sharon Gregory's parents, Kevin and Helen Cross, at an address in Basildon. According to the local police, the couple had just enjoyed a fortnight's river cruise the length of the Rhine, and arrived home to find a note asking them to telephone the police station. Fifteen minutes later two police officers had called at the Crosses' house and told them the sad news that their daughter had been murdered.

I decided that an interview with the bereaved parents was an unpalatable priority. I opted to take Kate Ebdon with me; it's always wise to be accompanied by a woman officer on these occasions.

ELEVEN

It was about forty miles from Earls Court to Basildon, but even with Kate's 'positive driving' skills, an expertise that was somewhat akin to Dave's, it took her nearly two hours to get us there. We arrived at a quarter past two.

The Crosses' house was a neat semi-detached three-up two-down property, of a style which pointed to it having been built before the Second World War. The front garden, in common with most of the houses in the street, had been paved over to accommodate the ubiquitous motor car. The vehicle outside the Crosses' house was an ageing Honda Civic fitted with manual controls.

A wreath was already hanging on the front door, an indication perhaps that Sharon Gregory's parents were very conventional people when it came to signs of mourning.

A woman answered the door. 'Are you from the press?' she asked. Although she was in plain clothes, I guessed who she was and why she was there. 'Because if you are—'

'No, we're police officers from the Met,' I said. 'Detective Chief Inspector Brock and Detective Inspector Ebdon.'

'Sorry about that, sir, but the vultures have started circling already. I'm PC Jacobs from Basildon police station, a victim support officer. You're here about the Crosses' daughter, I suppose.'

'Yes, we are.'

PC Jacobs beckoned us into the small hall and closed the front door. I noticed that a chair lift had been fitted to the staircase. Jacobs shut the door to the sitting room. 'It's not a happy state of affairs, sir,' she said in a low voice. 'Mrs Cross suffers multiple sclerosis. She's in a wheelchair, and her husband Kevin is severely disabled. He was badly crippled in a train crash some years ago.'

'Are they up to being interviewed?' It was not a pleasant task talking to people who had just lost a member of their family, but in these circumstances it would be doubly harrowing.

'I think they'd want to hear what happened, sir,' said Jacobs. 'I'll take you in. Incidentally, Sharon was their only child.'

The Crosses' sitting room was neatly furnished and clean, but it was fairly evident that they were not well off, despite having just returned from a cruise. There was a small television set in one corner, and a three-piece suite that had seen better days, as had the cheap carpet, now showing wear in places.

'These police officers are from London, Mr Cross,' said Jacobs. 'They've come to talk to you about Sharon.'

'I'm Kevin Cross,' said the man, pressing a button that raised him from a chair that was different from the others. He struggled into an upright position with some difficulty and leaned heavily on a walking stick. 'And this is my wife, Helen.' He indicated a grey-haired woman seated in a wheelchair. 'We got back from holiday first thing this morning only to find that our daughter had been murdered. Some homecoming this has turned out to be. It was the first holiday we've had in years and we'd been saving for it for ages.'

Mrs Cross gazed at us with red-rimmed eyes, but remained silent.

'You both have our deepest sympathy, Mr Cross,' I said. 'I know what it's like to lose someone close. I lost a son some years ago.'

Kate Ebdon glanced sharply in my direction. She obviously didn't know about young Robert, but it wasn't something I'd talked about. Although Dave knew the details, he obviously hadn't shared them with anyone else in the office.

'Can you tell us what happened, sir?' said Cross, sinking back into his chair and allowing his walking stick to fall to the floor unnoticed.

There was no way in which I could shield the Crosses from the truth of the matter; they were entitled to know the awful details.

'Sharon was found murdered at the Dickin Hotel near Heathrow Airport three days ago, Mr Cross,' I said. 'She'd been strangled.'

Helen Cross gave a convulsive sob and struggled to put a handkerchief to her mouth.

'But who would do such a thing?' Kevin Cross shook his head in bewilderment.

'That's what we're trying to find out,' I said.

'She was happily married, you know, and she had a very good job as an air hostess. It was always her ambition, even when she was a little girl. She always wanted to fly to wonderful places. Even when she was tiny we would take her on the bus to see the aeroplanes at Southend Airport as a treat.' Cross paused and looked sadly at the empty fireplace. 'Her husband must be devastated,' he mumbled, almost to himself.

This was getting even more difficult. 'I'm sorry to have to tell you that her husband has also been murdered, Mr Cross.'

'Oh good God!' Kevin Cross's whole demeanour registered extreme shock, and the blood drained from his face. For one awful moment I wondered if he was about to suffer a heart attack, but he recovered after a few seconds. 'Someone killed them both? Did this killer break into their house?'

'No, Mr Cross,' said Kate Ebdon, taking over from me. 'Mr Gregory was found murdered in the marital home at West Drayton last weekend. Sharon was murdered two days later in a hotel close to the airport. I think it was a hotel where the crew stayed,' she added, telling a white lie to avoid adding further grief to an already distressing situation.

'Was it the same person who murdered them both?' Kevin Cross was clearly having trouble absorbing the enormity of the crimes we were describing.

'It's possible, but that's something we're still looking into.' Kate decided that this was definitely not the moment to tell the Crosses that we had convincing evidence to indicate that Sharon had murdered her own husband.

'It's all quite dreadful. What is the world coming to?' Helen Cross spoke for the first time, her delivery halting and almost inaudible, as if she were actually talking to herself.

'Do you know of anyone who might've wanted to harm your daughter, Mr Cross?' I asked. It was a routine question and sounded crass in the circumstances, but it was one that had to be posed.

Cross didn't give it any thought. 'No, no one,' he said promptly. 'She was a lovely girl – the most popular girl at her school. Everyone who knew her liked her.'

But there's one person out there who obviously didn't like her that much, I thought.

'You say her marriage was a happy one, Mr Cross,' said Kate, taking up the questioning again.

'Very. They were devoted to each other. Admittedly Cliff was fourteen or fifteen years older than Sharon, but it made no difference. Their only disappointment was that they couldn't have children.'

There was also nothing to be gained by telling the Crosses that their daughter was two months pregnant when she died. Or that her late husband had had a vasectomy and could not therefore have been the father.

'Did Sharon visit you often?' asked Kate.

'No, young lady,' said Cross, 'but she had a very demanding job and a house and a husband to look after. I suppose you find it like that. Are *you* married?'

'Not yet, Mr Cross.' Kate smiled at the man. 'Did your daughter and her husband have any close friends?'

'I don't really know. As I said, she was a very busy girl and it's a long way from West Drayton to Basildon. We didn't see her that often.'

It was clear that we weren't going to get anything useful from the Crosses, particularly as they laboured under the illusion that she'd enjoyed a happy marriage. Our continued presence would only serve to exacerbate their grief.

PC Jacobs saw us to the door and turned to Kate. 'Have you any idea when and where the funeral will be, ma'am?'

'Not at this stage,' said Kate. 'I'll get someone to ring your nick at Basildon when we hear. I imagine that her funeral and Clifford Gregory's will take place together. It's probable that Sharon's parents will want to be involved, but it's all up in the air at the moment.'

'It seems that Sharon's parents didn't know anything about the murder of their son-in-law, ma'am,' said Jacobs.

'We'd automatically assumed that Sharon would've let them know,' said Kate, 'but then she too was murdered. As the Crosses were on holiday she was probably unsuccessful anyway.' But both Kate and I knew that Sharon wouldn't have bothered.

'I know what you said to Kevin, but do you think it *was* the same killer?'

'We've no idea,' said Kate, deeming it unwise to tell her that we were sure Sharon had killed her husband. Some things tend to slip out, even unintentionally, and she didn't want to add to the Crosses' distress.

*   *   *

On Friday morning, Dave came breezing into my office.

'What are we going to do about the other two men on Sharon's mobile phone list, guv? Max Riley in Guildford and Frank Digby out at Chalfont St Giles.'

'They're both within reasonable striking distance of Heathrow,' I said. 'We'll try and get to them later today, and we've got to fit in a visit to this place in Dorking to check Julian Reed's alibi. But first of all I think it's more important that we speak to Clifford Gregory's parents, wherever they live.'

'I found an address for a J. Gregory among the papers in Clifford Gregory's study,' said Dave, 'but there was nothing to indicate whether that's his father or his mother. It could be a brother or even a sister, I suppose.'

'We'll soon find out, Dave,' I said. 'Get the car.'

'I can't believe we're having this much bad luck,' I said, when we pulled up outside the address. 'It's a care home.' In its heyday the substantial property had probably been occupied by an affluent family.

'Definitely not our day, guv'nor,' said Dave.

The tall black woman who answered the door studied us both, and then concentrated her gaze on Dave.

'Can I help you?'

'We're police officers,' I said.

'I'm Daphne, the matron,' said the woman. 'Come in and tell me what I can do for you.'

We followed the matron into the spacious tiled hall. There was a large table on which were a vase of fresh flowers and a few magazines. The windows were open and the room smelled of polish and had a fresh, airy feel about it. This was obviously one of the better care homes.

'Hello, Daphne,' shouted a man with a walking frame as he shuffled across the hall, making for a door on the far side. 'You all right, then?'

'Hello, Jim. Yes, I'm fine.' The matron waved at the man. 'You'd better come into the office,' she said, turning back to me. She opened the door to a room on the front of the house. There were more flowers on a side table and a small potted plant on the desk.

'I'm Detective Chief Inspector Brock, Matron, and this is Detective Sergeant Poole.'

'May I ask what this is about?' The matron nodded briefly in Dave's direction and perched on the edge of her desk.

'I'm led to believe that you have a J. Gregory in your care, Matron,' I said.

'Please call me Daphne, everyone does. Yes, John Gregory is a resident here.'

'Are you able to tell us if he is Clifford Gregory's father? Or is he some other relative?'

'Just a tick. I'll have a look.' The matron crossed to a filing cabinet and pulled out a folder. 'Yes, he's Clifford Gregory's father,' she said, 'and Clifford Gregory, who has an address in West Drayton, is listed as John's primary next of kin. Is there a problem?'

'You could say that, Daphne,' said Dave. 'Clifford Gregory was murdered last Saturday at his home in West Drayton.'

'Oh crikey!' exclaimed the matron. 'You'd better sit down while we sort this out.' She waved a hand at a group of armchairs. 'I think we ought to have a cup of tea as well.' She picked up the telephone handset, tapped out a number and ordered tea for three. 'Presumably you've come with the intention of telling John about his son's murder.'

'We're not sure whether he knows already,' I said. 'Clifford's wife might've told him, but the problem is that she was murdered a day or so later.'

'Good grief! What a dreadful state of affairs. But I can tell you categorically that nobody got in touch with us here about this tragedy, Mr Brock. Not that it would've helped.'

'Why's that?'

'John Gregory is in the advanced stages of senile dementia. His short-term memory just doesn't exist any more. Mind you, he can tell you all about the air raids during the war when he was at school in Poplar. And one day he told us all about the Battle of Britain. Apparently he and his mates watched it from the local recreation ground.'

'I take it there'd be no point in telling him about his son, then?' said Dave.

'Not really. He wouldn't be able to take it in. He probably doesn't even know he's got a son. Not now, anyway.'

A young girl entered the room and placed a tray on the table near where we were sitting. She poured the tea and handed it round without a word.

'Does John Gregory have a wife?' I asked.

'No, Mr Brock,' said Daphne. 'According to our records, she died ten years ago.' She glanced at the folder again. 'I do have another name here, though. There's a Peter Gregory listed as John's other son. He lives in Bromley.'

'We'd better see him, then,' said Dave. 'Perhaps you'd give me the address, Daphne.'

'Someone will have to arrange the funeral,' I said. 'Well, both funerals, I suppose.'

The matron scribbled down the address and handed it to me. 'Good luck,' she said. 'It's not my problem, thank the Lord.'

We finished our tea and headed back to my favourite Italian restaurant in central London. As we were leaving, Dave got a call on his mobile.

'That was Colin Wilberforce, guv. Ben Donaldson rang from the embassy. He's got the information we wanted.'

'That's damned good going, Dave.' It had taken just two days for Ben Donaldson at the US Embassy to get a result. I glanced at my watch. 'Bromley will have to wait,' I said. 'We'll call at the embassy and then drive on from there to see Clifford Gregory's brother.'

Dave and I arrived at the US Embassy in Grosvenor Square twenty minutes later. Having once again been interrogated by a stern-faced and highly suspicious US Marine Corps corporal as to our reasons for being there, we eventually found our way to Donaldson's office.

I was tempted to refuse the obligatory cup of coffee, just for the hell of it, but decided that to do so might completely upset Darlene's routine.

'I'll give y'all a copy of this report, Harry, but to summarize what it says, one of the two guys you mentioned has been seen,' said Donaldson, once Dave and I were ensconced in his comfortable armchairs.

'One?' I queried.

'Yeah. Miles Donahue. He calls himself an entrepreneur, and admitted having had sex with your victim Sharon Gregory on quite a few occasions. He told the agent that he first picked her up in a bar in downtown Miami.' Donaldson glanced up. 'He told our agent that he was surprised that she refused to drink any alcohol. Probably knows all about date-rape drugs.'

She certainly does, I thought.

'No, she wouldn't have had a drink, Ben,' said Dave. 'If she'd had too much to drink before duty on the return flight, she'd get the bullet.'

'Sounds like she did anyhow,' commented Donaldson with a chuckle.

'No, she was strangled,' said Dave, matching Donaldson's quip with one of his own.

'Anyway,' Donaldson went on, 'after that, Donahue said he always arranged to meet her in her room at the Shannon Hotel. Reckons he shacked up with her at least three or four times in the past year.'

'Busy girl,' commented Dave drily, 'considering all the others she entertained. Did this guy have an alibi for the date in question?'

'Yep, sure did,' said Donaldson. 'He was in bed with a hooker at one of the other hotels in Miami Beach. Our man checked. He also made enquiries at the Shannon,' he continued, 'but no one there could recall anyone asking for Sharon Gregory. But that don't mean squat. If she's the sort of good-time girl you think she is, she probably called these guys on her cellphone and told 'em where to find her.' He shook his head slowly. 'I never managed to find a broad like that,' he added.

'What about Lance Kramer?' I asked.

Donaldson flipped over a page in the report he was reading. 'Kramer might interest you, Harry. He designs theatre sets and is here in London at the present time.'

'Was he over here on the twenty-ninth of July?' asked Dave.

'Sure was. According to the agent who made the enquiry, Kramer flew into London's Heathrow on Friday twenty-sixth. According to his office, he made a reservation at the Holiday Inn on Regents Park.'

'Did the person your agent saw in Kramer's office ask why he wanted that information, Ben?' I asked. I was concerned that Kramer's secretary might've called him and alerted him to our interest.

'No, sirree!' said Donaldson emphatically. 'FBI agents don't say why they're making an enquiry. They're Federal agents, for krissakes,' he added, as though that was sufficient explanation. 'Guess you'll go talk with him, huh?'

'Oh yes, we most certainly will,' I said. I paused as we turned to leave. 'If you're ever in touch with Joe Daly, give him my regards, and tell him I hope he's enjoying his retirement.'

'Retirement? Joe? No way. He's set up as a gumshoe in New York. Apparently he's working his butt off.'

'A gumshoe?' queried Dave. 'Is that something to do with the footwear industry?' he added, pretending naivety.

'Hell no! He's a private eye, a PI.' For a moment or two, Donaldson stared at Dave in disbelief. 'Hey, Dave, you're having me on,' he said, and laughed. 'Excellent!'

TWELVE

Having completed our business at the embassy, we drove out to Bromley. I didn't think we'd learn much from Clifford Gregory's brother, but we had to try. We also had to discover if he was prepared to deal with the question of the funerals, not that that was of any real concern to the police. If the worst came to the worst, the local authority would inter or cremate the Gregorys.

The woman who answered the door was wearing jeans and a white tee-shirt.

'Are you Mrs Gregory?' I asked.

'Yes, I'm Jill Gregory. Who are you?'

'Detective Chief Inspector Brock of Scotland Yard, Mrs Gregory, and this is Detective Sergeant Poole. Am I right in thinking that Peter Gregory is your husband?'

'Yes, but he's at work.' Jill Gregory's face suddenly assumed a worried look. 'Oh my God! Has something happened to him? A car accident?'

'No, nothing like that, Mrs Gregory,' I said. 'I hope we're not disturbing you.'

'Not at all. I'm a nurse, but I'm on night duty at the moment.'

'Oh, I'm sorry. Did we wake you up?' I was only too aware of what it was like to do shift work and to have one's sleep during the day broken by unthinking callers.

'No, it's all right. As a matter of fact I always sleep just before going on duty, rather than straight after I've finished,' said Jill Gregory. 'What's this about if it's not about Peter?'

'It concerns your brother-in-law, Clifford Gregory.'

'Has *he* had an accident?'

'No, Mrs Gregory, I'm sorry to have to tell you that he's been murdered.'

'Oh no, not Cliff!' said Jill Gregory. 'When did this happen?' She suddenly realized that she was carrying on the conversation on her doorstep. 'I'm so sorry, do come in.'

We followed her into the sitting room and accepted her offer of a seat.

'When did this happen?' Jill Gregory asked again. She sat on the edge of her chair, shoulders hunched and hands clasped together, an earnest expression on her face.

'On Saturday last, the twenty-seventh of July.'

'Was Sharon there?'

'Yes, Mrs Gregory. But two days later she was also murdered.'

'I don't believe it.' Jill Gregory gasped and shook her head in bewilderment. 'How on earth . . .? I mean, who would want to murder them?'

'That's what we're trying to find out, Mrs Gregory. Clifford was murdered at the marital home in West Drayton. Sharon was found strangled in a hotel room near Heathrow Airport.'

'Huh!' exclaimed Jill. 'I suppose I should be surprised by that, but I'm not. Did Sharon murder Cliff? What did she do, poison him?'

'We're still investigating both murders, Mrs Gregory,' I said diplomatically, 'but you don't seem at all surprised that Sharon was murdered.' I found it interesting that Jill Gregory had immediately jumped to the conclusion that Clifford Gregory had been murdered by Sharon.

'Not in the least. She was a slut, that one. Why on earth Cliff ever married her I shall never know. She'd readily sleep with any man who asked her. And you said she was murdered in a hotel room? No doubt she was there to have sex with one of her fancy men and it was he who killed her. Peter and I often said that she'd finish up with her throat cut, and it looks as though we were right. She didn't give a damn who she slept with, and she didn't give a damn about Cliff, either.'

'Did you know any of the men Sharon was seeing?' asked Dave, busily taking notes in his pocketbook.

'It would be a full-time occupation to list them all, I should think,' replied Jill Gregory cuttingly. 'But no, I don't know who any of them were. Cliff was a quiet sort of chap, an accountant, you know. All he wanted was an ordinary home life and children, but when he found out what Sharon was like he had a vasectomy. He confided in us that he wasn't going to have kids with a whore. It took an awful lot to rile Cliff, and an outburst like that was very much out of character, but that's how he described her. Frankly, I think Sharon drove him to the end of his tether.'

'He knew about her affairs, then?' queried Dave.

'Oh yes, he knew all right. Well, guessed anyway. But Cliff was a fool to himself. Peter and I told him he should get a divorce and start again. But he said he was too old. Mind you, he was only forty. So he didn't do anything about it. He was rather a weak man, was Cliff, and Sharon could twist him round her little finger. She treated him like dirt. The fact that she was an air hostess didn't help, either. Always jetting off to some foreign place and, no doubt, hopping into some man's bed whenever the mood took her. And I gather the mood took her quite often.'

'This morning we called at the care home where your father-in-law is living, Mrs Gregory,' I said. 'But after a conversation with the matron it was apparent that there would have been little point in talking to him.'

'No, there wouldn't be. He's suffering from Alzheimer's disease. The poor old chap is out of this world to all intents and purposes. I don't think he's got long, and if he'd been able to take in the news, which I doubt, the shock would probably have killed him.'

'There is the question of the funerals . . .' I began tentatively, loath to raise the matter. 'At the moment both bodies are in the public mortuary at Townmead Road, Fulham.'

'That's all we need,' said an exasperated Jill Gregory. 'My husband works for the local authority and my job as a nurse only pays a pittance, so we're not exactly rolling in money.' For a moment or two she paused, thinking. 'How much would a double funeral cost, I wonder?' she said eventually. A sudden thought occurred to her. 'But I think that Cliff had life insurance.'

'He did originally, for twenty thousand pounds, but it was cashed in when he and Sharon were married. As a deposit for the house, I understand.'

'Well, I don't know how Peter and I are going to foot the bill for two funerals.'

'We've also discovered that a month ago Sharon took out insurance on her husband's life in the sum of one hundred thousand pounds.'

'The cunning little bitch. It's obvious she did murder him, then. What happens to that money now?'

'Policemen are not experts on civil law, Mrs Gregory,' said Dave, 'but I imagine it will come to your husband or your father-in-law. It depends on whether Clifford Gregory made a will. But being an accountant I dare say he tied up all the loose ends. It's something your husband will have to take up with the insurance company.'

'If your husband will get in touch with me, Mrs Gregory,' I said, 'I'll give him all the details.' I handed her one of my cards. 'But I'd suggest that you and your husband speak to a solicitor. Despite what I just said, it's still possible that Clifford Gregory died intestate.' I paused. 'By the way, would you or your husband want to view the bodies?'

'No thank you,' said Jill Gregory emphatically. 'I see quite enough dead bodies at work, and Peter wouldn't have the time or the inclination.'

And that was that. We'd gleaned a little more about Sharon Gregory, but nothing that would advance our enquiries into her death. And what we had learned merely served to confirm what we knew already.

It was nearly fifty miles from Bromley to Dorking. Even by driving much of the way round the M25 – known as the biggest car park in England – we didn't arrive until half-past seven that evening.

The address at which Muriel Reed claimed that she and Julian had spent the evening, and indeed the night, of Sharon Gregory's murder was a large double-fronted detached house set back quite a way from the road. There were two or three cars parked on the drive. Even though it was bright sunshine, I was slightly puzzled to see that the Venetian blinds at every one of the windows were closed.

I rang the bell and moments later the door was opened by a grey-haired woman who must've been sixty if she was a day. She looked at each of us in turn and appeared slightly disconcerted that one of us was black and that both of us were male.

'I'm afraid we can't entertain singles. It upsets the balance, you see.'

'We're police officers from Scotland Yard, madam,' I said, and gave the woman our names.

'Oh my God!' The woman grasped the edge of the door for

support, her face blushing scarlet with embarrassment. 'We're not doing anything wrong, Officer.'

'I think it might be a good idea if we were to come inside, madam,' suggested Dave.

'Yes, yes, of course. Come in. I'll fetch my husband. I think it would be better if you spoke to him. Oh dear! I don't know what he'll say. I suppose we'll have to cancel.'

We entered the hall just in time to see a naked man rush out of a room, slam the door and run up the stairs.

'Was that your husband?' asked Dave.

'No, of course not. I've no idea who that was.' Mrs Simpson started to cross the hall. 'I'll fetch Jimmy now.'

But she had not gone more than a couple of paces when another man emerged from a different room. He too was in his sixties, but was fully dressed in red trousers, a short-sleeved yellow shirt and sandals.

'What's going on, Laura?' said the man, glaring at Dave and me.

'These gentlemen are from the police, Jimmy.'

'Oh Christ!' said the man. 'It's all above board, what we're doing here. It's just a bit of fun. All consenting adults and that sort of thing.'

'Perhaps we'd better start with who you are, sir,' said Dave with a smile. He had obviously worked out what was happening in this overtly respectable Surrey house and had difficulty in suppressing his amusement.

'I'm James Simpson and this is my wife Laura.'

'And what exactly is this bit of fun that you host here?'

'Well, it's a sort of club for couples,' said Simpson hesitantly. 'We provide an opportunity for like-minded people to meet others with similar interests and to get to know them.' But he didn't sound at all convincing.

'With no clothes on presumably?' queried Dave mischievously. 'Or is dress optional?'

'I really don't know what you mean,' protested Simpson, blinking at Dave through finger-marked spectacles and tweaking at his toothbrush moustache.

'Unless my eyes deceived me,' continued Dave, 'I saw a naked man legging it upstairs just now.'

'You'll have to tell them, Jimmy,' said Laura Simpson, resigned to what she believed would be a prosecution and a heavy fine. If not worse.

'It's not illegal,' said Simpson, trying desperately to avoid what he too believed to be his imminent arrest. And doubtless wondering what the neighbours would think if they saw him and his wife being escorted from their house in handcuffs. 'It's all very discreet.'

I decided to put Simpson on the spot. 'You're running a club for swingers, aren't you? And not licensed by the local authority, I imagine.'

'Yes,' admitted Simpson quietly, his shoulders sagging in defeat.

'Well, we're not here about that,' I said.

'You're not?' Simpson greeted that statement with obvious relief. 'What then?'

'Not unless the neighbours complain, but that would be a matter for the Surrey Police and the council,' I said. 'I'm investigating a double murder.'

'*Murder*!' exclaimed Laura Simpson, gasping and putting a hand to her mouth, convinced that their already precarious situation was getting even worse. 'Not here, surely?'

'No, Mrs Simpson, not here, but I need to know if a Mrs Muriel Reed was here last Monday evening. That was the twenty-ninth of July.' I deliberately didn't mention Julian Reed; I still had reservations about the story that his wife had told.

'I'm afraid our clients' names are confidential, Chief Inspector,' said Simpson, regaining some of his pomposity now that he believed himself to be in the clear.

'Are you a medical practitioner, a lawyer, or a clerk in holy orders?' Dave inclined his head, giving the impression that he was genuinely interested in Simpson's reply.

'No, of course not. I'm a retired bank officer. Why d'you ask?'

'In that case, you can't claim that such information is privileged. Of course, we could get the local police to obtain a warrant and seize your records, if you have any. And there's no telling what else they may find. Or for that matter what interest Her Majesty's Revenue and Customs may take in your activities. You do pay tax on your enterprise, I imagine?'

'Yes, Muriel was here on the twenty-ninth,' said Simpson, admitting defeat in the face of Dave's implied threat to involve the tax authorities. 'I seem to remember that she arrived at about half past seven and stayed all night.' He glanced at his wife. 'That would be right, Laura, wouldn't it?'

'Yes, I'm pretty sure that's right.'

'Your wife said you don't take singles,' I remarked. 'So Mrs Reed must've arrived with someone.'

'She was here with her husband, Julian, as far as I can recall,' said Simpson. 'To be honest, a lot of couples arrive at about the same time on the nights we hold a party, but I'm fairly sure he was here.'

'Yes, he was. Definitely,' said Laura Simpson.

'Thank you, Mr Simpson,' said Dave, barely able to conceal his mirth. 'I don't think we need to trouble you further.' He glanced at me. 'Do we, sir?'

'I don't think so, Sergeant,' I said, matching Dave's formality.

We had driven to the end of the Simpsons' road before Dave's reserve finally gave way to almost hysterical laughter. He stopped the car. 'Well, if that doesn't take the biscuit, guv, I don't know what does,' he said, hammering the steering wheel with his right hand. 'That Muriel Reed is one devious bitch. She spent half an hour telling us that her husband was the one who was over the side when all the time she's at it, too.'

'Why the hell couldn't she have said what they'd come here for when we interviewed them? It would have saved us a trip all the way to Dorking.'

'Perhaps he's shy, guv, and that's why Muriel didn't give us the address until we were at the top of the stairs. Anyway, you wouldn't have believed her without checking it out.'

'Well, that lets Julian Reed off the hook, Dave. And tomorrow we'd better have a look at the remaining two names on Sharon's mobile. But I somehow doubt we'll have any more luck than we've had so far.'

First thing on Saturday morning, DS Flynn came into my office clutching a fistful of computer printouts.

'This property development company of Julian Reed's, guv,' he began.

'I think I might've wasted your time, Charlie. Reed's probably in the clear, but do go on.'

'Julian Reed owns fifty-one per cent of the shares and his wife Muriel holds forty-nine per cent, not the other way round. But it looks as though the company's going down the tubes. It hasn't shown a profit for three years.'

'I'm not surprised, Charlie. Muriel Reed said that her husband couldn't afford to leave her. I reckon he's living on her money and she's bolstering up his company. Though God knows why.'

'That's not the case,' said Flynn. 'Muriel doesn't have a brass farthing of her own. And Julian Reed is due to inherit a very large estate from his father, the Right Honourable Earl Dretford, when the old boy snuffs it. In the meantime, the earl gives Julian a substantial allowance. And that's probably why he lives the life of a dilettante.'

'How on earth did you find out all that, Charlie?'

Flynn grinned. 'Ways and means, guv. Ways and means. I've still got friends on the Fraud Squad who know their way round the financial assault course.'

'Anyway,' I said, deciding not to enquire too deeply into Flynn's 'ways and means' of acquiring sensitive information, 'we've cleared Reed from the enquiry now. He was at a swingers' club in Dorking the night that Sharon Gregory was murdered, and his wife was with him.'

'Some people have all the luck.' Flynn flourished his bunch of printouts. 'I'll give this little lot to Colin Wilberforce to file away, guv, just in case.'

I decided that Saturday would be a good day to interview the other two names Dave found on Sharon's mobile. Most people don't work at the weekend, unless they happen to be policemen, that is. But then I decided I'd had enough of traipsing around London and its environs. I sent for Kate Ebdon.

'I've got a job for you, Kate,' I said, handing her details of those of Sharon's contacts who had yet to be interviewed. 'Speak to these two men, find out how well they knew Sharon and where they were on the night of her murder. And take Dave Poole with you.'

In the meantime, I intended to interview Gordon Harrison again. When Dave and I saw him previously, Sharon Gregory hadn't been murdered. I was now interested to know where he was when she was killed. It had been early evening when we'd interviewed him, on the day that Sharon Gregory had checked into the Dickin Hotel, and he would have had plenty of time to get to Heathrow from Fulham, a distance of about sixteen miles. I sent for Detective Sergeant Lizanne Carpenter.

'We're going to Fulham, Liz,' I said, 'to see a guy called Gordon Harrison. He claims to make his money by planning expensive holidays for rich businessmen who want some quality time with their girlfriends.' And I told her what had taken place on my last visit.

THIRTEEN

A girl with coffee-coloured skin, wearing nothing but a scarlet thong, opened the door to Harrison's house. She could not have been more than eighteen or nineteen and had long, black hair and a figure of which most women would have been jealous.

'Oh my God!' said the girl, putting her hand to her mouth and moving quickly behind the door. 'I thought you were Gordie.'

'So it would appear.' Lizanne surveyed the girl's figure with an envy that, in her case, was quite unnecessary.

'Oh hell!' exclaimed a familiar voice.

I turned to find that Harrison was standing behind me. 'So there you are,' I said.

'Shall we go in?' Harrison glanced nervously at the door of his neighbour's house and steered us quickly towards to the sitting room.

Lizanne paused in the hall to slip off her shoes. 'I don't want to damage your parquet flooring with my heels,' she said. Even without shoes she was an impressive height, and her well-cut blue jacket and skirt made her a woman who clearly took care over her appearance.

'Oh, it doesn't matter about the floor. I'm thinking of having it carpeted anyway.' Looking at the girl, he said, 'And for God's sake, Shona, go and put some clothes on, quickly.'

The girl called Shona dashed upstairs, only to reappear in the sitting room a minute or two later. 'Can I get anyone a drink?' Her idea of putting on some clothes had been to don a short, diaphanous negligee over her thong.

'Go away, Shona.' Harrison spoke sharply. He was obviously displeased that we'd caught him out. 'I need to talk to these police officers.'

'Is it about your car again?' asked Shona innocently.

'It's nothing to do with my car,' said Harrison.

'But I thought you said—'

'Go!' said Harrison. He took hold of the girl's shoulders, spun her round and gave her bottom a sharp slap.

The girl pouted and sashayed provocatively from the room, making a point of slamming the door.

'Sorry about that. I'd just popped out for a packet of cigarettes.' Harrison did not seem at all surprised to see me again. 'You were lucky to find me still here. I'm about to throw a few things into a grip before I take off for Los Angeles. I'm catching the fourteen-thirty flight from Heathrow.'

'Another executive holiday to arrange?' I asked.

'Something like that,' said Harrison, without elaborating.

'We'll not keep you too long,' I said, as Liz and I settled into the armchairs. 'This is Detective Sergeant Lizanne Carpenter.'

'Hi!' said Harrison, nodding in Lizanne's direction.

We took a seat and waited while Harrison moved his computer chair to face us and sat down.

'I take it that Shona is your wife, Mr Harrison,' I said, knowing damned well that she wasn't.

'Er, no, not exactly.'

Lizanne said nothing, but fixed Harrison with a quizzical gaze, forcing him into saying something.

'My wife's visiting her folks. Well, she's my partner; we're not actually married. She's a Romanian called Krisztina Comaneci.' Harrison seemed at pains to explain his marital status.

'Oh, I see. And Shona's your housekeeper, I suppose.' But I smiled as I said it.

'Oh, what the hell! While the cat's away . . .'

It was some time before I discovered that even that was not the truth.

'However, we've not come here to discuss your domestic arrangements, Mr Harrison,' I said.

'So, what can I do for you, Chief Inspector?' Harrison was more relaxed now that we'd dealt with the matter of Shona's status. And his demeanour was certainly not that of someone who thought he was about to be arrested for murder. But I'd met cool killers before and I recalled one in particular who was eventually convicted of murdering three women in various parts of London. Almost cherubic in appearance, he had remained unperturbed throughout the two days of interviews I'd conducted with him. And he hadn't displayed any emotion when he was eventually sentenced to life imprisonment with a tariff of thirty years before he could apply for parole.

'We came to see you last Monday,' I began.

'Yes, I remember,' said Harrison, leaning forward and linking his hands between his knees.

'Would you mind telling me how you spent the rest of that evening?'

'Does that have something to do with Sharon Gregory?' asked Harrison, the trace of a frown on his face.

'Yes, it does, but I'll explain why in a moment.'

'As a matter of fact, I was here all evening. I watched *The Cruel Sea*: Jack Hawkins, Donald Sinden and the delectable Virginia McKenna. I once nurtured the idea of going into the navy, but eventually opted for making money instead.'

That all came out like a well-rehearsed alibi, I thought.

'Was it on TV or was it a DVD?' asked Liz casually.

'A DVD,' replied Harrison immediately.

'Were you alone?'

'No. Shona was here.'

Really? I couldn't imagine Shona settling down to watch a war film. A porn video maybe, but not The Cruel Sea. That idle thought was interrupted by Harrison speaking again.

'But you still haven't told me why you want to know.' Harrison spent a few seconds discreetly appraising Lizanne's nylon-clad legs before switching his gaze back to me.

'That was the evening Sharon Gregory was murdered,' I said.

'Murdered? My God! What happened to the poor little bitch?' Harrison shook his head. 'But it can't be true . . .'

It's strange the way people always say that when a police officer has just related an incontrovertible fact to them.

'That's why I'm interested in your whereabouts that evening, Mr Harrison.'

'Hey, whoa, hold on! Surely you can't think I had anything to do with that?' Harrison's protest sounded genuine, but murderers are often good actors, which is how they manage to persuade their victims into vulnerable situations where help is far from hand.

'D'you think I could use your bathroom, Mr Harrison?' asked

Lizanne, affording Harrison a shy smile before giving me a knowing glance.

'Yeah, sure. It's up the stairs and first door on the right. That's the bedroom. The bathroom leads off it. If Shona's in there, chuck her out.'

'Thank you.' Lizanne stood up and made for the door.

'What happened, Mr Brock? To Sharon, I mean.'

'Someone strangled her,' I said.

'Why the hell would anyone want to do that? She was a sweet girl and very . . .' Harrison paused. 'How can I put it . . . amorous.' He smiled boyishly.

'And when did you last have contact with Sharon?' I knew what he had said previously, but wanted to find out if he would say the same again.

'A month ago, I think I said, the last time you were here. Yes, it was at least a month.'

'Do you happen to know the name of anyone else she might've been seeing?' I asked.

'No, I'm afraid not. Mind you, knowing what sort of girl she was, it wouldn't surprise me to know that she had a string of lovers.' Harrison glanced out of the window before looking back at me. 'As well as a husband,' he added ruefully. 'And you told me that he was murdered too.' He shook his head as he tried to absorb a situation that was entirely outside his own experience.

Lizanne came back into the room and gave me a discreet nod just as I stood up.

'We'll not delay you any further, Mr Harrison,' I said, 'but I might need to see you again.'

'Of course.'

'Enjoy your trip,' said Lizanne, as she stopped in the hall to pick up her shoes.

Shona, having abandoned her negligee, returned to the sitting room.

'Who is this Sharon Gregory they were talking about, Gordie?'

'Were you listening, you little bitch?'

'Of course I was. You said last time that they'd come about your car, but they hadn't, had they?'

'It's nothing to do with you, Shona, my pet. It was about a girl I knew ages ago.'

'That policeman said something about her being murdered. Do they think you did it?'

'Of course not. They're talking to everyone who might have known her.'

'Why did you tell them that you were here with me that night, Gordie?'

'For God's sake stop calling me Gordie. My name's Gordon,' snapped Harrison. 'I told them that because otherwise they'll start making enquiries. And they might find out what I really do on these trips of mine. And that'd be a damned nuisance because I didn't have anything to do with her murder. But I told them I was here with you, so don't forget to back me up.'

'Too late,' said Shona, throwing herself into a chair and hooking one leg over the arm. 'When that policewoman came upstairs she asked me if I was here that night, and I told her I was at work. Well, they check on these things, don't they?'

'You did *what*? You silly little cow. Now they'll think I was mixed up in Sharon's murder.'

'Where were you, then, *Gordon*?' asked Shona.

'None of your damned business. But when they start probing they might uncover things that I don't want uncovered. Now get yourself up to the bedroom. It seems to me that it's the only place where you know what you're doing.'

'What did you make of that, Liz?' I asked, as we drove out of Glenn Road.

'As I went into the hall, Shona shot upstairs. She'd obviously been standing in the hall listening to our chat with Harrison. Anyway, I cornered her in the bedroom and asked her about the night Sharon Gregory was murdered. She said she wasn't here at all that evening. Her full name's Shona Grant and she claimed to be employed as a West End nightclub hostess most evenings, including the twenty-ninth of July. Personally I think she's a stripper in this nightclub, but I'll check it out. I thought that Harrison came up with what he was doing that night just a bit too glibly, sir; it's bound to be untrue.'

'I thought so too, but we'll need a lot more evidence before we can think about arresting Harrison. It's just possible that he had another bird with him. But if that was the case, why not say so?'

'Perhaps he got confused.' Lizanne laughed, and without taking her eyes off the road, took a small plastic envelope from her jacket pocket and handed it to me. 'This might help,' she said. 'I took a couple of hair samples from his comb when I used his bathroom. The boffins should be able to get a DNA sample from those.'

'And if it matches the DNA from the fetus that Doctor Mortlock found when he did the post-mortem on Sharon, we might be getting somewhere.'

'But you said that Harrison had admitted having sex with her, sir.'

'Yes, he did.'

'And from what we know about her, so did a hell of a lot of other men. So that doesn't necessarily make Harrison her killer, does it, sir?'

Frank Digby lived in what was known as a chalet bungalow in a quiet road in Chalfont St Giles. Predominantly white, the house had brown windows and doors, and decorative brown shutters that were fixed permanently to the walls.

It was half past midday when Dave pulled up on the drive next to a Ford Galaxy, and he and Kate Ebdon alighted.

Kate rang the bell and waited for some two or three minutes. She was on the point of giving up when a man opened the door. A good-looking thirty-something, he was tall and muscular, and had a clipboard in one hand and a pen lodged behind an ear.

'Good morning.' The man glanced at his watch. 'Or, should I say, good afternoon.'

'Mr Frank Digby?'

'Yes, I'm Frank Digby. Sorry to have kept you waiting, I was dealing with an order on my computer. How can I help?' Digby smiled at Kate and rapidly appraised her figure, his glance travelling from head to toe and back again.

'We're police officers, Mr Digby. I'm Detective Inspector Ebdon and this is Detective Sergeant Poole.'

'Oh! I was hoping you'd come to buy some wine.' Digby laughed nervously. 'But if it's about the licences, I can assure you that all the paperwork is in order.'

'I take it you're a wine merchant, Mr Digby.'

'Yes, I am.'

'It's not about wine or the relevant paperwork; that's nothing to do with us. We're from Scotland Yard and we'd like to speak to you concerning another matter.'

'This is all very mysterious. You'd better come in,' said Digby, as he showed the two detectives into a living room at the front of the house. A young woman in a plain cream dress was reclining on a sofa, her feet tucked up beneath her. She put down the magazine she was reading, lowered her feet and pushed them into a pair of mules. 'The police have come to see us, Fi.' He turned to Kate. 'Fiona Douglas is my partner. And my business partner.'

'How d'you do?' said Fiona.

'Ripper, thanks,' said Kate.

'Ah, you're Australian,' said Digby, as he recognized the accent and the colloquial response. Kate, as she always did, had mistaken the customary English greeting for a question. Brock thought she did it on purpose. 'You have some fascinating wines Down Under. There's quite a market for them here these days.'

'Yes, I'm sure there is, but as I said just now, we haven't come here to talk about wine.' Kate shot a glance in Fiona Douglas's direction. 'D'you travel to Miami very often, Mr Digby?'

'Occasionally,' said Digby, but the response was guarded, hesitant almost. It was a loaded question and he recognized it as such. 'I more often go to California. The New World wines have become increasingly popular over here. But what's with Miami? I think I've only been there two or three times.' As if sensing what was coming next, he glanced at his partner. 'Be a pet, Fi, and check on the orders and send them to the warehouse. Practically all our wine business is online, Inspector,' he explained, as his partner left the room. 'If we don't keep up with the orders, it quickly gets out of hand. Now, then, what's this interest in Miami?'

'Sharon Gregory, a cabin attendant on the Heathrow to Miami service,' said Kate bluntly.

'Oh God!' exclaimed Digby with a hunted look. He pushed a hand through his hair. 'What about her?'

'We understand from our enquiries that you and she were rather close.'

Digby glanced at the door. 'Yes, I've met her a couple of times. Why?'

'I was also told that you and she had a sexual relationship,' said

Dave, hazarding a guess at the reason Digby's phone number was on Sharon's mobile phone list of contacts.

'Now look here,' said Digby, displaying a hint of steel. 'I don't see that this has anything to do with the police. Is adultery a criminal offence all of a sudden?' he asked sarcastically.

'Not any more,' said Dave. 'But it might reach the divorce courts if you're actually *married* to your business partner.'

'I'm not,' snapped Digby.

'You admit to having sex with Sharon Gregory, then,' said Kate, getting none too subtly to the nub of the matter.

'I'm not admitting anything. I have nothing further to say and I'd be grateful if you left. Now! If you come back again, you'd better have a warrant.'

'I think you've touched a nerve, ma'am,' commented Dave quietly.

'Where were you on the twenty-ninth of July, Mr Digby?' Kate ignored Digby's request to leave, and her Australian accent became a little sharper. 'That was last Monday.'

'I don't have to answer that.'

'In that case,' said Dave, 'we *will* come back with a warrant and we'll turn this place upside down. And we might just bring Revenue and Customs with us. They're always interested in online businesses.'

'Fiona and I went to the Royal Opera House to see *Swan Lake*.' Digby caved in.

'Really? My wife is in that,' said Dave quietly.

'Doing what?'

'She's a principal dancer,' said Dave.

'Oh!' said Digby. Unaware that Dave's wife was white, he was obviously trying to recall whether he had ever seen a black ballet dancer. 'But you still haven't told me what's so important about last Monday.'

'It's the night that Sharon Gregory was murdered. Two days after her husband was murdered,' said Kate, and was pleased to see the shocked expression on Digby's face. But, being the cynic she was, she was uncertain whether it was shock at the death of someone he had slept with, or the fact that the victim had been married, or that the police had arrived at his front door in connection with the woman's murder. Or even that of her husband.

'That's terrible,' said Digby. But there was no sign of guilt, just transparent insincerity.

'I'll ask you again,' said Kate. 'Did you have sex with Sharon Gregory?'

'Yes, a couple of times in Miami. We met on a flight and she made it fairly clear that she was—'

Kate held up a hand. 'We get the picture, Mr Digby. As a matter of fact, we've heard it all before. From the numerous other men she slept with.'

'Good God!' exclaimed Digby. 'There were others?' he asked, rather naively.

'Oh yes, there were dozens,' said Dave. 'Do you still have the ticket stubs for your visit to Covent Garden?' he asked. 'Or perhaps you'd rather we checked with Miss Douglas.'

'I'd prefer that you didn't speak to Fiona, Sergeant,' said Digby hurriedly. 'But I'm afraid I don't have the ticket stubs any more.'

'Did you throw them away?' Kate posed the question innocently, but she didn't believe that Digby had been to the ballet at all.

'Not exactly, Inspector,' said Digby. 'Fiona has them. She keeps a scrapbook and pastes them in. Do you *really* have to talk to her about it?' he implored.

'There is a way round that, Mr Digby,' said Dave.

'Yes? Anything,' pleaded Digby.

'You can give us a DNA sample.'

'Certainly, if that means you don't have to speak to Fiona.'

Dave produced a DNA kit from his briefcase and took a swab from inside Digby's mouth. It would have no evidential value without the authorization of a superintendent, but it may help to eliminate Digby from their enquiries.

'Oh, you're still here.' Fiona Douglas came back into the room just as Dave was putting the kit back into his briefcase.

'We were just leaving, Miss Douglas.' Kate turned to Digby. 'Thank you for your help,' she said. 'We'll see ourselves out.'

Fiona Douglas stood at the window and watched as the police car pulled off the drive. 'What did they want, Frank?' She turned to face Digby, her arms folded and a suspicious expression on her face. 'Have you been out kerb-crawling again?'

'Certainly not. And you know that that was a case of mistaken identity. The police were collecting car numbers that night. Everybody's car number. But you'll never let me forget it, will you?'

'What *did* they want, then?'

Digby paused before answering. 'Er, they wanted to know if we'd seen a hit-and-run accident in Bow Street outside the Royal Opera House last Monday,' he said eventually. 'But I told them we hadn't seen a thing.'

'What the hell made them think we were at Covent Garden last Monday? Is there something you're not telling me? What have you been up to, Frank?'

'Nothing, darling, and I don't know why they thought that,' said Digby lamely. 'I suppose the police have access to all sorts of records these days. They're probably interviewing everyone who had tickets to *Swan Lake*. After all, I did book them online.'

'What, all two thousand of them?' asked Fiona sarcastically. 'But I don't suppose you mentioned to them that we didn't see it anyway. Or that you cancelled at the last minute because you told me that you had to see someone who wanted to place a large wine order for their restaurant. An order that didn't materialize. So, where the hell were you?'

'Well, I was—'

'O what a tangled web we weave, when first we practise to deceive!' quoted Fiona, and turned on her heel. 'I'm going to take a shower. Alone!'

It wasn't until Dave had steered the car on to the A413 that Kate mentioned the interview with Frank Digby.

'What d'you reckon, Dave?'

'Same problem as with all the others, guv. If his DNA shows that he's the father of Sharon's unborn child, it merely means he joins the merry band of men who had sex with her. It doesn't mean he murdered her.'

'Did you notice the perfume that Fiona was wearing?'

'I'm no good at identifying perfumes. All I know is that they cost an arm and a leg.'

'It was Lancôme Trésor.'

'Is that important, guv?'

'It's the perfume that Sharon Gregory was wearing when she was found at the Dickin Hotel.'

'A coincidence?' asked Dave.

'Could be. Anyway, we'll see what Max Riley has to say,' said Kate. 'And he's the last of the names on Sharon's contact list. I don't know where the hell the guv'nor will go after that.'

'He'll think of something,' said Dave, and accelerated to overtake a dithering pensioner wearing a flat cap and doing twenty-five.

FOURTEEN

After Kate and Dave had left to interview more of our 'suspects', I spent some time going over the statements we had accrued so far.

I hadn't been at it long before I was interrupted by the arrival of a detective inspector from the Serious Organized Crime Agency.

'Good morning, sir. I'm DI Ken Sullivan from SOCA.'

'Take a seat,' I said, pushing aside the pile of statements, 'and tell me what I can do for SOCA.'

'Gordon Harrison, boss.' Sullivan was obviously from a northern force where 'boss' was an informal alternative to 'guv'.

'You've got my interest. What about him?'

'I picked up that you'd put his name on the PNC, and I'm interested to know whether it has any relevance to the current enquiries my agency is making.'

I explained briefly how we had come to interview Harrison, but were still undecided about whether he had been involved in the murder of Sharon Gregory, or indeed had been her accomplice on the night of Clifford Gregory's murder.

'But what is SOCA's interest in him?' I asked.

'Drug smuggling,' said Sullivan. 'He has a Romanian girlfriend called Krisztina Comaneci.'

'Yes, that much he told us, Ken. He actually said that she was his partner.'

'In more ways than one,' said Sullivan. 'We believe her to be a courier, taking heroin into Romania from the Czech Republic. All we've learned so far is that Harrison imports antique statuary from Romania, and we're pretty sure that those items contain the drugs that Comaneci obtains. The story is that she legitimately buys these so-called artefacts and brings them back to the UK.'

'But hasn't customs examined them at the point of entry?' I asked.

'Oh, sure. Discreetly, of course, but Harrison's a smart guy and the statues don't always contain drugs. So far, customs haven't struck lucky. But they have to be careful because we'd like to know the origin and where those statues containing drugs go once they're in this country.'

'He told us that he planned holidays for tired executives who wanted to get away with their girlfriends. He also told us that in furtherance of that business, he travels quite often to the States. Florida and California mainly.'

'That's interesting,' said Sullivan, 'and will be of even greater interest to the FBI or the DEA. If he's taking drugs into America, that is. On the other hand, that might be a smokescreen for his drug activities.'

'We called on him this morning,' I said, 'for the second time, but that was strictly in connection with the murder of Sharon Gregory. He knew her and had had sex with her on several occasions in Miami. There was a young black girl there by the name of Shona Grant. He told us that he was with her, at home, at the time of the murder. But when my sergeant spoke to her alone, she claimed that she was at work as a hostess in a nightclub. I'm having one of my officers checking her story.'

'I'd rather you didn't, boss,' said Sullivan. 'A number of possibilities open up here. We know about Shona Grant and it's possible that she might be another of his couriers.' He paused. 'D'you think it's possible that Sharon Gregory was involved in his drug-smuggling activities and that's what got her killed?'

'I don't know, Ken,' I said, 'but we've scientific evidence that leads us to believe that one of her many male friends, and there were quite a few, might have been responsible. The best I can offer is to keep you informed of anything we find out.'

'I'm grateful, boss,' said Sullivan. 'And if I find anything that points to her killer being tied up in our enquiries, I'll let you know.'

Sullivan departed, leaving me to ponder yet another twist in the murder of Sharon Gregory.

It was forty miles from Chalfont St Giles to Guildford, and it was nearing five o'clock before Kate and Dave arrived at Max Riley's top-floor apartment not far from the ruins of the eleventh-century Guildford Castle.

'Hello. I hope you're not selling something.' The woman who

came to the door had smooth black skin and softened her statement with a radiant smile. She was about forty, tall, and dressed
in a tight-fitting red woollen dress that accentuated every contour
of her shapely figure. Her black hair was flecked with grey and
cropped very short. Higher-than-usual cheekbones lent a diamond-
shaped, almost sculpted appearance to her face. Most men would
doubtless find her sexually compelling, but she could not be
described as a beauty.

'We're police officers,' said Kate. 'I'm Detective Inspector
Ebdon and this is Detective Sergeant Poole. We'd like to have a
word with Mr Max Riley if he's at home.'

The woman threw back her head and burst out laughing. It was
an infectious, bubbly sort of laugh. 'I'm Max Riley,' she said.
'Actually, my name's Maxine, but I've only ever used Max and
that's what everyone calls me. There is no *Mr* Riley. Anyway, you'd
better come in and explain why you wanted to talk to this fictitious
Mr Riley.' She spoke with mellifluously rounded, educated tones.

The two detectives followed Maxine into a large airy studio
at the back of the apartment. It had a picture window running
almost the length of the room, and close to it, where it would
receive the maximum light, was an easel on which was a canvas
covered with a cotton sheet. A nearby paint-spattered bench bore
a number of paint pots, several palettes, a maulstick and a jar of
brushes. And a dirty coffee cup. A painter's smock had been thrown
carelessly over a stack of canvases leaning against the wall on the
far side of the studio.

'Take a seat.' Maxine pointed at a sofa. 'It's old, but it's clean
and comfortable. I cover it with a red velvet shawl whenever I do
the occasional life study.'

'You're an artist,' said Dave, as he and Kate sat down.

'I can tell you're a detective.' Maxine smiled mockingly. 'Now,
what's this all about?'

'Sharon Gregory. We found your phone number on her mobile,'
said Kate.

'I'm not surprised,' said Maxine. 'We had a relationship for a
while, Sharon and I.'

'Would you care to explain?'

'May I ask why you're interested in my relationship with
Sharon?'

'She was murdered last Monday,' said Dave.

'Oh my God, how awful!' Maxine was clearly shocked at the news of Sharon's murder and sat down heavily in a director's chair. 'D'you know who did it?'

'Not at the moment,' said Dave, 'which is why we're making enquiries of anyone who knew her. When did you last see her?'

'It must've been all of six months ago, I should think,' said Maxine, 'and then our affair sort of fizzled out. By unspoken mutual consent, if you know what I mean. Mind you, I know that I wasn't the only lover in her life, male or female. As a matter of fact, she talked quite openly about her affairs. She'd often tell me about her conquests, as she called them, both here and in the States. I told her she was being too reckless for her own good and that such irresponsible behaviour would get her into trouble one day.' Her face took on a sad expression. 'And it looks as though I was right,' she added, unaware that she was echoing what Jill Gregory had said about her late sister-in-law's promiscuity.

'How did you meet Sharon?' asked Kate.

'On a flight to Miami. I'd treated myself to a rare holiday. I thought that to have a look at America would be a change from my usual jaunts to Europe.'

'When was this?' asked Dave.

'About a year ago, I suppose, maybe eighteen months. It was a night flight, but I can never sleep on an aeroplane, so I went up to the first-class lounge for a few drinks. There was no one else there and Sharon was on duty, and we got talking. I could see straightaway that she had a good figure and a vibrant personality, and my artist's eye told me that she'd make a good nude study. I do the occasional life painting, although landscapes and seascapes are my usual métier.'

'And did she pose for you?' enquired Kate.

'Yes, she did, but only once.'

'Why was that?'

'I'm afraid the sight of a naked Sharon was just too much of a distraction for me, and the next time she came we finished up in the bedroom for a couple of passionate hours.' Maxine smiled, but displayed no sign of embarrassment at her admission. She crossed to the pile of canvases, sorted through them and selected one that depicted an unclothed Sharon reclining elegantly on the very couch Kate and Dave were occupying. It was unfinished.

'Was that the last time you saw her?'

'No, she came to the studio quite a few times after that, but not to pose. At least, not for a painting.' Maxine smiled at the recollection. 'She even turned up uninvited on one occasion when my boyfriend was here. That was a fun few hours, I can tell you.'

'Did she ever mention any of her male friends by name?' asked Kate.

'No, and I didn't ask. But I think she was too discreet to name names. Oh, what a loss. We had some good times together.'

'Did you know that she was married?' asked Dave.

'No, I didn't. What does it matter, anyway?'

'When you said that your boyfriend was here on one occasion, Miss Riley . . .' began Kate.

'Please call me Max, Inspector. In fact, Jonno – his name's actually Jonathan – was here more than once.'

'And did Sharon meet him here more than once?'

'Yes, several times. I think Jonno took quite a shine to her. She certainly did to him. I could see there was chemistry between the two.'

'Didn't that worry you?' asked Kate, seeking a motive for murder.

'Why should it? We were all free spirits and I haven't got a jealous bone in my body.'

'Do you think she and Jonathan were ever alone, away from here perhaps?'

'It's possible, I suppose. As I said, it wouldn't have bothered me. Neither of us was married – Jonno and I – and we enjoyed a fairly free lifestyle. And I wouldn't have blamed him for having sex with Sharon; as I said, she was a very passionate woman.'

'Are you still seeing this boyfriend?' asked Dave.

'He was killed in a car accident three months ago.' Maxine grabbed a tissue from the box on the table and dabbed at her eyes. 'I'm sorry,' she said, 'but I still miss him. He was a good artist, painted portraits mainly. It seems that everyone in my life is getting killed.'

'I apologize for having to ask this, Max, but where were you last Monday?' asked Kate, conscious of the fact that evidence of another woman's involvement had been found at the scene of Sharon's murder.

'I suppose that's what you police persons call a routine enquiry,' said Maxine, quickly recovering her composure and smiling. 'Actually I was in Southampton. I spent all that day and the following painting the *Queen Mary 2*. Not painting the ship itself,' she added, with a laugh, 'painting a depiction of it.' She crossed to the easel and whipped off the cloth to reveal an almost finished study of Cunard's flagship cruise liner. 'I stayed at the Hilton Hotel in Southampton that night and the night after, and came home on Wednesday. I can finish the rest of the painting here.'

'I understand that you don't own a car, Max,' said Dave.

'My word, you have been doing your homework. I used to own a vintage MG, but it got stolen about six months ago. The police told me that it was probably well on its way to Eastern Europe before I'd even noticed it gone. I haven't bothered to get another; it doesn't seem worth it. I hire a car if I need one, but most of the time I take taxis. As a matter of fact, it's worked out cheaper in the long run.'

'Thank you, Max,' said Kate. 'I don't think we need to trouble you further.'

'I suppose you wouldn't like to sit for me, Inspector, would you?' asked Maxine, appraising Kate's figure with an artist's eye.

'No thanks,' said Kate. 'I don't think that would be a very good idea.'

'No, I didn't think you would, Inspector. I should think you're all hetero.' Nevertheless, there was an element of regret in Maxine's reply. 'I'll show you out.'

'I reckon you had a lucky escape there, guv,' said Dave, as they drove away from Maxine Riley's apartment.

'So do I, Dave,' said Kate. 'But I wonder what Max's boyfriend was like,' she said, almost to herself.

Kate and Dave got back to the office at about half past six.

'How did you get on?' I asked.

'Frank Digby's a bit sussy, guv,' said Kate, 'but Dave got his DNA. Voluntarily. Well, with a little gentle persuasion.'

'And Max Riley turned out to be Maxine Riley, a bisexual artist,' said Dave. 'Miss Ebdon had to do a bit of verbal tap-dancing when she was propositioned.'

'Like hell I did,' said Kate. 'She didn't stand a chance – but I notice she didn't ask you to pose, Dave.'

'No, a pity that,' said Dave, a dreamy look in his eye.

'You say that this Max Riley is bisexual, Kate. D'you think that—'

'No,' said Kate firmly. 'She has an alibi for the night of Sharon's murder – it'll have to be checked out, of course, but she seemed genuinely shocked when I told her that Sharon had been murdered.'

I took the opportunity to brief Kate and Dave about the visit of DI Ken Sullivan.

'Blimey!' said Dave. 'If that's true we've been looking in the wrong direction.'

'I don't think so, Dave,' said Kate. 'I'm convinced that Sharon Gregory's murder is down to one of her lovers.'

'So am I,' I said. 'But there's one other thing we've got to do, Dave. Get on to Richie at Sharon's airline and find out where her friend Cindy Patterson lives and when she's likely to be there. I think it's time we had a word with her. She might have something useful to tell us. In the meantime, I think we'll have a word with Lance Kramer. I just hope he's not out painting the town red.'

The Holiday Inn, Regents Park, was in Carburton Street off Great Portland Street.

'We're police officers, miss,' I said to the receptionist. 'I understand that you have a Mr Lance Kramer staying here.'

The receptionist turned to her computer and keyed in the name. 'He's in room 314,' she said.

'Is he in the hotel now?'

'As far as I can tell. I can call him for you if you like.'

'No thanks, we'd like to surprise him,' said Dave.

'Take the lift to the third floor,' said the receptionist helpfully.

'I'd more or less worked that out,' said Dave.

We made our way to Kramer's room and knocked.

'Mr Kramer?'

'Yep, in person.' The man who answered the door of room 314 was not very tall, probably the same height as Sharon had been: about five foot seven. He was clearly a devotee of permatan;

probably an 'all-over' guy. He was wearing a half-open orange shirt and light-coloured slacks. A gold medallion was around his neck, nestling in his hairy chest, and an ostentatiously chunky gold watch adorned his right wrist. *Possibly left-handed,* I thought. Not that that meant anything; Mortlock had said that Sharon's killer had used both hands. Apart from which, I'd often noticed that 'arty' people, particularly actors, were left-handed.

'We're police officers, Mr Kramer. I'm Detective Chief Inspector Brock, and this is Detective Sergeant Poole.'

'Come right on in, gentlemen, have yourselves a seat and tell me how I may help you.' Kramer perched on the edge of the bed, his face expressing curiosity.

I decided to get straight to the point.

'How often did you sleep with Sharon Gregory, Mr Kramer?'

'Jesus! You London cops don't go in for the small talk, do you?'

'We found your number on her cellphone,' I said, using the American term for a mobile, not wanting Kramer to be under any illusion as to what we were talking about. 'To start with, can you account for your movements on the evening of Monday the twenty-ninth of July?'

'If it's not a rude question, Detective, why are you interested in what I was doing last Monday evening?' Kramer sat forward, hands linked loosely between his knees, perfectly relaxed.

'Because we're investigating her murder, Mr Kramer.'

'You're joking, right?' Kramer smiled.

'It's not our custom to make jokes about murder, Mr Kramer,' said Dave, speaking for the first time. His educated English accent seemed to surprise the man.

'No, I guess not. Sorry,' said Kramer. 'Sharon Gregory. Yes, I met her on a flight, maybe a year back. I'd been here in London and was on my way home to Miami Beach. That's where I live,' he added. 'But, hell, man, I don't sleep around. I've got me the cutest little wife and two adorable kids back in Miami. Why would I want to risk that?' He leaned across for his wallet and promptly produced a photograph of his family to back up his story.

'Have you any idea why she should have had your cellphone number?' asked Dave.

'Sure. We got to talking and she asked me if I'd been in London on vacation. I told her I was a designer of theatre sets, and she said that she loved the theatre. I gave her my cellphone number and told her any time she wanted to go to a theatre in Miami she was to call me. I get plenty of free tickets and I said she'd be welcome to have a couple for herself and a friend. That's all there was to it. She never did call me, though. But now you tell me she was murdered. Any idea who did it?'

'No, Mr Kramer,' I said. 'That's why we're talking to you.'

'Well, sure as hell, I had nothing to do with it. As a matter of fact, I was having dinner at your Savoy Hotel that night, with some guys from the production I'm working on. If you want, I can give you their names.'

'That would be helpful,' I said. 'You see, I've got this boss who insists on me covering all the bases.'

'Yeah, I get your drift, Detective. I worked on a TV cop show once, and the police adviser – a guy from the LAPD – told me that those shows are nothing like the real thing.' Kramer took one of the hotel's complimentary notepads from the bedside cabinet and scribbled three names on it together with their office addresses. I noticed that he wrote with his left hand. 'There y'go,' he said, tearing off the sheet and handing it to me. 'I hope you catch the guy. She was a sweet kid, but not my type.'

'And now I think we'll call it a day, Dave,' I said, as we left the Holiday Inn. 'See you Monday, and we'll sit down and rethink our strategy.'

'What strategy, sir?' asked Dave.

It was ten past nine that evening by the time I opened the door of my flat in Surbiton. I was looking forward to a shower and a whisky, but didn't fancy cooking anything for myself. I was no good at cooking anyway, the cooker and I being natural enemies. And, as Mrs Gurney had pointed out, the microwave had broken down. I decided that I would send out for a Chinese, and then I'd go to bed.

But all my plans were set at nought when I shut the front door.

'I'm in the kitchen, darling.' And there was Gail in a red tee-shirt, white slacks and an apron. She turned and gave me a kiss. 'I rang your office, but they told me you'd left for home, so I decided to come round and get supper for you. I knew your fridge and freezer would be empty,' she said, making a sour face, 'so I brought a few things in with me. *And you haven't got a wok!*' She pointed a spatula at me and made the accusation sound as though I was guilty of serious criminal negligence.

'Sorry about that,' I said, with feigned contrition. 'I'd be no good at using it anyway, even if I had one. I'll open the champagne. At least I've got some of that.'

'I'd rather have a G-and-T, if you don't mind,' said Gail, waving away the idea of bubbly with the spatula.

'Good,' I said, 'because I'm going to have a Scotch.' I put the champagne back in the fridge.

I don't know how Gail does it, but the meal was amazing. In no time at all, she had produced chicken breasts coated in flour and lightly fried, boiled rice and stir-fried vegetables that, as she pointedly observed, she had been obliged to cook in a frying pan. *Because I hadn't got a wok!* I provided a bottle of Gewürztraminer, one of the few commendable wines that Helga, my ex, had introduced into our sixteen years of marriage. Finally, Gail rounded off the meal by producing a tub of Häagen-Dazs mint and chocolate ice cream. She's all class, that girl.

'That was superb, darling,' I said, sitting back with a satisfied smile. 'Cognac?'

'Please.'

As usual Gail stayed the night, and I was hoping that we might spend Sunday lazing around and doing nothing in particular. It was at times like that I tended to forget I was a detective.

At nine-thirty on that Sunday morning, while we were still in bed, the dream was shattered by a phone call. I disentangled myself from Gail and reached for my mobile, which, as ever, was never far away from me.

'Good morning, guv. It's Dave.'

'Don't tell me, Dave. You've arrested our murderer, but you've mislaid the phone number of the Crown Prosecution Service.'

Dave laughed. 'I'd like to mislay the CPS altogether, guv. No, it's about Cindy Patterson, Sharon Gregory's crewmate. The incident room got a call from Ted Richie last night to say that the Patterson girl is at home today, but is flying off to Miami early tomorrow morning. She'll be leaving home very early, like zero-five-hundred. Unless we see her today, we won't get a chance to speak to her for another four days.'

'Give her a ring, Dave, and tell her we'll be there to see her this afternoon, if she's free to see us. Where does she live?'

'Feltham, guv. Richie said that she shares a flat with two other airline girls. I'll pick you up at about two. Is that all right?'

I sighed. 'It'll have to be, I suppose.'

'Work?' asked Gail, as I cancelled the call.

'I'm afraid so,' I said. 'I've got to see a ravishing air hostess this afternoon.'

'Oh, have you indeed?' said Gail apprehensively.

FIFTEEN

The door to Cindy Patterson's Feltham flat was opened by a plain, leggy girl with straggly shoulder-length chestnut hair. She was casually dressed in a sloppy cream sweater and green leggings.

'Hi,' she said with a smile. She shot an appraising glance in Dave's direction and swept her hair back behind her ears. Why do girls do that?

'Cindy Patterson?'

'No, I'm Liz, one of her flatmates.'

'We're police officers,' I said. 'We've arranged to have a word with her.'

'Sure. Come on in. She is expecting you.' Liz showed us into a comfortable but cluttered living room. 'You'll have to excuse the mess,' she said, rushing around and gathering up magazines and items of female apparel that were spread over the armchairs and sofa. 'We're always coming and going at odd hours and never seem to have the time to clear up,' she added breathlessly, before turning off the TV. 'I'll fetch Cindy for you.'

The girl who entered a few moments later was of medium height and her jet-black hair was gathered into an untidy ponytail. She was wearing a full-length cotton skirt and a green polo-necked jumper. 'Hi! I'm Cindy.'

'We'd like to talk to you about Sharon Gregory, Miss Patterson,' I said, and told Cindy who we were and why we were there.

'Oh, for goodness sake, it's Cindy, there's no need to stand on ceremony. And please sit down.' She seated herself in an armchair and crossed her legs. 'It was awful, hearing that Sharon had been murdered,' she said. 'We'll miss her terribly. She was great fun to be with.'

'From what we've learned about Sharon, it seems that she had quite a few lovers, Cindy,' I began, getting straight to the point. 'I'll be quite frank with you: a number of witnesses we've interviewed have led us to the conclusion that she'd happily share a bed with anyone who asked her.'

'They weren't lying,' said Cindy. 'And I reckon that Miami was usually the place where she spent time in the sack with most of them.'

'And you know this for certain,' said Dave.

'Sure do. There was one occasion when I'd asked her if she fancied a swim and she agreed to meet me on the beach ten minutes later. I got so annoyed when she didn't show after half an hour that I left the beach and went up to her room. She was in bed with a man.' Cindy wrinkled her brow. 'Actually, they were on it rather than in it.'

'When was this?'

'It must've been a couple of months ago. Yes, it was the beginning of June. In fact, it was an incident almost identical to one that occurred a year ago.'

'How did you get in? From what I know of hotel doors they can only be entered with a keycard.'

'That's true,' said Cindy. 'Anyway, there was a "Do Not Disturb" sign on the door, a dead giveaway, that. But my room was next to Sharon's, so I went along the balcony. It was a hellishly hot day and she'd left the doors open. It was no problem because we were on the fifth floor and there was only a low wall between the two rooms and I vaulted over it. I swim a lot and work out whenever I get the chance, so I keep myself in pretty good shape. Mind you, I did bark my shin,' she added ruefully.

'Did she say anything when you barged in?'

'No, but the man she was on the bed with did. The saucy bastard asked if I'd come to join in. But I was only wearing a bikini, so I suppose he thought I was up for it. Or that Sharon had arranged a threesome. It's the sort of thing she might've have done. I don't mean she'd ever done it before, but I wouldn't've put it past her.'

'What did this man look like, Cindy?' asked Dave, pocketbook at the ready.

'Dishy,' said Cindy.

'Could you be a bit more specific than that? How tall was he?'

'He must've been about six-three, I should think,' said Cindy. 'Well, I guess he was. It was a bit difficult to tell because he was lying down. He was well-built – very well-built, if you know what

I mean.' She flashed Dave a mischievous smile. 'To be honest, I didn't stay long enough to take too much notice of the rest of him. I wasn't surprised that Sharon was having it off with some guy, particularly that one. But I was annoyed that she'd stood me up. If she'd told me what she was going to get up to, I wouldn't've bothered to ask her for a swim.'

'What was he wearing?' asked Dave, pretending to be naive.

Briefly puzzled by the question, Cindy stared at Dave for a moment or two and then laughed when she realized he was teasing her. 'Nothing, of course,' she said, and giggled. 'Neither was Sharon. Mind you, as I said, it was a very hot day.'

'Did Sharon say who this man was?' I asked. 'Did she tell you his name or whether he was English or American? In fact, did she say anything at all about him?'

'Not until we were on the flight home and she had a little dig at me for barging in on the two of them. She told me that he was British and a frequent flyer, but that was all she said.'

'Was he on that return flight?'

'He may have been, I don't know. But if he was, Sharon was careful not to pay any more attention to him than to the other passengers.'

'Because of you having caught them in the act?'

'No, that didn't worry her, but because chatting up the passengers is a sacking offence in our airline. I'm not saying that it doesn't go on – the girls hooking up with passengers, I mean – but they don't brag about it and they certainly don't show out when they're on duty. It's OK for us to meet a guy away from the job, and a few of the girls have married men they've met on flights, but you don't make a song and dance about it. Anyway, I don't think I'd've recognized the guy again, not once he had his clothes on.' Cindy giggled again; she seemed to giggle a lot.

'Was that all Sharon said about it?' asked Dave.

'Yes, she never mentioned the incident again, and I didn't either. After all, she was entitled to fuck anyone she liked. It's just that I was a bit pissed off that she'd agreed to come for a swim and then didn't show. Like I said just now, if she'd refused and told me that she was having it off with a guy instead, I couldn't have cared less about it. And I certainly wouldn't've gone looking for her.'

'You did know she was married, I suppose?' said Dave.

'*Married*! What, Sharon? I don't believe it.'

'She was,' I said. 'What's more, her husband was murdered two days before Sharon.'

'Bloody hell! I never knew she was married. What a deceitful little bitch.' Cindy shook her head in disbelief. 'I must say she kept that pretty quiet. She never mentioned a husband and she didn't wear a wedding ring. Is there a connection between Sharon and her husband both being murdered?'

'We're still working on it,' said Dave, unwilling to disclose that we had sufficient evidence to leave us in little doubt that Sharon was responsible for the death of her husband.

'About this man you saw Sharon in bed with, Cindy,' I said. 'D'you think she was seeing him on a regular basis?'

Cindy shrugged. 'I really have no idea. I know one shouldn't speak ill of the dead, but Sharon was very much someone who put herself first. And she was a bit of a loner, too. She only very occasionally socialized with the crew on stopovers. The rest of us would spend most of our free time beside the pool or down on the beach soaking up the sun. Not Sharon, though. As I said, she'd sometimes join me for a swim, but I think she probably spent most of the time in bed, and not by herself either. One thing's for sure: if she did shack up with a guy, he'd have to have been filthy rich. She always said that she was on the lookout for a man who could afford to give her the high life.'

'Do you happen to know any of the other men she was seeing?'

'No. I certainly didn't blunder in and find her at it. Not after that time in Miami.' Cindy paused. 'Hang on, though. I've just remembered. It was about a year ago. Same hotel, of course, and I'd called her and suggested a swim, just like I did last June. But I told you about that just now. She agreed to meet me on the beach in ten minutes' time, but she never showed up. After about an hour, I rang her from the beach and she said something about having had to take a call.'

We hadn't learned anything we didn't already know. Sharon indulged in serial promiscuity. That she was looking for a rich man didn't narrow the field either; the men who had been interviewed were all well-heeled. We thanked Cindy for her time and wished her a safe flight.

*   *   *

On Monday morning I received a report from the forensic science laboratory. The DNA sample taken from Sharon Gregory's unborn child had been compared with the swab taken from Frank Digby, the wine merchant from Chalfont St Giles, but had proved not to be a match. Not that that took him out of the frame for her murder.

Later that day we received similarly depressing information: the sample that Lizanne Carpenter had taken from the hairbrush in Gordon Harrison's bathroom at Fulham didn't match either. As with Digby, that didn't mean that he hadn't murdered her. But from what Ken Sullivan of SOCA had said, Harrison was probably heavily engaged in some other nefarious activity at the time of the murder.

There was one piece of encouraging news. The DNA of a hair that Linda's people had found on the pillow at the Dickin Hotel *had* been found to match that of the father of Sharon's child. We were getting closer, but not close enough to make an arrest.

That apart, it looked very much as though our enquiry had stalled. We'd gathered all these DNA samples, but they meant nothing until we actually found the man who's DNA could be matched to them, and none of them was on the database. We might get somewhere once we'd identified the fingerprints found in the room, but those could, of course, belong to anyone who had used the room over the preceding weeks.

I walked out to the incident room.

'Dave, I think we'll have another run out to the Gregory house and have a look around. What's the position? Is it still under police guard?'

'No, guv. It was handed over to Peter Gregory shortly after we'd interviewed Jill Gregory on Friday. But I've kept a key, just in case we needed it.'

'Give him a ring, or Mrs Gregory, and ask one of them if it's all right for us to have another poke around.'

We arrived at West Drayton at about eleven o'clock. It was immediately apparent that Clifford Gregory's brother and sister-in-law had paid a visit. The house had been cleared up and there was no sign of the chaos that we'd encountered on the night of Clifford's murder, apart from the wine stain on the dining room carpet and the broken television set.

'Are we looking for something in particular, guv?' asked Dave.

'I wondered if there was a laptop computer anywhere here that might shed some light on more of Sharon's bed mates, Dave. More than we've turned up so far.'

'We didn't find one the night Clifford Gregory was murdered, and we didn't find one when we came back looking for Sharon. Why should we find one now . . . sir?'

'It was just a thought,' I said.

'We examined the one in Clifford's study,' said Dave, 'but the only files on it were those connected with his job as an accountant. Anyway, Sharon wouldn't have been stupid enough to put details of her extramarital affairs on a computer that her husband might find, would she? And there wasn't one in her locker at Heathrow.'

I still wasn't convinced. 'Nevertheless, we'll have a last look round, Dave. When the house was searched, Sharon was still alive, and we were only looking for evidence in connection with her husband's murder.'

'Very good, sir,' said Dave.

That was the second time he'd called me 'sir' in a short space of time. However, he was right to doubt the value of conducting a second search. We went through the house – even the loft and the garage – but didn't find another computer or anything else that would help us to identify who had killed Sharon Gregory.

'Give Peter Gregory a call, Dave, and ask him if he's removed a computer. And while you're at it, ask him if a date's been set for the funerals.'

'Yes, sir,' said Dave. I think he thought I was becoming obsessed about finding another computer.

We left, just as an estate agent was erecting a 'For Sale' board in the front garden.

'Good luck,' said Dave. 'They'll have a job selling a house where a murder's been committed.'

Dave and I had not long returned to ESB from West Drayton when Colin Wilberforce burst into my office. It is extremely rare for Colin to make a hurried entry without knocking, and I knew instinctively that he had something to say that was both important and urgent.

'What is it, Colin?'

'Two minutes ago I received a call from a traffic unit in Saint James's Street off Pall Mall, sir. They're in the process of arresting Julian Reed for driving under the influence.'

'Interesting.' It was just after two o'clock in the afternoon. 'I thought it was only ladies-who-lunch who got caught. And they usually say, "But I've only had one glass of white wine, Officer."'

'It happens, sir. But I dare say Mr Reed had a few lunchtime bevvies at the Dizzy Club,' said Wilberforce. 'One of the PCs did a PNC check and found that we were interested.'

'Are they still at the roadside?'

'Yes, sir.'

'Get back to them and ask them to do a fingerprint check on that magic machine they carry with them these days.'

'I did that already, sir.' Wilberforce gave a smile of satisfaction. 'They're a match for one of the prints found at the scene of Sharon Gregory's murder at the Dickin Hotel.'

Give or take a few hours, it was now exactly a week since Sharon Gregory had been murdered. All we had found so far were an unidentified vaginal fluid, a few fingerprints and a few hairs on a pillow, one of which was a DNA match to whoever was the father of her unborn child. And in all probability it was he who was her killer. Maybe.

But now, it seemed, we'd had that stroke of luck that so often results in the apprehension of someone whom CID officers have spent hours trying to identify. And, as not infrequently happens, it was a uniformed constable, albeit in this case a specialist, who was almost accidentally responsible. This sort of extrinsic contribution to solving a murder, although not exactly commonplace, occurs more often than is realized.

When I did a senior investigators' course at the Detective Training School, I remember being told of at least two examples of it happening in the past. In 1961 a man named Edwin Bush murdered a woman, Elsie Batten, in an antique shop in Cecil Court off Charing Cross Road, and an Identikit likeness was prepared from the descriptions of witnesses. Four days later a young uniformed PC was patrolling the Soho area of London and arrested the murderer whom he'd identified from that depiction.

And twenty-two years later, a drain-clearance operative had found human remains in the blocked drain of a house in North

London, resulting in the arrest of Dennis Nilsen, a multiple murderer.

Now it was my turn. Perhaps.

'Where are they taking him, Colin?'

'Charing Cross nick, sir.'

'Ask them to take Reed's car there, too. I presume it was his Mercedes that he was driving?'

'It was, sir, and they're taking it in anyway.'

'Tell them that they're not to search it. We'll do that when we arrive. And just to be on the safe side, ask Linda Mitchell to get a team down there.'

'Right, sir.'

'And advise the nick that we'll be there as soon as possible.'

'I'll get a car, sir,' said Dave. 'Looks as though we might've cracked it.'

'Maybe, Dave,' I said cautiously. All too often in the past I'd believed myself to be on the point of solving a murder, only to find that I was wrong. 'There's one problem. The Simpsons, they of the swingers' club in Dorking, were certain that Julian Reed was there with his wife at the time of Sharon's murder.'

'People have been known to make mistakes, guv.'

'Yes, and I'm not usually one of them.'

'No, sir,' said Dave. 'By the way, guv, I checked with Peter Gregory and he didn't remove a laptop from the West Drayton house.'

SIXTEEN

By some method I didn't wish to know about, Dave had laid hands on an unmarked police car that was fitted with a siren, and flashing blue lights positioned behind the radiator grille. He made good use of this equipment and we covered the five or so miles from Earls Court to Charing Cross police station in just over as many hair-raising minutes. It was one of the few occasions on which I would rather have been driven by a traffic unit officer.

I identified myself to the custody sergeant and enquired about Julian Reed.

'He's providing a second breath test at the moment, sir,' said the sergeant. 'I've no doubt it'll be positive. According to the arresting officers, he was slightly more than twice over the legal limit when they breathalysed him at the roadside.'

'Julian Reed is a strong suspect for a murder that I'm investigating, Skip,' I said, 'and I should like him to be kept in custody until he's sober enough to be interviewed.'

'I presume there's sufficient evidence to support the allegation, sir.' The custody sergeant was only doing his job; in normal circumstances the responsibility for deciding whether a prisoner should be admitted to bail rested with him. Nevertheless, I could overrule him if I thought that detention was warranted.

'There is,' I said, 'substantial fingerprint and forensic evidence.' I thought it better not to mention that Reed had furnished an alibi which, on the face of it, appeared to place him at a swingers' party in Dorking at the time of Sharon Gregory's murder. But I still had reservations about that.

'Right, sir. In any case, he'll have to be detained until he's sober enough to be released.' The sergeant paused as a traffic officer entered the custody suite. 'Got a result?' he asked him.

'The lowest reading was eighty micrograms, Skip. Just over twice the limit.'

'That settles it, sir,' said the custody sergeant, turning back to me. 'We'll have to keep him in custody for at least eight hours before he can safely be released.'

All of which was a confounded nuisance. If I were to interrogate a man with that amount of alcohol in his system, anything he said would undoubtedly be challenged by his solicitor, to say nothing of defence counsel. If we ever got to court on a murder charge, that is. Given that I accepted the custody sergeant's prediction, which I was bound to do, it would be at least eleven o'clock this evening before we could speak to him. And as the Police and Criminal Evidence Act stipulated that a prisoner must be afforded rest, usually at night, we would be unable to talk to him before tomorrow.

'We'll be back in the morning, Skip,' I said. 'In the meantime, I'd like to have a look at his car.'

'No problem, sir. It's in the yard. I'll get a PC to show you the way. Incidentally, a couple of forensic examiners are out there already. They said they were meeting you here.'

Linda Mitchell and an assistant were waiting for us as Dave and I walked out to the station yard.

For a moment or two, Dave stood in open-mouthed admiration of Julian Reed's silver-grey C-Class Mercedes.

'That is some car, guv,' said Dave. 'It must've set him back at least thirty-five grand, possibly more. And presumably Mrs Reed paid for it.'

'She didn't,' I said. 'According to Charlie Flynn's sources, she's not worth a bean.'

'All right for me to take a look inside, Mr Brock?' asked Linda, donning a pair of latex gloves.

'Yes, go ahead, Linda.'

For the next twenty minutes, Linda conducted a meticulous examination of the car's interior before emerging with a mobile phone.

'This was in the glove compartment,' she said. 'I've examined the calls register on it and it shows that a call was made to Reed's landline from this phone at twelve minutes past twelve on the afternoon of Monday the twenty-ninth of July.'

'The call was made *to* Reed?' I queried. 'Not *from* Reed?'

'That's right,' said Linda, and paused while she referred to her notes. 'The number called was one of those in Sharon Gregory's contact list, which is the one Dave obtained from her SIM card. That means that this is *her* mobile phone, and the one we found in her room at the Dickin Hotel most likely belongs to the murderer.'

'That must mean that Julian Reed, if he's Sharon's killer, took her phone with him by mistake,' said Dave. 'I reckon we've got him, guv. It's got to be down to him.'

'It certainly looks like it, Dave,' I said, 'but there's still the question of the swingers' club at Dorking. The Simpsons said he was there with his wife. Ask the custody sergeant if they've photographed Reed yet. If they have, get a copy and we'll have a run to Dorking again. There's nothing else we can do for the time being.'

'Wonderful,' said Dave. 'I love Dorking,' he added sarcastically.

We arrived at the Simpsons' house in Dorking at just after six o'clock. This time there was only one car on the drive. But I expected more would arrive before long.

'Hello! Welcome to our little soirée,' said a beaming Laura Simpson, at first failing to recognize who was standing on her doorstep. But then she did recognize us. 'Oh, my God, it's you.'

When we'd called last Friday Mrs Simpson had been soberly dressed, but now she was attired in a short black basque, a thong, and black stockings held up with suspenders. It was one of the most ridiculous visions I'd seen in years. Particularly as I'd decided, the last time we were there, that Laura Simpson must be at least sixty. Disregarding her age, she was certainly too plump to get away with such an outrageous costume. If it was an attempt at sexual allure, it failed miserably; she had merely succeeded in becoming a rather ludicrous and pathetic figure. I could only conclude that she intended to take an active part in that night's proceedings.

'Yes, it's us, Mrs Simpson,' said Dave. 'We'd like a word with you.'

'But when you came the last time I thought you said that what we were doing here was all right.' Laura Simpson reluctantly admitted us, at the same time trying unsuccessfully to hide behind the front door.

'We didn't actually say that, Mrs Simpson,' I said. 'Merely that what you were doing here was of no interest to us in our murder investigation. Is your husband here?'

'Yes, he is.'

'We'd like a word with him as well as with you.'

'I'll fetch him.' Laura Simpson hurried away, unsteady on the stiletto heels to which she was clearly unaccustomed, and trying desperately to cover her wobbling naked buttocks with her hands.

We had to wait for some time before James Simpson appeared. I presumed that the delay was caused by the need for him to dress in presentable clothing. Laura Simpson had certainly taken the time to don an all-embracing pink candlewick dressing gown and exchange her high heels for fluffy bedroom slippers. The result was that she looked even more absurd than she had done previously.

'What is it this time?' James Simpson spoke with impatient arrogance. 'We're expecting guests.'

'You can come off your high horse right now, Simpson,' said Dave, who was clearly irked by the man's lofty attitude and what he saw as prevarication. 'My chief inspector only has to make one phone call and you'll be having a visit from the local police. Tonight.'

'So, er, how can I, um, help you, gentlemen?' In the face of Dave's uncompromising threat, Simpson capitulated, and immediately became a stuttering sycophant.

'Have a look at this photograph, Mr Simpson,' I said, taking the print from Dave, 'and tell me if you've ever seen this man before.'

Simpson studied the image closely. 'I think that's Julian Reed,' he said, and then passed the photograph to his wife.

'Yes, that's Julian,' said Laura Simpson, handing the print back to Dave. 'Why d'you ask?'

'Julian Reed is the man you said was here with his wife Muriel on the night of the twenty-ninth of July.'

'I'm sure they were here,' said Simpson. 'He and his wife are regular visitors. But I suppose it's possible that I was confused.'

'Really?' said Dave sarcastically. 'Then perhaps you can tell me what sort of car this couple, who might or might not have been the Reeds, arrived in.'

'I think it was a Lexus, a new one by the look of it,' said Simpson.

In my book that confirmed that the Reeds had not been at Dorking on the night of Sharon Gregory's murder. Julian Reed did not own a Lexus; his car was a Mercedes.

Dave marked the photograph of Julian Reed as an exhibit and took a statement from each of the Simpsons, testifying that it was not a likeness of the man who'd come to their swingers' party on the night of Sharon's murder, but adding that they recognized Reed as a previous caller at their house.

We arrived at Charing Cross police station early on Tuesday morning. I had to go through the whole business of explaining to a different custody sergeant why we were there and what we wanted.

'I'll have him brought up, sir,' said the sergeant. 'Interview Room Three.'

Julian Reed carved a sorrowful figure as he was escorted into the interview room. Deprived of his belt and tie – I presumed he was one of those rare men who actually wore a tie these days – he was clearly showing signs of having been on a bender the previous day.

He put on his spectacles and took some time to focus on Dave and me, but eventually recognition dawned.

'What are you doing here, Chief Inspector?' It was an odd question for Reed to have asked. After all, it wasn't unusual for policemen to be in a police station.

'We've some questions to put to you, Mr Reed,' I said, as Dave broke the seals of the tapes, inserted them into the recording equipment and turned it on.

'Interview at Charing Cross police station commencing at oh-nine-twelve,' said Dave, and added the date. 'Present are Mr Julian Reed, Detective Chief Inspector Harry Brock and Detective Sergeant David Poole.'

'What's this about, Mr Brock?' Reed's vacant expression implied that he was totally bemused by all this legalistic mumbo-jumbo.

'It's about this for a start, Mr Reed.' I produced the mobile phone – now sealed into a plastic bag – that Linda Mitchell had found in his Mercedes. 'I am showing Mr Reed a mobile telephone marked Exhibit LM Forty-One,' I said, for the benefit of the tape. 'This was found in your car, Mr Reed.'

Reed picked it up and examined it. 'I've never seen it before,' he said, putting it back on the table. 'Does it have something to do with my being arrested yesterday?'

I couldn't work out whether Reed's response to this first question meant that he intended to deny everything, or that he was so naive that he didn't realize why we were questioning him.

'Where were you during the afternoon and evening of Monday the twenty-ninth of July, Mr Reed?' I asked.

'I know I told you that I was at the Dizzy Club in the afternoon, and that I was at home with my wife that evening, but that's not true. I was at an address in Dorking that evening.' Reed may have been suffering from a hangover, but his recall wasn't lacking.

'We've visited that address,' said Dave. 'It was a swingers' party. We have statements from Mr and Mrs Simpson who were shown the photograph of you taken when you were arrested yesterday. The Simpsons are prepared to testify that you were not there on that occasion. They did, however, state that you had been there on previous occasions. We've also visited the Dizzy Club and your favourite stripper told us that you weren't there that afternoon.'

'What has any of this to do with my being arrested for being drunk yesterday?' Reed stared at me through his heavy-rimmed spectacles, the innocent Boy Scout image that had been apparent at our previous interview still prevailing.

'Are you willing to give a sample of your DNA, Mr Reed?' I asked.

'Of course, if you think it'll help whatever it is you're enquiring into. But I don't understand what this has to do with drink-driving.'

'It has nothing to do with it,' I said. 'I have sufficient evidence to suspect you of the murder of Sharon Gregory on the night of Monday the twenty-ninth of July.'

'My God! That's absurd. I didn't kill her. I loved her. We were going to get married,' exclaimed Reed, clearly shocked by my bald accusation. 'I've hardly been sober since I heard that awful news when you came to the house the other day.' For a moment or two he stared at me before sinking his head into his hands. It was some time before he looked up again. 'I told you where I was. I was at Dorking.'

'And I've already told you that the Simpsons will testify that you weren't there.' I was beginning to wonder what clever game Reed was playing. Perhaps the innocent Boy Scout image was a charade.

'I suppose I'd better tell you the truth then,' said Reed, his shoulders slumping. 'I was certainly with Sharon Gregory at the Dickin Hotel at Heathrow, but I didn't kill her. Why would I? I went there at about a quarter past one on that day and we spent an hour or so in bed.'

'One question, Mr Reed,' said Dave. 'Is your wife Muriel bisexual?' He was obviously thinking of the unidentified vaginal fluid found on Sharon's body.

Reed stared at Dave in astonishment. 'Muriel, bisexual? D'you know I haven't the faintest idea. I never asked her.'

There was now no alternative but to caution Reed, and I did so, and went on to tell him that he was entitled to the services of a solicitor. 'I shall now obtain the authority of a superintendent to take a DNA sample from you. Are you also prepared to consent to having your fingerprints taken?'

'Of course,' said Reed, 'if it'll help to prove that I didn't kill Sharon. You've got to understand, Chief Inspector, that I loved her. I told my wife I was leaving her and it was our intention, Sharon's and mine, to get married as soon as I could get a divorce.'

'You told your wife that you were divorcing her?' It was a rhetorical question, but it revealed a situation I hadn't foreseen, and it opened up another field of possibilities. 'I still think it would be a good idea for you to speak to a lawyer, Mr Reed.'

'What, about the divorce?'

This man's continuing naivety astounded me. 'No, about the fact that I believe you murdered Sharon Gregory.'

'Well I didn't, but I'll send for my own lawyer, if you think I need one.'

'That's entirely a matter for you,' I said, becoming increasingly frustrated with what I saw as a feigned innocence. 'However, Julian Reed, I am arresting you on suspicion of murdering Sharon Gregory on or about the twenty-ninth of July.' And I cautioned him.

'Am I going to get bail?' Reed posed the question rather like a small boy asking if he could get down from the dining table. I was utterly mystified by his total lack of alarm at being arrested for murder, and I was beginning to wonder if he actually was innocent. Either that or he was a damned good actor.

'That's not in my discretion,' I said. But I saw no reason why he shouldn't be bailed; he was too ingenuous to run. That said, it was always possible that he might be tempted to go to Miami. 'However, I will require you to surrender your passport.'

Without querying why I wanted it, Reed took the document from his pocket and handed it over.

I went upstairs to the chief superintendent's office and briefly explained the circumstances that had led to my suspecting Julian Reed of murder.

'It's essential that I obtain Mr Reed's DNA, sir,' I said, 'and I'd be obliged if you'd authorize the taking of an intimate sample. He has given his consent.'

'No problem, Mr Brock.'

I handed the chief superintendent the appropriate form and waited while he filled in the details and signed it.

I returned to the interview room and told Dave to go ahead. He produced the necessary kit and took a sample of Reed's saliva from inside his mouth. Then he escorted him to the custody suite where his fingerprints were taken.

'What now, guv?' asked Dave, as we returned to our car.

'Get that sample of Reed's DNA off to the lab immediately and the fingerprints to Linda.' I glanced at my watch. 'We'll go back to the office and get Charlie Flynn to do urgent background checks on Reed. And then, this afternoon, we'll pay a visit to Muriel Reed to see if she confirms this story about a divorce.'

'I suppose that'll help . . . sir,' said Dave. 'But his fingerprints were taken by the traffic guys.'

'Just do it, Dave.'

A surprise in the shape of DI Ken Sullivan of SOCA awaited me when Dave and I got back to ESB. And he brought news that I hadn't expected.

'An interesting development, boss,' Sullivan began, as he seated himself in my office. 'It's about Gordon Harrison, one of your suspects in the case of the Sharon Gregory murder.'

'I think we have our murderer, Ken, so Harrison can be ruled out of it now,' I said.

'In more ways than one,' said Sullivan. 'He's been murdered.'

'Where and when?' I had a nasty feeling about this.

'Wandsworth, boss.'

'Oh, that's all right, then,' I said, with a feeling of relief.

Sullivan raised his eyebrows. 'Any particular reason you should be pleased by that?' he asked.

'Yes,' I said, 'that means the investigation's down to Homicide and Serious Crime Command *South*.'

'Yes, it is.' Sullivan laughed. 'They already have a man in custody.'

'Good, but what's the SP?'

'The what?' queried Sullivan.

'What happened?' I asked, realizing that the term 'SP' was probably unknown to officers in northern forces.

'Oh, I see. I'll remember that,' said Sullivan, with a grin. 'I'm slowly getting used to the language of the Met.'

Wait until you meet Kate Ebdon, I thought.

'We've had an observation on Harrison for the last couple of days and he met with a man in a bar in Putney,' continued Sullivan. 'There was obviously some sort of falling out, and the next thing our obo team knew was that Harrison had been shot dead. The shooter ran for it, but he was promptly arrested by our chaps. They handed him over to your HSCC guys; an open-and-shut case. He's a Nigerian called Emedubi Anubi, a known drug dealer. We also arrested Shona Grant, who we're satisfied was one of Harrison's couriers. And the day before that, customs officers at Manchester Airport were lucky enough to pick up Harrison's partner, Krisztina Comaneci, arriving with a statue filled with heroin. Case closed. So, all in all, a good result.'

'Thanks for that,' I said, standing up to shake hands with Sullivan. But the murder of Gordon Harrison was of no real interest to me.

'It turns out that Anubi is wanted for murder in Nigeria. So, rather than mounting a costly trial followed by appeals, the powers-that-be will probably deport him.'

'You must be joking,' I said. 'We seem to find it impossible to deport people from this country. Anyway, Nigeria still has the death penalty, and no doubt our brave politicians will have a touch of the vapours at the mere suggestion that we send him back to be hanged. That's what they do with murderers.'

SEVENTEEN

'If you want to speak to my husband, he's not here. In fact I've no idea where he is.' Muriel Reed, her arrogance no less apparent than before, was attired in a mauve maxi kaftan below which her bare feet peeped out.

'He's just been released from Charing Cross police station, Mrs Reed. He was arrested yesterday afternoon for driving under the influence of alcohol.'

'Oh, what a stupid man.' Muriel opened the door wide. 'You'd better come in.'

We followed her upstairs to the sitting room and accepted her offer of a seat.

'Where did this happen, Chief Inspector?' Muriel raised her eyebrows and paused. 'But surely you're not dealing with that, are you?' She opened her hands in a theatrical gesture; she knew perfectly well that the CID didn't normally deal with drunken drivers. Unless there was more to it than that.

'He was arrested in Saint James's Street by traffic unit officers,' said Dave. 'At about two o'clock yesterday afternoon.'

'Surely you haven't come here just to tell me that, have you?' Muriel adopted an amused expression. 'And if this happened yesterday, why hasn't he come home? He's not at another strip club, is he?'

'He's been arrested for the murder of Sharon Gregory on the twenty-ninth of July,' I said.

'Murder?' exclaimed Muriel, and after a moment's hesitation, added, 'But it's absurd to think that Julian's capable of murdering anyone. Anyway, he was with me on that date. All day.'

'But the last time we were here, he told us that he'd gone to the Dizzy Club in Soho, but only in the afternoon.' We'd confirmed that he hadn't been there on that day, and I knew what he'd told us earlier, but I wanted to see what his wife said about that.

'You're quite right. I was confused,' said Muriel. It was almost an apology. 'In the evening we went to a swingers' club in Dorking for the sole purpose of having sex with other people.' There was no embarrassment about her admission as she pointed an accusing finger at Dave. 'And I gave you the address.'

'How did you get there, Mrs Reed?' asked Dave.

'By car, of course.'

'The Mercedes?'

'Of course the Mercedes. We don't have another car.'

'We've checked with the Simpsons, the couple who run that club, and they seemed to be under the impression that you'd arrived in a Lexus, and that you'd parked on their drive.'

'They must've made a mistake. There were quite a few cars there that night and there was no room on the drive. We had to park on the road, some way away.' Despite providing what must have seemed to her a reasonable explanation, Muriel Reed was suddenly neither as composed nor as disdainful as she had been when we'd first arrived. 'Ah!' she said, having come up with another excuse, 'I realize how the Simpsons' confusion must've arisen. We were there with some friends of ours. They own a Lexus.' She looked at me, almost imploring me to believe her.

'What are the names of these friends?' I asked.

'I'm sorry, but I'm not prepared to tell you.'

'You're not helping your husband, Mrs Reed,' I said.

'I don't see how telling you the names of our friends is going to help Julian in any way, Chief Inspector. I refuse to tell you who they were. They might not wish it to be known that they're swingers. They certainly wouldn't appreciate being questioned by the police about what is an innocent if unconventional pastime. What *would* their neighbours think?'

I heard the front door slam and seconds later Julian Reed burst into the room. He looked at me and then addressed his wife.

'I suppose they've told you that they think I murdered Sharon, Muriel.'

'Yes, they have,' said Muriel. 'And who exactly is this Sharon?'

'You know bloody well who she is,' said Reed, shaking his head at his wife's duplicity. 'Sharon Gregory's the stewardess I met on a flight to Miami. But I told you that, and I told you I was going to divorce you and marry her.' This was an entirely new Julian Reed, one that I'd never before seen standing up to his wife.

'I've no idea what you're talking about, Julian. But did you murder her?'

'Of course not.' Reed stared at his wife in disbelief before switching his glance to me. 'She knew all about Sharon,' he said. 'I told Muriel everything. She knew where I'd been.'

Despite what Muriel Reed had said previously – that she rather liked having Julian around – I detected a distinct lack of warmth in the relationship. And I'd noticed that neither Julian nor Muriel ever used terms of endearment when speaking to each other.

'Your wife has just told us that you and she were at a swingers' party in Dorking the night that Sharon was murdered, Mr Reed,' I said.

There was but a moment's hesitation before Reed clutched at the lifeline that had been extended to him by his wife. 'Yes, we were.'

'We both enjoy having sex with other people, Chief Inspector,' said Muriel, clearly relieved that her husband had confirmed her story. 'It livens up our own sex lives. Julian is always on the lookout for an attractive and willing girl and I simply love getting laid by a younger virile man.' She lifted her chin as if defying me to criticize her behaviour. 'I suppose I'm what you might call a cougar.'

Once again I was surprised at the woman's willingness to discuss her sex life quite openly with a complete stranger. But I also got the impression that Muriel Reed now found herself in a corner and was trying desperately to find a way out of it.

'I thought you preferred playing tennis, Muriel,' said Reed sarcastically, continuing to stand up to his wife. He looked at me. 'She's got a wicked forearm smash, Chief Inspector.' He paused before adding what, for him, was an unusually subtle remark. 'Especially when she's playing with new balls.'

'I think that's all for the time being,' I said. 'We'll let ourselves out.' I decided that Julian Reed would have to be questioned further, but not in the presence of his wife.

Dave and I hadn't reached the front door before we heard a monumental screaming match breaking out between Julian and Muriel Reed.

On the way back to the office, I mulled over the claim by Muriel Reed that she and her husband had been to the Dorking swingers' party with friends. But despite her candid admission as to what she was doing there, I was intrigued that she refused to tell us who the friends were. She must've known that it would be simplicity itself to discover their identity. More to the point, she probably feared that they would not support her story.

When we arrived at ESB, I asked Dave to come into the office.

'Give the Simpsons a call, Dave, and persuade them to shed some light on the identity of the people who Muriel Reed claims that she and Julian met there on the twenty-ninth of July.'

'Are the Simpsons likely to know the names of these people, guv? I got the impression that anyone could turn up there and use any name they liked.'

'Yes, I realize all that, but they might've heard one of the Reeds use their names.'

Dave did not seem at all enamoured of the idea, and probably wondered whether discovering the Reeds' friends identity would help our investigation.

'But we've got Julian Reed bang to rights, sir.'

'Maybe,' I said pensively, 'but it's the only way to break his alibi. I can already hear defence counsel asking if we'd identified these other people, and if not why not. They might've been more than just swinging partners; they could be implicated.'

With a certain element of bad grace, Dave retired to the incident room to make the call.

Fifteen minutes later he was back.

'You were right, guv,' he said, somewhat grudgingly. 'The Reeds weren't there at all.'

'How did you get that out of them, Dave?'

'I spoke to James Simpson. He wasn't very forthcoming to start with until I threw in a few threats about conspiracy, perjury and perverting the course of justice. I also explained the penalties that went with them, and hinted that if peers of the realm and MPs could get done for it, he stood no chance.'

'And I presume that had the desired effect, Dave?'

'Oh yes.' Dave laughed. 'He couldn't admit fast enough that on reflection he didn't think that Julian and Muriel Reed were there that night. He said it was a much younger couple who came in the Lexus, and that the man paid by credit card. His name is Adrian Curtis, and Simpson described the woman as being in her early twenties with a good figure and short blonde hair. I got Adrian Curtis's address from the credit card company and he lives in Effingham, eight miles from Dorking.'

'Did you ask when the Reeds had previously been to Dorking?' I asked.

'According to Simpson, about a week previously. In fact he said they were regulars, but he'd said that before.'

'Did Simpson explain why he was so confused?'

'After a fashion, guv. He made some lame excuse about people not always giving their real names for fear of embarrassment if it ever got out that they'd been swinging. But it was plain that he was bobbing and weaving, right from the start. I think he's still terrified he might finish up in court.'

'He's right, Dave. I think I will have a word with the Surrey Police after all,' I said. 'I doubt that the CPS would be interested in doing the Simpsons for conspiracy, but at least the local law can put them out of business.' I glanced at my watch. 'Get the car, Dave, we're going to Effingham.'

'But what for, guv?'

'To interview Adrian Curtis, of course.'

It was eight o'clock by the time Dave and I arrived at the cottage where Adrian Curtis lived on the outskirts of Effingham in Surrey. A red Lexus was parked outside. Without doubt, and in view of what we now knew, it was the one that the Simpsons had said was parked at their Dorking house on the night of Sharon Gregory's murder.

'Adrian Curtis?' I asked, when a young man, attired in jeans and a rugby shirt, answered the door.

'Yes?' Curtis gazed at us apprehensively, but maybe that was because I was accompanied by a tall, well-built black man of menacing appearance.

'We're police officers, Mr Curtis, and we'd like a word with you. May we come in?' In no mood for prevarication, I took a step towards him.

'What's this about?' Curtis continued to display nerves as he showed us into his sitting room. 'This is my girlfriend, Donna Webb,' he said, indicating a young blonde seated in an armchair. A plain-looking girl, dressed in shorts and a crop top, was watching a wildlife programme on television, but grabbed the remote and switched it off as we entered.

'I'm Detective Chief Inspector Brock of New Scotland Yard and this is Detective Sergeant Poole. I have it on good information, Mr Curtis, that you and Miss Webb attended a swingers' party in Dorking on the night of Monday the twenty-ninth of July. I've also been told that you were there with friends of yours, a Mr and Mrs Reed.'

'Donna and I were certainly there, but Julian and Muriel weren't, not that night,' said Curtis. 'Anyway, what's this about? It's not a crime to go to a party of that sort, is it?' His question wasn't so much a protest as a concerned enquiry. Perhaps he thought he was about to be prosecuted for it.

'No, not at all,' I said. 'What you do in your private lives is none of our business. Except when it involves murder.'

'*Murder*?' Curtis stared at me open-mouthed. 'What murder? I don't know anything about a murder. Are you sure it's me you want to speak to?'

'Julian Reed has been arrested on suspicion of murdering a woman named Sharon Gregory at a hotel near Heathrow Airport on the night you were at this swingers' party in Dorking.' I glanced briefly at Donna Webb, whose face bore a similar expression of shock.

'Julian? Murder?' exclaimed Curtis. 'I don't know anyone called Sharon. I think there's been some sort of mix-up here. Surely Julian didn't murder anyone.'

'What sort of mix-up would that be, Mr Curtis?' asked Dave.

'We were supposed to meet the Reeds at Dorking that night, but they never showed up.'

'Perhaps you'd better explain,' said Dave.

But it was Donna Webb who explained. 'We've often "swapped" with the Reeds: Adrian and Muriel, and Julian and me. And we've been to Dorking with them on quite a few occasions. On the night you mentioned, Muriel rang and said they were going to the Simpsons' place and they'd like to meet us there. Well, we always enjoyed a bit of fun with those two, so we jumped into the car and off we went. But, as Adrian said, the Reeds didn't show up.'

Even though Muriel Reed must've been at least ten years older than Adrian Curtis, I could quite see that he would have found her attractive enough to want to have a sexual encounter with her; she was certainly possessed of a compelling ice-cold allure and had admitted having an appetite for younger men. But I found it difficult to envisage the apparently gormless Julian Reed appealing to Donna, given that he must've been at least fifteen years older than she was.

'Are you absolutely certain that the Reeds were not there? This is vitally important, Mr Curtis.'

'I'm adamant,' said Curtis. 'The four of us had been there often, and when Donna and I arrived that evening, I asked Jimmy if the Reeds had arrived yet, but he said they hadn't.'

'You say that Muriel telephoned you that evening, Miss Webb,' said Dave. 'At what time?'

'I'm not sure. I was having a bath and Adrian took the call. What time was it, darling?' Donna glanced at Curtis.

'It was certainly after five o'clock,' said Curtis. 'Perhaps quarter past, even half past. But to tell you the truth, I'm not really sure.'

'Did this happen often, that they'd ring you at a moment's notice and suggest a meeting at Dorking?' I asked, and noted that Dave had begun writing in his pocketbook.

'Yes. As a matter of fact, that was the way we usually fixed our get-togethers,' said Donna. 'All four of us liked the idea of a spur-of-the-moment arrangement like that; it added to the excitement. Spiced it up, if you know what I mean.'

Actually, I didn't know what she meant, but I invited her to continue.

'Sometimes they'd suggest coming here or they'd ask us to their place in Chelsea,' said Donna. 'Sometimes they'd just arrive and we'd indulge our fantasies here, or they'd give us a lift to Dorking. We've been there quite often. Sometimes we dress up to act out a game, but it's all innocent fun. The Simpsons sometimes join in, too.'

Donna Webb appeared to be quite uninhibited as she described the arrangements that she and Curtis had made for their orgies with the Reeds. But that aside, I thought that Adrian Curtis and Donna Webb were too honest to have been part of a complex plot whereby they'd been used by the Reeds to cover up the murder of Sharon Gregory. And I had to be satisfied with their account of what had happened on that night.

*　　*　　*

On Wednesday morning, Linda Mitchell reported the result of the forensic science laboratory's tests on the DNA sample taken from Julian Reed.

'Julian Reed is definitely the father of Sharon's unborn child, Mr Brock, and the hairs found on the pillow and elsewhere on the bed at the Dickin Hotel also match his DNA. But there were several other hairs present on the bed that are neither Reed's nor Sharon's. And of course, the vaginal fluids.'

'Any result on fingerprints, Linda?' I asked.

'The fingerprints don't help much,' said Linda. 'There is, however, a set on the mobile phone that Dave found in the hotel room, but they're not Sharon's.' She paused. 'They're Julian Reed's.'

'Forgetting the phones for a moment,' I said, 'I reckon the DNA clinches it. In my book it confirms that Julian Reed's the killer and was in such a hurry to leave that he picked up the wrong phone.'

'In addition to the phone, we found some other prints in the hotel room that match the set that were taken from Reed yesterday,' continued Linda, 'but there were a hell of a lot more that we couldn't identify, including a set on the mobile phone found in Reed's car. But it's no surprise that Sharon's prints *are* on it.'

'It looks as though I was right,' I said. 'In his hurry to get the hell out of there, Reed picked up Sharon's phone by mistake and left his own. Which just goes to show that a killer can usually be relied upon to make a mistake.'

'There was one other set found in the room that might interest you, Mr Brock.' Linda shuffled through her sheaf of papers and handed me a criminal record printout. 'They go out to a Paul Matthews with an address in Sheffield. He's got a previous conviction for false accounting and theft. He was a bank clerk and stole funds from the account of one of the bank's customers. He got three years.'

'I told you they didn't clean those hotel rooms properly,' commented Dave.

'This Matthews doesn't sound like a murderer,' I said, 'but ask Sheffield Police to check on his whereabouts when Sharon was topped, Dave. And then we'll get a search warrant for the Reeds' house in Chelsea.'

'We don't need one, guv,' said Dave, 'now that we've arrested Reed for Sharon's murder.'

'I know we don't need one, Dave, but I'd rather have a district judge who can be blamed if it all goes pear-shaped. And right now I've got a nasty feeling it might.'

'Got a minute, guv?' Detective Sergeant Flynn hovered in the doorway of my office clutching his large daybook.

'What is it, Charlie?'

'The Honourable Julian Reed, guv. Turns out his property development business is going down the tubes. Of course, it could be some tax avoidance scheme,' said Flynn. 'There's a lot more to it all than meets the eye, but it's beginning to look like some sort of scam. I think it might finish up in the Fraud Squad's lap. But my take on it is that he has substantial funds in offshore accounts – tax havens probably. Mind you, it'll probably turn out to be legit.' He looked a bit disappointed.

Flynn had obviously been making further use of his clandestine sources to obtain that information, but who was I to question it.

'I'm sure it will, Charlie,' I said. 'The bloody man's too naive to be cunning.'

'That's very nearly a truism, sir,' murmured Dave. 'If it's not an oxymoron.'

'Keep me posted, Charlie,' I said, ignoring Dave's little sideswipe.

'Yes, guv. I reckon that Reed employs a creative accountant.'

'What d'you think about that, Dave?' I asked, once Flynn had departed.

'It puts a different slant on Muriel's claim that Julian couldn't afford to leave her, guv. If Charlie's right about Julian's financial affairs being a bit dodgy, Muriel might've been putting the black on him. After all, it wouldn't do for a future earl to be done for fraud, tax evasion and anything else the Fraud Squad might dig up, would it?'

'You could well be right,' I said, as I absorbed this latest twist in our investigation. 'But that's better than a future earl being charged with the murder of his extramarital sleeping partner.'

'Excuse me, sir, but I was looking for Sergeant Poole,' said DC Appleby, glancing at Dave as he hesitated in the doorway of my office. 'He asked me to do some urgent checking.'

'Come in, John. What did he ask you to do?' I knew that when Dave gave a DC an urgent job he usually had a very good reason for wanting it done.

'I suggested that John did a check on the cameras on the A4, guv,' said Dave. 'As we've nicked Julian Reed on suspicion of murdering Sharon, I thought it might be useful to see if we could get a fix on the exact time his car was on its way back from Heathrow Airport to Chelsea. If that's the route he took.'

'And did he, John?' I asked Appleby.

'That was certainly the route, sir. At eighteen-forty-one Reed's Mercedes was clocked by the speed camera near Hatton doing eighty-seven miles an hour.'

'He must've stayed there quite a long time if that's the time he returned to Chelsea,' I said.

'He wasn't going home, sir. The vehicle was actually travelling westbound. In other words, *towards* Heathrow Airport.'

'What the hell was it doing going that way at that time?' I said, half to myself.

'We could ask him,' said Dave.

'Oh, we will,' I said, and turned back to Appleby. 'You've done a good job there, John.'

'Thank you, sir,' said Appleby

'And now, Dave, you and I are going to spin the Honourable Julian Reed's drum.'

EIGHTEEN

I t was half past one by the time we'd finished filling in all the necessary forms and had journeyed to Marylebone Road to obtain a search warrant from the district judge at Westminster Magistrates' Court.

We arrived at the Reeds' Chelsea house at just after two. I had decided to take Linda Mitchell with us, and thought it would be a good idea to have Kate Ebdon along as well. But I told Linda to remain outside in her van until we needed her and her team of forensic examiners. If we needed them.

Muriel Reed opened the door. 'Oh, it's you again.' There was a resigned note in her voice.

'Yes, it's us, Mrs Reed. Is your husband at home?'

'Yes, he is. He's not long back from Chelsea police station. For some ridiculous reason he has to report there every day as part of his bail conditions. This whole business is rapidly becoming most intolerable.'

If you think that's intolerable, the worst is yet to come, I thought.

'I have a warrant to search these premises, Mrs Reed.'

'Oh my God! When is all this going to end? It's absolutely farcical that my husband should be suspected of murdering that tart, whatever her name is.'

'It's Sharon Gregory, Mrs Reed, as you well know.' I was tired of the woman's prevarication, and of standing on the doorstep. I pushed past her.

'Oh, come in, why don't you?' Muriel's response was bitingly sarcastic.

Accompanied by Dave and Kate Ebdon, I walked upstairs to the sitting room, followed by Mrs Reed.

'Hello, Chief Inspector.' Julian Reed was sitting in an armchair reading a copy of *The Times*. He looked tired, but his face expressed no surprise at our being there.

'I was just explaining to your wife, Mr Reed, that I have a warrant to search this house.'

'I suppose that's what you have to do in cases like this,' said Reed, standing up and casting the newspaper untidily to the floor.

'Are you just going to stand there and let them ransack my house, Julian?' Muriel Reed's whole body seemed to vibrate with fury at our intrusion. Reaching back, she undid the clasp that was holding her titian hair in a ponytail, and shook it free so that it cascaded around the shoulders of her well-cut grey trouser suit.

'We've no option, Muriel,' said Reed mildly. 'If they have a warrant there's nothing we can do about it, except cooperate. And it's *my* house, not yours.'

'Well, you can cooperate if you like. I'm going to lie down. I've got a migraine coming on.'

'My sergeant has some questions for you before you go, Mrs Reed,' I said.

'Has he indeed?' Muriel glanced imperiously at Dave and sat down in the chair furthest from where her husband was standing.

'What time did Mr Reed arrive home on the evening of Monday the twenty-ninth of July?' asked Dave.

'I got in just before five o'clock,' said Reed.

'The sergeant was asking me, Julian,' snapped Muriel. 'And the answer is I don't know. I was downstairs having a swim.' Noticing Dave's expression of surprise, she added, 'We have our own pool in the basement.'

'No you weren't, Muriel,' said Reed. 'You were sitting in that chair.' He waved a hand at the uncomfortable white armchair in which his wife was now nonchalantly reclining. 'And you were reading a magazine. It was much later that you had a swim.'

'You're wrong, Julian, and anyway I do occasionally have more than one swim in a day,' said Muriel cuttingly. 'Particularly when the weather's as hot as it was at the end of July.'

Dave ignored this inconsequential tiff and got to the crux of the matter. 'Did you go out again that night, Mr Reed?'

'No, I didn't. What makes you ask?'

'Because a Mercedes car registered in your name was recorded by a speed camera on the A4 – that's the Great West Road – at six-forty-one that evening, and its speed was logged at eighty-seven miles an hour. So, if it wasn't you driving, who was it?'

'I must've got home later than I thought, then,' said Reed thoughtfully. 'I don't really remember.'

'It has nothing to do with your returning here,' said Dave, 'because your car was travelling in a westbound direction. In other words, it was going *towards* Heathrow, not away from it.'

This awesome announcement was followed by a second or two of complete silence.

Clenching his fists, but otherwise controlling the anger he must've felt, Reed stared at his seated wife. 'It was *you* who murdered Sharon,' he said in a remarkably restrained voice. Despite his apparent absent-mindedness, he was obviously quick to grasp the implications of this latest revelation.

'Don't try and swing this on me, Julian,' said Muriel, matching her husband's mildness with her own calm response. 'Do you really think I could be that bothered about one of your tarts? It was you who killed her, wasn't it? Just be honest for once in your life.'

'I wasn't driving the bloody car, Muriel,' said Reed, 'so it must've been you.'

And I believed him. It was time for me to put a stop to this argument before it damaged our case.

'Stand up, Mrs Reed,' I said. 'Muriel Reed, I am arresting you on suspicion of murdering Sharon Gregory on or about the twenty-ninth of July. You do not have to say anything, but it may harm your defence if you do not mention when questioned something you later rely on in court. Do you understand the caution?'

'Of course I do,' snapped Muriel. 'I've watched police programmes on television often enough, but you should know that you're making a big mistake.' Apart from that statement, she was remarkably unmoved by her arrest. 'And I warn you, Chief Inspector, that I shall instruct my solicitor to take proceedings for wrongful arrest.'

'Put your hands behind your back, Mrs Reed,' said Kate Ebdon, and promptly handcuffed her.

'Is that really necessary?' asked Julian Reed.

'Yes, it's for your wife's own safety, Mr Reed,' I said. But I was nevertheless surprised that Reed was concerned for Muriel's reputation and the indignity of seeing her taken out to a police car in handcuffs. I don't think he was too worried about what the neighbours might think; he wasn't that sort of man. Apart from which, the residents of Chelsea were occasionally arrested, but usually as a result of holding heroin parties. It was that sort of area.

'Would it be all right if I came with you to the police station, Chief Inspector?' asked Reed.

'Yes, in fact it's necessary for you to come with us, Mr Reed.'

Leaving Dave to oversee a search of the house – not that I thought anything useful would be found – Kate and I escorted the Reeds out to the car. The street was quiet and none of the neighbours seemed to notice that Muriel Reed was handcuffed. Or if they did, they were observing this minor melodrama from behind Venetian blinds or net curtains.

It was past four o'clock by the time we arrived at Charing Cross police station and got the Reeds booked in with the custody sergeant. I decided to interview Julian Reed first.

'I have to remind you that you're still under caution, Mr Reed,' I said, once Kate Ebdon had gone through the procedure of setting up the recording machine and announcing the names of those who were present. 'And I also have to tell you that you are under no obligation to answer any or all of my questions.' I had yet to satisfy myself that he had played no part in the murder of Sharon Gregory, but I hoped that he would be prepared to tell me more about what led up to it. 'I must also remind you that you are entitled to have a solicitor present during this interview.'

'I don't mind what you ask.' Reed appeared to be in shock after seeing his wife arrested for the murder of Sharon Gregory. 'And no, I don't want a solicitor. Anyway, Brian's only good at conveyancing and drawing up wills and that sort of thing.'

'How long had you known Sharon Gregory?' I asked.

'It must've been getting on for two years, I suppose,' said Reed. 'She was an air hostess on the flight to Miami that I regularly travelled on, and it was on about my second trip out there that we got talking.' He paused and smiled shyly. 'And one thing led to another. After that our meetings became a regular thing, and I'd call her in advance and ask her which flight she was on so that I could book on the same one. We'd usually have dinner in the evening at a discreet restaurant in Miami, away from her colleagues in the crew – she preferred to keep her personal relationships private from her friends – and then we'd spend the night together either in her hotel room or mine. It was some time after that that we began to meet at the Dickin Hotel near Heathrow Airport.'

Reed could still not see – or preferred not to see – that Sharon had been a conniving woman with an eye to the main chance. Had she known, I wondered, that he was heir to an earldom? And had she deliberately failed to take birth-control precautions so that she would become pregnant by him?

'What can you tell me about the day Sharon was murdered?' I asked.

'I got a phone call from her at just after midday telling me that she was at the Dickin Hotel, which is where, as I said, we usually met, and that she wanted to see me.'

'Did she ring you on your landline at Chelsea?'

'Yes, she did on this occasion. Muriel knew that I played around, but she didn't seem to care. Anyway, I knew that she had her admirers, too. Sometimes she would be out all night and I guessed that she'd be in some young man's bed.'

'Did Sharon say why she wanted to see you?' I asked, steering him away from talking about his wife's extramarital trysts.

'It was the usual: a pleasant afternoon in bed with her.'

'What time did you arrive at the hotel?' I asked.

'It must've been about an hour after Sharon called. It was sometime after one o'clock, anyway.'

'Did she tell you later if there was a particular reason for her wanting to see you on that day?' asked Kate.

Reed smiled at her. 'Yes, there was. She told me that she was pregnant and that the baby was mine.'

'Was there any doubt in your mind that it was your child?'

Reed gave the question some thought. 'There was always the possibility that it was someone else's,' he said thoughtfully. 'We both slept around, you see.' It didn't seem to worry him that Sharon was promiscuous. I suppose he took the view that if he had other partners, it was only fair to accept that she did too.

'Well, I can tell you from the pathologist's post-mortem report, and a DNA comparison, that the child was yours,' I said.

'Was it a boy or a girl?'

'A boy.'

Reed looked immensely sad. 'He would've been my heir.' He picked at an imperfection on the table, as though trying to remove

it with his fingernail. 'My father is the eighth earl, and if I don't
sire an heir the earldom will become extinct. I don't want that to
happen . . . but now the title will die out, I suppose,' he added
with obvious regret.

'Was it your intention to marry Sharon Gregory, then?' asked
Kate.

'Yes, definitely. We'd actually talked about it for some time,
but when she told me she was pregnant that settled it. I proposed
to her that afternoon, and she accepted. I said that I was going
home to tell my wife that our marriage was over and that I intended
to marry the girl who was carrying my child. My life with Muriel
had become a sham.' Reed glanced up and stared at Kate. 'It was
Muriel who first introduced me to the Simpsons at Dorking. And
to Adrian and Donna.' He stared out of the window for a second
or two, a wistful expression on his face. 'Donna was a nice girl,'
he said, looking back at Kate.

That last statement seemed to be an irrelevancy, and Kate didn't
question it. Julian Reed was so naive at times – childlike almost
– in his approach to life that I was beginning to wonder if he was
suffering from some form of arrested development. An article I'd
read some years ago about the effects of interbreeding among the
aristocracy flitted briefly through my mind.

'And did you tell your wife that you were going to divorce her?'
I asked.

Reed chuckled. 'Yes, and I made no secret of the fact that I'd
spent the afternoon in bed with Sharon at the Dickin Hotel and
that I intended to marry her. Muriel didn't like it much.' Reed
described his wife's reaction with breathtaking simplicity. 'You
see, one of the things that she coveted, apart from my money of
course, was the prospect of becoming a countess when eventually
I succeeded to the earldom. She'd've loved that.'

'You say she didn't like the idea of being divorced by you, Mr
Reed. That, surely, is putting it mildly.'

'Yes, I suppose it is.' This time Reed laughed outright. 'Actually
she went ballistic. I don't suppose it helped much when I told
Muriel that Sharon was pregnant and that I was the father. And I
reminded Muriel that she wasn't able to conceive, although I did
at times wonder if she'd made sure that she wouldn't become
pregnant. I don't think the idea of childbirth appealed to her very

much; she was always worrying about her figure. And she often said that being a domesticated housewife wasn't her scene. However, that no longer matters.' He brushed aside his wife's objections with a brief wave of the hand.

'What was your wife's actual response to your statement?' asked Kate. 'Apart from going ballistic, as you put it.'

'She said she'd fight a divorce all the way, and I said I hoped she could afford to, because I wasn't going to pay for a barrister for her. By then I was becoming a bit annoyed by her reaction.'

'What happened next?'

I had decided to let Kate continue with the interview. She seemed to be getting more out of Reed than I had been able to. But I put that down to Kate being an attractive woman, and there was little doubt that Reed was a pushover when confronted by a pretty girl. Even if she was a detective inspector.

'I had a shower.'

'*You had a shower*?' Kate was unable to hide her astonishment at Reed's cavalier reaction to the acrimonious discussion with his wife that he'd just described.

'Yes. It was a very hot day,' he said, as though that were sufficient reason. 'And when I came downstairs Muriel had gone. I didn't know where, but I assumed she'd gone out somewhere in a fit of pique, probably to seek solace in the bed of some male friend. She had quite a few.'

'And did she take the Mercedes?' Kate asked, not that there was much doubt about that now.

'I imagine so. It certainly wasn't outside the house when I'd finished showering,' said Reed. 'We've got a resident's parking permit, you see,' he added unnecessarily.

'How did she know where Sharon was?'

'I told her I'd been at the Dickin Hotel, and when I'd taken Sharon's call I'd jotted down the room number on the pad beside the telephone. We always keep a pad by the phone, it's handy for jotting things down.' Reed seemed to think it necessary to describe in detail his actions that day. 'Bit careless of me really.' It seemed that Reed was not one disposed to take any precautions. About anything.

I was surprised that Sharon had still been at the hotel when Muriel arrived, but then I recalled that she'd booked the room for the night. Given that she must've realized by then that we suspected her of murdering her husband Clifford, I wondered what she'd intended to do next. That, however, was no longer of any importance.

'Did you, by chance, leave your mobile phone in Sharon's room at the Dickin Hotel, Mr Reed?' asked Kate.

Reed looked mystified, but only for a moment. 'I must've done,' he said. 'I wondered what I'd done with it. I'm always losing the wretched things. I must've bought half a dozen of them over the past year.'

'When did your wife get back?'

'I don't know really. I suppose it must've been about nine o'clock. I'd spent the evening reading in my study and I first saw her at about half past nine, I think. I remember that she appeared in the study door wearing a swimsuit.'

'Did she say anything?'

'Only that she was going for a quick swim and then she'd go to bed. But apart from that, hardly anything. It was a very short conversation. She certainly didn't mention anything about the divorce or my plans to marry Sharon. Anyway, I didn't see her again until the following morning. We don't sleep together any more, you see – there'd be no point – and we have separate bedrooms.'

'Did you ask Mrs Reed where she'd been when she came home that evening?'

'Yes. She said she'd been to the Dorking swingers' party with Adrian and Donna. But I thought that was unlikely; she usually insisted on staying the night whenever we went there together. I've never known her to leave as early as she said she had.'

'Did Sharon say what she was going to do after you left her at the Dickin Hotel?'

'No, she said she'd be flying most of the time. She mentioned visiting her parents in Basildon to tell them of our engagement.'

I knew that that was unlikely. We'd interviewed Kevin and Helen Cross and knew that they'd been on holiday at the time. But perhaps Sharon didn't know; the Crosses had told me that they didn't see their daughter very often. However, it didn't matter what Sharon had told Julian Reed; she was dead within a few hours of talking to him.

'But then, of course, you brought the dreadful news that she'd been murdered,' continued Reed.

'I don't think there's anything else, Mr Reed. You will remain on bail for the time being, but I'll arrange for the requirement to report daily to Chelsea police station to be lifted. We'll advise you if and when your bail is rescinded altogether.'

I'd come to the conclusion that Julian Reed had not played any part in the murder of Sharon Reed, and recalled what Muriel Reed had said when we'd first interviewed her and her husband. '*To be quite frank,*' she'd said, '*he hasn't got the guts for that sort of thing.*' But it seemed that what Julian lacked in that sort of twisted resolve was more than compensated for by his wife.

I escorted Julian Reed to the door of the police station and watched as he wandered aimlessly down Agar Street towards Trafalgar Square, hands in pockets. I'd come to the conclusion, all things considered, that he was quite a decent man, but now doubtless a very sad and broken one. It was rare, but probably not unique in the annals of crime, for a man to have contemplated divorce from one murderess in order to marry another one. Not that he knew that Sharon had killed her husband; he probably hadn't even known that she was married. He was that naive.

NINETEEN

K ate Ebdon had already arranged for Muriel Reed to be brought into the interview room that her husband had just vacated. She was an entirely different character from Julian Reed. Whereas he was naive and had a tendency to gaze at the world through rose-tinted spectacles, his wife was cold, calculating and avaricious for anything upon which she set her mind.

When we had spoken to her earlier, Muriel Reed had vehemently denied any involvement in the murder of Sharon Gregory. I had already obtained the chief superintendent's authority to take an intimate sample from her to determine her DNA, but the results would take time.

'Muriel Reed, I put it to you that on the twenty-ninth of July this year you murdered Sharon Gregory at the Dickin Hotel near Heathrow Airport.'

'Nonsense,' said Muriel, her steely gaze switching from me to Kate Ebdon and back again.

'I have the authority of a senior officer to take a sample of your saliva, Mrs Reed.' I had decided on a saliva sample to avoid the necessity of involving a medical practitioner. But if more were required, that could be dealt with later.

'Well, if you must, you must, I suppose,' she said resignedly.

I took that statement to be one of tacit consent.

'And I am quite satisfied that once that sample has been analysed and compared with evidence found at the Dickin Hotel, it will prove beyond all reasonable doubt that you murdered Sharon Gregory.'

'That's it then, I suppose.' Muriel paused for a second or two and glanced up at the barred window of the interview room. Then she lifted her chin slightly and finally gave in. 'Of course I murdered the little slut. You don't really think that I was going to stand by and see that tramp take everything away from me, do you? Can you imagine that Essex trollop flaunting herself as a countess and having everyone bowing and scraping and addressing her as "Lady Dretford"?'

And that was that. Nevertheless, I had to admire her vocabulary; she possessed a mastery of English that was capable of deploying three different adjectives with which to denigrate her victim.

'You will now be charged with that murder, Mrs Reed,' I said, 'and will be detained here until your remand appearance at court tomorrow morning.'

'I haven't finished yet,' said Muriel Reed, as I stood up.

'You're not obliged to say any more,' I reminded her.

'She was a pushover, you know, Chief Inspector,' she continued, ignoring my words of caution. 'I went up to her room and knocked, but I have to admit that I was surprised she was still at the hotel. When she opened the door she was stark naked except for a pair of black nylons. I imagine that she thought Julian had come back for seconds.' She laughed, a grating, humourless laugh. Now that she had confessed, she seemed to be enjoying relating her account of how she had murdered Sharon and continued with spine-chilling deliberation. 'I told her who I was and that Julian had sent me because he'd said that she liked to have fun with women as well as men, and that's why I was there. She was more than willing and I spent a happy half hour making love to her. *And then I strangled her.* I expect you remember Julian telling you that I had a good forearm smash. Well, with that and my daily swimming, that little hussy was physically no match for me. I got dressed, picked up my mobile phone and went home.'

That was all I needed, and it was all on the tape.

'But it wasn't your mobile phone,' said Kate, careful not to make it sound like a question, 'it was Julian's.'

'I know that now. It wasn't until much later that I realized I hadn't even taken my own phone with me. And then I picked up her phone, thinking it was mine. That was my one mistake,' admitted Muriel ruefully.

That wasn't the only mistake you made, I thought.

I had a short discussion with the Crown Prosecution Service lawyer who was resident at the police station, and laid my evidence before him. It took him only a matter of minutes to formulate the charge, following which Kate and I escorted Muriel Reed to the custody suite where she was 'put on the sheet' for the murder of Sharon Gregory.

I was now faced with the onerous task of writing a report

detailing everything connected with the enquiry, and ensuring that all the relevant statements were attached. When prosecuting counsel received his brief, which would be based on that report, he should have no problem in securing a conviction. I hoped. But, as I've said many times before, there is nothing quite as fickle as an English jury.

A month later, Muriel Reed was arraigned in Court Number Three at the Central Criminal Court at Old Bailey in the City of London. There was only one count on the indictment: the wilful murder of Sharon Gregory.

She was escorted into the dock by two stern-faced women prison officers, but stood erect, her expressionless gaze fixed firmly on the Royal Arms above the judge's chair. As befitted the occasion, she was smartly dressed in a matching grey jacket and skirt, and a high-collared white blouse. She wore no jewellery, not even earrings.

Had she looked up at the public gallery above and behind her, she would have seen her husband. Julian Reed was seated in the front row, leaning forward with his arms folded on the edge of the balcony and studying the proceedings with great interest.

As the usher shouted 'All rise', the red-robed judge appeared and bowed to counsel. They bowed back.

With a shout of 'Oyez, oyez!' the usher had his real moment of glory, and went on to mumble something about 'oyer and terminer and general gaol delivery'.

Then it began.

Muriel wanted to plead guilty, but the judge was having none of it. This was fairly common practice in murder trials; Her Majesty's Justices rightly wanted to make sure that defendants knew what they would be signing up for. Either that or there was some conspiracy between the bench and the bar to make sure that counsel would be able to milk the legal aid system for all it was worth. Whatever the reason, the judge directed that a plea of not guilty should be entered.

At this point, I leaned forward and whispered in prosecuting counsel's ear. He nodded and stood to address the judge.

'My Lord, I have just been informed that the defendant's husband is in the public gallery. I'd be obliged if Your Lordship direct that he be removed. I intend to call him as a witness.'

The judge looked up. 'Mr Reed, be so good as to wait outside the court until you are called.'

That little piece of procedural correctness accomplished, the jury was empanelled and the theatre of British justice lumbered slowly into action. One almost expected to hear the usher shout, 'Overture and beginners, please,' to herald the opening addresses by counsel for the Crown and for the defence respectively.

It was at that point that I, as a witness, was also obliged to leave.

It was not until the afternoon that the usher opened the door and bellowed, 'Detective Chief Inspector Brock' in a voice that would have been heard in Ludgate Circus.

I took my place in the witness box, swore to tell the truth and waited for prosecuting counsel to earn his fee.

He took me through all the investigations that had led to the arrest of Muriel Reed until we reached the important bit.

'Chief Inspector, did Mrs Reed state that she had murdered Sharon Gregory?'

'She did, sir,' I replied.

'What exactly did she say?'

I repeated Muriel's statement, word for word.

'And was that confession made under caution and was it recorded?' asked counsel.

'It was, sir.'

'And did the defendant say anything else?'

'She did, sir. She made a voluntary statement describing her visit to the hotel room where the body of Sharon Gregory was later discovered.' I went on to tell the court exactly what Muriel Reed had said.

Prosecuting counsel went through the rigmarole of having the tape-recording entered as an exhibit, asked a few more banal questions and sat down.

Defence counsel, a youngish Queen's Counsel, rose and made an elaborate charade of finding the right page in her brief.

'Inspector Brock, did you—?'

'I'm a chief inspector, madam,' I said. 'A *detective* chief inspector.'

'Quite so. I do apologize, Chief Inspector. I have you down in my brief as an inspector.'

That was always a show-stopper, one that threw her for a moment or two, and I could foresee a junior in her chambers getting a flea in his ear for making that mistake. But she quickly recovered and embarked upon a curious line of questioning.

'Chief Inspector, did you form any opinion about my client?'

'What sort of opinion, madam?' I thoroughly enjoyed this sort of forensic jousting.

'Well now, let me see.' Pushing back her gown, the woman placed her left hand on her hip while holding her brief loosely in her other hand. 'Do you think that Mrs Reed's behaviour was entirely rational?' she asked, as though that question had just popped into her head.

The judge raised his eyebrows and peered at counsel over his spectacles, but I was able to get my answer in before he queried whether her client's defence was to be one of diminished responsibility.

'I can't answer that question, madam. I'm not qualified in psychiatry.' I had to admit, but only to myself, that the cold way in which Muriel Reed had described how she'd murdered Sharon Gregory made me wonder about her sanity.

'No, I appreciate that,' said the lady barrister, a syrupy smile masking her disappointment that I'd not fallen into her rather obvious little trap. 'But surely the crime of which she stands accused was not the action of a rational person.'

Oh, well, you asked for it. 'In my experience, madam, no murderer or murderess is a rational being, otherwise they would not commit murder. But, as I said, I'm not a psychiatrist.'

The judge smiled, but said nothing.

Defence counsel tried one or two other well-known ploys, but had no greater success than she had with the first one. But she had to try; that's what she was paid for.

And so it ground on, day after day. Testimony was given by Dr Mortlock, Linda Mitchell, Kate Ebdon and everyone else who had been involved in the investigation.

But the evidence that clinched it came from a forensic scientist who testified that the DNA sample taken from Muriel Reed matched the vaginal fluid found on Sharon's body. A fingerprint officer assured the court that Muriel Reed's fingerprints had also been found in room 219 and on the phone in the glove compartment of the Reeds' Mercedes.

Julian Reed's evidence was interesting. He recounted his conversation with his wife when he'd told her he was leaving her for
Sharon Gregory, but altogether he didn't contribute much. I don't
know why the prosecution bothered to call him at all.

Defence counsel made several attempts to undermine the
evidence, but rather reminded me of a small dog angrily snapping
at the witnesses' heels. Wisely, she decided against putting her
client into the witness box, probably assuming that Muriel Reed
would merely repeat what she had said to me: '*Of course I murdered
the little slut.*'

After thirteen days filled, for the most part, with technical
evidence that would neither have excited nor interested aficionados
of crime fiction, the jury retired to consider their verdict.

Despite Muriel Reed's confession, it took the twelve upright
citizens two hours to find her guilty. God knows what they were
talking about during that time. Perhaps they were considering
adding a rider for mercy.

Fourteen days after the verdict, we were back at the Old Bailey
to hear the sentence.

Personally, I think the judge was a trifle soft in expressing the
view that Muriel Reed had been betrayed by her husband. I'm not
quite sure how that could've justified cold-blooded murder, but he
imposed a life sentence with a tariff of just fifteen years before
she could apply for parole.

After several weeks of deliberation, the Crown Prosecution
Service decided that Julian Reed shared no culpability in the
murder of Sharon Gregory. It was a conclusion at which I had
arrived within seconds of finishing my interview with him. But
then I'm not a lawyer and I didn't know that it should have taken
weeks to arrive at such a decision.

The resumed inquest into the death of Clifford Gregory took place
a week after the sentencing of Muriel Reed.

Dave and I attended the Hammersmith coroner's court at nine
o'clock on the morning of Monday the thirtieth of September. The
weather was dull and overcast; a suitable climate, I thought, for
the final act in the murders of Clifford and Sharon Gregory.

I entered the witness box and told the court that Muriel Reed had been convicted of the wilful murder of Sharon Gregory. But then came the difficult part. I outlined the evidence that had been amassed regarding the death of Clifford Gregory and the inference I had drawn that he'd been murdered by his wife. I was followed by Henry Mortlock who gave the medical details.

After a summing-up by the coroner, his jury brought in a verdict that Clifford Gregory had been murdered by his wife, and that Sharon Gregory had been murdered by the Honourable Muriel Reed. Not that any of it meant anything now, but it tied up the loose ends.

I hadn't told Julian Reed when the inquest was to take place and I didn't tell him the verdict. I reckoned he'd suffered enough.

It was August, just over one year after the murder of Sharon Gregory.

The Miami flight had taken off from Heathrow Airport on time. Once it was airborne – and the seat-belt warning light had been extinguished – the cabin staff set about tending to the needs of the passengers.

'Good morning.' The smiling man seated in the first-class section of the aircraft was forty-one years of age and a frequent traveller to Miami where he had interests, business and social – but one in particular. 'It's nice to see you again . . .' He paused while pretending to read the stewardess's name badge. 'Cindy.'

'Good morning, sir.' The stewardess's name was Cindy Patterson. She was twenty-seven years of age, shapely, and her long jet-black hair was fashioned into a French roll. She returned the man's smile. 'Would you care for coffee, sir?'

'Thank you, Cindy. Decaf, black, no sugar.'

'I know, sir.' Cindy smiled. 'Breakfast will be served shortly.'

'Thank you. That'll be nice,' said the man.

'Will you be staying in Miami long, sir?' Although it sounded like the normal trite enquiry that a stewardess would make to pass the time of day, there was more to it than that. And the man knew it.

'Just for twenty-four hours. I should've had a business meeting later, but just as I arrived at Heathrow, I got a phone call to say that it was cancelled. But I decided to come anyway.'

Cindy leaned closer. 'Liar!' she whispered, and smiled. 'What are you going to do here, then, sir?' she asked, raising her voice again.

'I'll think of something,' said the man. Now it was his turn to lean closer and whisper. 'Usual hotel?'

'Of course,' said Cindy.

'Call me with the room number.'

Nine hours later, the huge aircraft touched down at Miami International, taxied to the walkway and the passengers began to alight.

'Enjoy your stay, sir,' said Cindy to the man from first class. She was standing at the exit, a fixed smile on her face, bidding farewell to the disembarking passengers. 'I hope we'll see you again soon.'

'You know jolly well you will. Quite soon,' said the man in a voice that only Cindy heard.

Once the enormous airliner was empty of passengers, the crew gathered their overnight suitcases and disembarked, making their way to customs and thence to the crew bus that awaited them outside the airport terminal.

Once in her room at the Shannon Hotel, Cindy made a phone call, stripped off her clothes and took a shower. Returning to the bedroom, she dabbed Lancôme Trésor on her neck and between her breasts. Next, she donned frilly white underwear and a summer dress. Finally she slid her bare feet into a pair of high-heeled mules.

She had to wait only fifteen minutes before the expected knock came at her door.

'Just coming, darling.' Cindy opened the door and the passenger she had served on the flight that morning entered the room. But before locking the door, he hung a 'Do Not Disturb' sign outside. As he always did on these occasions.

Later, when the couple were lying side by side and perspiring freely from the exertions of their lovemaking, the man raised himself on one elbow and gazed down at the girl.

'You are a thoroughly wanton woman, Cindy Patterson,' he said, tracing little patterns on her damp breast with a finger. 'But you know that, don't you?'

'Only when I'm with you, darling.' Cindy placed her hands behind her head and stretched sensuously.

'Oh, come on,' said the man teasingly. 'I'd bet you'd jump into bed with any man who asked you.'

'You know that's not true.' Cindy lowered her arms and prodded him gently in the chest.

'Of course I do, darling.' The man laughed and relaxed against the pillows.

'But you'd hop into bed with any available woman.'

'There was a time when I would've done,' said the man. 'But not any more, because there's something important I want to ask you about. Something really important.'

It was a good eighteen months after the murder of Sharon Gregory that Kate came into my office flourishing a copy of the *Daily Telegraph*.

'There's an interesting piece in the paper this morning, guv.'

'Oh? What's that?'

Kate opened the newspaper and read the piece that had caught her eye in the Court and Social Section. '"The marriage took place quietly in Capri last week between Julian, Earl Dretford, son of the late Earl and the dowager Countess Dretford, of London, and Miss Cindy Patterson, daughter of Ralph and Elizabeth Patterson of Truro, Cornwall."' She looked up. 'Isn't that the air hostess who was Sharon Gregory's crewmate, guv?'

'Yes,' I said. 'It seems that Julian Reed, now the Earl Dretford, has a liking for air hostesses.'

'I hope the new Countess Dretford will enjoy swingers' parties,' said Kate.